CARL HIAASEN

HOOT

MACMILLAN CHILDREN'S BOOKS

First published 2002 by Alfred A. Knopf, a division of Random House, Inc., USA

This edition published 2019 by Macmillan Children's Books
an imprint of Pan Macmillan
20 New Wharf Road, London N1 9RR
Associated companies throughout the world
www.panmacmillan.com

ISBN 978-1-5290-2085-4

3 5 7 9 8 6 4 2

A CIP catalogue record for this book is available from
the British Library.

Typeset by Intype Libra Ltd
Printed and bound by CPI Group (UK) Ltd, Croydon CR0 4YY

*For Carly, Ben, Samantha, Hannah,
and, of course, Ryan*

ONE

Roy would not have noticed the strange boy if it weren't for Dana Matherson, because Roy ordinarily didn't look out the window of the school bus. He preferred to read comics and mystery books on the morning ride to Trace Middle.

But on this day, a Monday (Roy would never forget), Dana Matherson grabbed Roy's head from behind and pressed his thumbs into Roy's temple, as if he were squeezing a soccer ball. The older kids were supposed to stay in the back of the bus, but Dana had snuck up behind Roy's seat and ambushed him. When Roy tried to wriggle free, Dana mushed his face against the window.

It was then, squinting through the smudged glass, that Roy spotted the strange boy running along the sidewalk. It appeared as if he was hurrying to catch the school bus, which had stopped at a corner to pick up more kids.

The boy was straw-blond and wiry, and his skin was nut-brown from the sun. The expression on his face was intent and serious. He wore a faded Miami Heat basketball jersey and dirty khaki shorts, and here was the odd part: no shoes. The soles of his bare feet looked as black as barbecue coals.

Trace Middle School didn't have the world's strictest dress code, but Roy was pretty sure that some sort of footwear was required. The boy might have been carrying sneakers in his backpack, if only he'd been wearing a backpack. No shoes, no backpack, no books – strange, indeed, on a school day.

Roy was sure that the barefoot boy would catch all kinds of grief from Dana and the other big kids once he boarded the bus, but that didn't happen . . .

Because the boy kept running – past the corner, past the line of students waiting to get on the bus; past the bus itself. Roy wanted to shout, 'Hey, look at that guy!' but his mouth wasn't working so well. Dana Matherson still had him from behind, pushing his face against the window.

As the bus pulled away from the intersection, Roy hoped to catch another glimpse of the boy farther up the street. However, he had turned off the sidewalk and was now cutting across a private yard – running very fast, much faster than Roy could run and maybe even faster than Richard, Roy's best friend back in Montana. Richard was so fast that he got to work out with the high school track squad when he was only in seventh grade.

Dana Matherson was digging his fingernails into Roy's scalp, trying to make him squeal, but Roy barely felt a thing. He was gripped with curiosity as the running boy dashed through one neat green yard after another, getting smaller in Roy's vision as he put a wider distance between himself and the school bus.

Roy saw a big pointy-eared dog, probably a German shepherd, bound off somebody's porch and go for the boy. Incredibly, the boy didn't change his course. He vaulted over the dog, crashed through a cherry hedge, and then disappeared from view.

Roy gasped.

'Whassamatter, cowgirl? Had enough?'

This was Dana, hissing in Roy's right ear. Being the new kid on the bus, Roy didn't expect any help from the others. The 'cowgirl' remark was so lame, it wasn't worth getting mad about. Dana was a well-known idiot, on top of which he outweighed Roy by at least fifty pounds. Fighting back would have been a complete waste of energy.

'Had enough yet? We can't hear you, Tex.' Dana's breath smelled like stale cigarettes. Smoking and beating up smaller kids were his two main hobbies.

'Yeah, OK,' Roy said impatiently. 'I've had enough.'

As soon as he was freed, Roy lowered the window and stuck out his head. The strange boy was gone.

Who was he? What was he running from?

Roy wondered if any of the other kids on the bus had seen what he'd seen. For a moment he wondered if he'd really seen it himself.

That same morning, a police officer named David Delinko was sent to the future site of another Mother Paula's All-American Pancake House. It was a vacant lot at the corner of East Oriole and Woodbury, on the eastern edge of town.

Officer Delinko was met by a man in a dark blue pickup truck. The man, who was as bald as a beach ball, introduced himself as Curly. Officer Delinko thought the bald man must have a good sense of humour to go by such a nickname, but he was wrong. Curly was cranky and unsmiling.

'You should see what they done,' he said to the policeman.

'Who?'

'Follow me,' the man called Curly said.

Officer Delinko got in step behind him. 'The dispatcher said you wanted to report some vandalism.'

'That's right,' Curly grunted over his shoulder.

The policeman couldn't see what there was to be vandalized on the property, which was basically a few acres of scraggly weeds. Curly stopped walking and pointed at a short piece of lumber on the ground. A ribbon of bright pink plastic was tied to one end of the stick. The other end was sharpened and caked with grey dirt.

Curly said, 'They pulled 'em out.'

'That's a survey stake?' asked Officer Delinko.

'Yep. They yanked 'em out of the ground, every damn one.'

'Probably just kids.'

'And then they threw 'em every which way,' Curly said, waving a beefy arm, 'and then they filled in the holes.'

'That's a little weird,' the policeman remarked. 'When did this happen?'

'Last night or early this morning,' Curly said. 'Maybe it don't look like a big deal, but it's gonna take a while to get the site marked out again. Meantime, we can't start clearin' or gradin' or nuthin'. We got backhoes and dozers already leased, and now they gotta sit. I know it don't look

4

like the crime of the century, but still—'

'I understand,' said Officer Delinko. 'What's your estimate of the monetary damage?'

'Damage?'

'Yes. So I can put it in my report.' The policeman picked up the survey stake and examined it. 'It's not really broken, is it?'

'Well, no—'

'Were any of them destroyed?' asked Officer Delinko. 'How much does one of these things cost – a buck or two?'

The man called Curly was losing his patience. 'They didn't break none of the stakes,' he said gruffly.

'Not even one?' The policeman frowned. He was trying to figure out what to put in his report. You can't have vandalism without monetary damages, and if nothing on the property was broken or defaced . . .

'What I'm tryin' to explain,' Curly said irritably, 'it's not that they messed up the survey stakes, it's them screwing up our whole construction schedule. That's where it'll cost some serious bucks.'

Officer Delinko took off his cap and scratched his head. 'Let me think on this,' he said.

Walking back toward the patrol car, the policeman stumbled and fell down. Curly grabbed him under one arm and hoisted him to his feet. Both men were mildly embarrassed.

'Stupid owls,' said Curly.

The policeman brushed the dirt and grass burs off his uniform. 'You say owls?'

Curly gestured at a hole in the ground. It was as big around as one of Mother Paula's famous buttermilk flapjacks. A mound of loose white sand was visible at the entrance.

'That's what you tripped over,' Curly informed Officer Delinko.

'An owl lives down there?' The policeman bent over and studied the hole. 'How big are they?'

''Bout as tall as a beer can.'

'No kidding?' said Officer Delinko.

'But I ain't never seen one, officially speakin'.'

Back at the patrol car, the patrolman took out his clipboard and started writing the report. It turned out that Curly's real name was Leroy Branitt, and he was the 'supervising engineer' of the construction project. He scowled when he saw the policeman write down 'foreman' instead.

Officer Delinko explained to Curly the problem with filing the complaint as a vandalism. 'My sergeant's going to kick it back down to me because, technically, nothing really got vandalized. Some kids came on the property and pulled a bunch of sticks out of the ground.'

'How do you know it was kids?' Curly muttered.

'Well, who else would it be?'

'What about them fillin' up the holes and throwin' the stakes, just to make us lay out the whole site all over again. What about that?'

It puzzled the policeman, too. Kids usually didn't go to that kind of trouble when pulling a prank.

'Do you have any particular suspects?'

Curly admitted he didn't. 'But, OK, say it was kids. That means it's not a crime?'

'Of course it's a crime,' Officer Delinko replied. 'I'm saying it's not technically vandalism. It's trespassing and malicious mischief.'

'That'll do,' Curly said with a shrug. 'Long as I can get a copy of your report for the insurance company. Least we'll be covered for lost time and expenses.'

Officer Delinko gave Curly a card with the address of the police department's administration office and the name of the clerk in charge of filing the incident reports. Curly tucked the card into the breast pocket of his foreman shirt.

The policeman put on his sunglasses and slid into his patrol car, which was as hot as a brick oven. He quickly turned on the ignition and cranked the air conditioner up full blast. As he buckled his seat belt, he said, 'Mr Branitt, there's one more thing I wanted to ask. I'm just curious.'

'Fire away,' said Curly, wiping his brow with a yellow bandanna.

'It's about those owls.'

'Sure.'

'What's gonna happen to them?' Officer Delinko asked. 'Once you start bulldozing, I mean.'

Curly the foreman chuckled. He thought the policeman must be kidding.

'What owls?' he said.

*

All day long Roy couldn't stop thinking about the strange running boy. Between classes he scanned the faces in the hallways on the chance that the boy had come to school late. Maybe he'd been hurrying home, Roy thought, to change clothes and put on some shoes.

But Roy didn't see any kids who resembled the one who had jumped over the big pointy-eared dog. Maybe he's still running, Roy thought as he ate lunch. Florida was made for running; Roy had never seen anyplace so flat. Back in Montana you had steep craggy mountains that rose ten thousand feet into the clouds. Here the only hills were man-made highway bridges – smooth, gentle slopes of concrete.

Then Roy remembered the heat and the humidity, which on some days seemed to suck the very meat out of his lungs. A long run in the Florida sun would be torture, he thought. A kid would have to be tough as nails to make a routine of that.

A boy named Garrett sat down across from Roy. Roy nodded hi and Garrett nodded hi, and then both of them went back to eating the gooey macaroni on their lunch trays. Being the new kid, Roy always sat alone, at the end of the table, whenever he was in the cafeteria. Roy was an old pro at being the new kid; Trace Middle was the sixth school he had attended since he'd started going to school. Coconut Cove was the tenth town his family had lived in since Roy could remember.

Roy's father worked for the government. His mother said they moved so often because Roy's father was very good at his job (whatever *that* was) and frequently got promoted. Apparently that's how the government rewarded good work, by transferring you from one place to another.

'Hey,' said Garrett. 'You got a skateboard?'

'No, but I've got a snowboard.'

Garrett hooted. 'What for?'

'Where I used to live it snowed a lot,' Roy said.

'You should learn to skateboard. It's awesome, man.'

'Oh, I know how to skateboard. I just don't have one.'

'Then you should get one,' Garrett said. 'Me and my friends, we do the major malls. You should come.'

'That'd be cool.' Roy tried to sound enthusiastic. He didn't like shopping malls, but he appreciated that Garrett was trying to be friendly.

Garrett was a D student, but he was popular in school because he goofed around in class and made farting noises whenever a teacher called him out. Garrett was the king of phoney farts at Trace Middle. His most famous trick was farting out the first line of the Pledge of Allegiance during homeroom.

Ironically, Garrett's mother was a guidance counsellor at Trace Middle. Roy figured she used up her guiding skills every day at school and was too worn out to deal with Garrett when she got home.

'Yeah, we skate hard until the security guards run us off,' Garrett was saying, 'and then we do the parking lots until we get chased out of there, too. It's a blast.'

'Sweet,' Roy said, though cruising a mall seemed like a

pretty dull way to spend a Saturday morning. He was looking forward to his first airboat ride in the Everglades. His dad had promised to take him, one of these weekends.

'Are there any other schools around here?' Roy asked Garrett.

'Why? You sick of this one already?' Garrett cackled and plunged a spoon into a lump of clammy apple crisp.

'No way. The reason I asked, I saw this weird kid today at one of the bus stops. Except he didn't get on the bus, and he's not here at school,' Roy said, 'so I figured he must not go to Trace.'

'I don't know *anyone* who doesn't go to Trace,' Garrett said. 'There's a Catholic school up in Fort Myers, but that's a long ways off. Was he wearing a uniform, this kid? Because the nuns make everybody wear uniforms.'

'No, he definitely wasn't in a uniform.'

'You're sure he was in middle school? Maybe he goes to Graham,' Garrett suggested. Graham was the public high school nearest to Coconut Cove.

Roy said, 'He didn't look big enough for high school.'

'Maybe he was a midget.' Garrett grinned and made a farty noise with one of his cheeks.

'I don't think so,' said Roy.

'You said he was weird.'

'He wasn't wearing any shoes,' Roy said, 'and he was running like crazy.'

'Maybe somebody was after him. Did he look scared?'

'Not really.'

Garrett nodded. 'High school kid. Betcha five bucks.'

To Roy, that still didn't make sense. Classes at Graham High started fifty-five minutes earlier than the classes at Trace; the high school kids were off the streets long before the middle school buses finished their routes.

'So he was skippin' class. Kids skip all the time,' Garrett said. 'You want your dessert?'

Roy pushed his tray across the table. 'You ever skip school?'

'Uh, yeah,' Garrett said sarcastically. 'Buncha times.'

'You ever skip alone?'

Garrett thought for a moment. 'No. It's always me and my friends.'

'See. That's what I mean.'

'So maybe the kid's just a psycho. Who cares?'

'Or an outlaw,' said Roy.

Garrett looked sceptical. 'An outlaw? You mean like Jesse James?'

'No, not exactly,' Roy said, though there *had* been something wild in that kid's eyes.

Garrett laughed again. 'An outlaw – that's rich, Eberhardt. You got a seriously whacked imagination.'

'Yeah,' said Roy, but already he was thinking about a plan. He was determined to find the running boy.

TWO

The next morning, Roy traded seats on the school bus to be closer to the front door. When the bus turned on to the street where he had seen the running boy, Roy slipped his backpack over his shoulders and scouted out the window, waiting. Seven rows back, Dana Matherson was torment-ing a sixth grader named Louis. Louis was from Haiti and Dana was merciless.

As the bus came to a stop at the intersection, Roy poked his head out the window and checked up and down the street. Nobody was running. Seven kids boarded the bus, but the strange shoeless boy was not among them.

It was the same story the next day, and the day after that. By Friday, Roy had pretty much given up. He was sit-ting ten rows from the door, reading an X-Men comic, as the bus turned the familiar corner and began to slow down. A movement at the corner of his eye made Roy glance up from his comic book – and there he was on the sidewalk, running again! Same basketball jersey, same grimy shorts, same black-soled feet.

As the brakes of the school bus wheezed, Roy grabbed his backpack off the floor and stood up. At that instant, two big sweaty hands closed around his neck.

'Where ya goin', cowgirl?'

'Lemme go,' Roy rasped, squirming to break free.

The grip on his throat tightened. He felt Dana's ashtray breath on his right ear: 'How come you don't got your boots on today? Who ever heard of a cowgirl wearing Air Jordans?'

'They're Reeboks,' Roy squeaked.

The bus had stopped, and the students were starting to board. Roy was furious. He had to get to the door fast, before the driver closed it and the bus began to roll.

But Dana wouldn't let go, digging his fingers into Roy's windpipe. Roy was having trouble getting air, and struggling only made it worse.

'Look at you,' Dana chortled from behind, 'red as a tomato!'

Roy knew the rules against fighting on the bus, but he couldn't think of anything else to do. He clenched his right fist and brought it up blindly over his shoulder, as hard as he could. The punch landed on something moist and rubbery.

There was a gargled cry; then Dana's hands fell away from Roy's neck. Panting, Roy bolted for the door of the bus just as the last student, a tall girl with curly blonde hair and red-framed eyeglasses, came up the steps. Roy clumsily edged past her and jumped to the ground.

'Where do you think you're going?' the girl demanded.

'Hey, wait!' the bus driver shouted, but Roy was already a blur.

The running boy was way ahead of him, but Roy figured he could stay close enough to keep him in sight. He knew the kid couldn't go at full speed for ever.

He followed him for several blocks – over fences, through shrubbery, weaving through yapping dogs and lawn sprinklers and hot tubs. Eventually Roy felt himself tiring. This kid is amazing, he thought. Maybe he's practising for the track team.

Once Roy thought he saw the boy glance over his shoulder, as if he knew he was being pursued, but Roy couldn't be certain. The boy was still far ahead of him, and Roy was gulping like a beached trout. His shirt was soaked and perspiration poured off his forehead, stinging his eyes.

The last house in the subdivision was still under construction, but the shoeless boy dashed heedlessly through the lumber and loose nails. Three men hanging drywall stopped to holler at him, but the boy never broke stride. One of the same workers made a one-armed lunge at Roy but missed.

Suddenly there was grass under his feet again – the greenest, softest grass that Roy had ever seen. He realized that he was on a golf course, and that the blond kid was tearing down the middle of a long, lush fairway.

On one side was a row of tall Australian pines, and on the other side was a milky man-made lake. Roy could see four brightly dressed figures ahead, gesturing at the barefoot boy as he ran by.

Roy gritted his teeth and kept going. His legs felt like wet cement, and his lungs were on fire. A hundred yards ahead, the boy cut sharply to the right and disappeared into the pine trees. Roy doggedly aimed himself for the woods.

An angry shout echoed, and Roy noticed that the people

in the fairway were waving their arms at him, too. He kept right on running. Moments later there was a distant glint of sunlight on metal, followed by a muted *thwack*. Roy didn't actually see the golf ball until it came down six feet in front of him. He had no time to duck or dive out of the way. All he could do was turn his head and brace for the blow.

The bounce caught him squarely above the left ear, and at first it didn't even hurt. Then Roy felt himself swaying and spinning as a brilliant gout of fireworks erupted inside his skull. He felt himself falling for what seemed like a long time, falling as softly as a drop of rain on velvet.

When the golfers ran up and saw Roy facedown in the sand trap, they thought he was dead. Roy heard their frantic cries but he didn't move. The sugar-white sand felt cool against his burning cheeks, and he was very sleepy.

The 'cowgirl' jab – well, that was my own fault, he thought. He'd told the kids at school he was from Montana, cattle country, when in fact he'd been born in Detroit, Michigan. Roy's mother and father had moved away from Detroit when he was only a baby, so it seemed silly to call it his hometown. In Roy's mind, he didn't really have a hometown; his family had never stayed anywhere long enough for Roy to feel settled.

Of all the places the Eberhardts had lived, Roy's favourite was Bozeman, Montana. The snaggle-peaked mountains, the braided green rivers, the sky so blue it seemed like a painting – Roy had never imagined anywhere so beautiful. The Eberhardts stayed two years, seven months and eleven days; Roy wanted to stay for ever.

On the night his father announced they'd be moving to Florida, Roy locked himself in his bedroom and cried. His mother caught him climbing out the window with his snowboard and a plastic tackle box in which he had packed underwear, socks, a fleece ski jacket, and a $100 savings bond his grandfather had given him as a birthday present.

His mother assured Roy that he would love Florida. Everybody in America wants to move there, she'd said, it's so sunny and gorgeous. Then Roy's father had poked his head in the door and said, with somewhat forced enthusiasm: 'And don't forget Disney World.'

'Disney World is an armpit,' Roy had stated flatly, 'compared to Montana. I want to stay here.'

As usual, he was outvoted.

So when the homeroom teacher at Trace Middle asked the new kid where he was from, he stood up and proudly said Bozeman, Montana. It was the same answer he gave on the school bus when Dana Matherson accosted him on his first day, and from then on Roy was 'Tex' or 'cowgirl' or 'Roy Rogers-hardt.'

It was his own fault for not saying Detroit.

'Why did you punch Mr Matherson?' asked Viola Hennepin. She was the vice-principal of Trace Middle, and it was in her dim office cubicle that Roy now sat, awaiting justice.

'Because he was choking me to death.'

'That's not Mr Matherson's version of events, Mr

Eberhardt.' Miss Hennepin's face had extremely pointy features. She was tall and bony, and wore a perpetually severe expression. 'He says your attack was unprovoked.'

'Right,' said Roy. 'I always pick the biggest, meanest kid on the bus and punch him in the face, just for fun.'

'We don't appreciate sarcasm here at Trace Middle,' said Miss Hennepin. 'Are you aware that you broke his nose? Don't be surprised if your parents get a hospital bill in the mail.'

Roy said, 'The dumb jerk almost strangled me.'

'Really? Your bus driver, Mr Kesey, said he didn't see a thing.'

'It's possible he was actually watching the road,' Roy said.

Miss Hennepin smiled thinly. 'You've got quite the snippy attitude, Mr Eberhardt. What do you think ought to be done with a violent boy like you?'

'Matherson is the menace! He hassles all the smaller kids on the bus.'

'Nobody else has complained.'

'Because they're scared of him,' Roy said. Which was also why none of the other kids had backed up his story. Nobody wanted to nark on Dana and have to face him the next day on the bus.

'If you did nothing wrong, then why'd you run away?' Miss Hennepin asked.

Roy noticed a single jet-black hair sprouting above her upper lip. He wondered why Miss Hennepin hadn't removed the hair – was it possible that she was letting it grow?

'Mr Eberhardt, I asked you a question.'

'I ran because I'm scared of him, too,' Roy replied.

'Or perhaps you were scared of what would happen to you when the incident was reported.'

'That's totally not true.'

'Under the rules,' said Miss Hennepin, 'you could be suspended from school.'

'He was choking me. What else was I supposed to do?'

'Stand up, please.'

Roy did what he was told.

'Step closer,' Miss Hennepin said. 'How does your head feel? Is this where the golf ball hit you?' She touched the tender purple lump above his ear.

'Yes, ma'am.'

'You're a lucky young man. It could've been worse.'

He felt Miss Hennepin's bony fingers turn down the collar of his shirt. Her chilly grey eyes narrowed and her waxy lips pursed in consternation.

'Hmm,' she said, peering like a buzzard.

'What is it?' Roy backed out of her reach.

The vice-principal cleared her throat and said, 'That knot on your head tells me you've learned your lesson the hard way. Am I right?'

Roy nodded. There was no use trying to reason with a person who was cultivating one long oily hair on her lip. Miss Hennepin gave Roy the creeps.

'Therefore, I've decided not to suspend you from school,' she said, tapping a pencil on her chin. 'I am, however, going to suspend you from the bus.'

'Really?' Roy almost burst out laughing. What a fantastic punishment; no bus ride, no Dana!

'For two weeks,' Miss Hennepin said.

Roy tried to look bummed. 'Two whole weeks?'

'In addition, I want you to write a letter of apology to Mr Matherson. A *sincere* letter.'

'OK,' said Roy, 'but who's going to help him read it?'

Miss Hennepin clicked her pointy yellow teeth. 'Don't press your luck, Mr Eberhardt.'

'No, ma'am.'

As soon as he left the office, Roy hurried to the boys' bathroom. He climbed up on one of the sinks that had a mirror and pulled down his shirt collar to see what Miss Hennepin had been staring at.

Roy grinned. Plainly visible on each side of his Adam's apple were four finger-sized bruises. He swivelled around on the rim of the sink and, craning over his shoulder, spotted two matching thumb marks on the nape of his neck.

Thank you, dumb-butt Dana, he thought. Now Miss Hennepin knows I'm telling the truth.

Well, *most* of the truth.

Roy had left out the part about the strange running boy. He wasn't sure why, but it seemed like the sort of thing you didn't tell a vice-principal unless you absolutely had to.

He had missed his morning classes and most of lunch hour. He hurried through the cafeteria line and found an empty table. Sitting with his back to the doors, he wolfed down a chilli burger and a carton of lukewarm milk. Dessert was an overbaked chocolate chip cookie the size of a hockey puck and just about as tasty.

'Gross,' he muttered. The inedible cookie made a thud when it landed on the plate. Roy picked up his tray and rose to leave. He jumped when a hand landed forcefully on his shoulder. He was afraid to look – what if it was Dana Matherson?

The perfect ending, Roy thought gloomily, to a perfectly terrible day.

'Sit down,' said a voice behind him, definitely not Dana's.

Roy brushed the hand off his shoulder and turned. Standing there, arms folded, was the tall blonde girl with the red-framed eyeglasses – the one he'd encountered on the school bus. The girl looked extremely unhappy.

'You nearly knocked me down this morning,' she said.

'Sorry.'

'Why were you running?'

'No reason.' Roy tried to get past her, but this time she sidestepped in front of him, blocking his path.

'You could've really hurt me,' she said.

Roy felt uncomfortable being confronted by a girl. It wasn't a scene you wanted the other boys to see, for sure. Worse, Roy was truly intimidated. The curly-haired girl was taller than he was, with wide shoulders and tanned muscular legs. She looked like an athlete – soccer, prob- ably, or volleyball.

He said, 'See, I punched a kid in the nose—'

'Oh, I heard all about it,' the girl said snidely, 'but that's not why you ran off, was it?'

'Sure it was.' Roy wondered if she was going to accuse him of something else, like stealing the lunch money out of her backpack.

'You're lying.' The girl boldly seized the other side of his lunch tray, to prevent him from leaving.

'Let go,' Roy said sharply. 'I'm late.'

'Take it easy. There's six minutes to the bell, cowgirl.' She looked as if she wouldn't mind socking him in the stomach. 'Now tell the truth. You were chasing somebody, weren't you?'

Roy felt relieved that he wasn't being blamed for a serious crime. 'Did you see him, too? That kid with no shoes?'

Still gripping Roy's tray, the girl took a step forward, backing Roy up.

'I got some advice for you,' she said, lowering her voice.

Roy glanced around anxiously. They were the only ones left in the cafeteria.

'You listening?' The girl shoved him once more.

'Yeah.'

'Good.' She didn't stop pushing until she had Roy pinned to the wall with his lunch tray. Glaring balefully over the top of her red-framed eyeglasses, she said, 'From now on, mind your own damn business.'

Roy was scared, he had to admit. The edge of the tray was digging into his rib cage. This girl was a bruiser.

'You saw that kid, too, didn't you?' he whispered.

'I don't know what you're talkin' about. Mind your own business, if you know what's good for you.'

She let go of Roy's tray and spun on her heels.

'Wait!' Roy called after her. 'Who is he?'

But the curly-haired girl didn't answer or even look back. Stalking off, she simply raised her right arm and reproachfully wagged a forefinger in the air.

THREE

Officer Delinko shielded his eyes against the noon glare.

'Took you long enough,' said Curly, the construction foreman.

'There was a four-car pile-up north of town,' the police officer explained, 'with injuries.'

Curly huffed. 'Whatever. Anyways, you can see what they done.'

Again the trespassers had methodically removed every survey marker and filled in the stake holes. Officer Delinko wasn't the sharpest knife in the drawer, but he was beginning to suspect that this wasn't the random work of juvenile pranksters. Perhaps somebody had a grudge against Mother Paula and her world-famous pancakes.

'This time you got a actual vandalism to report,' Curly said pointedly. 'This time they messed up some private property.'

He led Officer Delinko to the south-west corner of the site, where a flatbed truck was parked. All four tyres were flat.

Curly raised the palms of his hands and said, 'There you go. Each a them tyres is worth a hundred and fifty bucks.'

'What happened?' the policeman asked.

'The sidewalls was slashed.' Curly's shiny head bobbed in indignation.

Officer Delinko knelt down and studied the truck's tyres.

He couldn't see any knife marks in the rubber.

'I think somebody just let the air out,' he said.

Curly muttered a reply that was difficult to hear.

'I'll make a report, anyway,' the policeman promised.

'How about this?' Curly said. 'How about you put some extra patrols around here?'

'I'll speak to my sergeant.'

'You do that,' Curly grumbled. 'I got some people I can speak to myself. This is gettin' ridiculous.'

'Yes, sir.' Officer Delinko noticed that three portable latrines were strapped on the back of the flatbed truck. He caught himself smiling at the name painted on the blue doors: TRAVELLIN' JOHNNY.

'For the construction crew,' Curly explained, 'for when we get this project started. *If* we ever get started.'

'Did you check 'em out?' asked the policeman.

Curly frowned. 'The johns? What for?'

'You never know.'

'Nobody in their right mind's gonna fool around with a toilet.' The foreman snorted.

'Can I have a look?' Officer Delinko asked.

'Be my guest.'

The policeman climbed up on the bed of the truck. From the outside, the portable latrines appeared untouched. The cargo straps were cinched tight, and the doors to all three units were closed. Officer Delinko opened one and peeked his head inside. The stall smelled heavily of disinfectant.

'Well?' Curly called up to him.

'A-OK,' said the policeman.

'Truth is, there ain't much to wreck on a port-a-potty.'

'I suppose not.' Officer Delinko was about to shut the door when he heard a muffled noise – was it a splash? The policeman stared uneasily at the blackness beneath the plastic seat. Ten seconds passed; then he heard it again.

Definitely a splash.

'What're you doin' up there?' Curly demanded.

'Listening,' replied Officer Delinko.

'Listenin' to *what*?'

Officer Delinko unclipped the flashlight from his belt. Edging forward, he aimed the light down the toilet hole.

Curly heard a cry and watched in surprise as the policeman burst from the doorway of the latrine, leaping off the flatbed like an Olympic hurdler.

What now? the foreman wondered unhappily.

Officer Delinko picked himself off the ground and smoothed the front of his uniform. He retrieved his flashlight and tested it to make sure the bulb wasn't broken.

Curly handed him his hat, which had come to rest near an owl burrow. 'So. Let's hear it,' the foreman said.

The policeman nodded grimly. 'Alligators,' he declared.

'You're kiddin' me.'

'I wish I was,' said Officer Delinko. 'They put alligators in your potties, sir. Real live alligators.'

'More than one?'

'Yes, sir.'

Curly was flabbergasted. 'Are they... big 'gators?'

Officer Delinko shrugged, nodding toward the Travellin'

Johnnys. 'I imagine all of 'em look big,' he said, 'when they're swimming under your butt.'

Miss Hennepin had notified Roy's mother, so he had to repeat the story when he got home from school, and once more when his father returned from work.

'Why was this young man choking you? You didn't do something to provoke him, did you?' asked Mr Eberhardt.

'Roy says he picks on everybody,' Mrs Eberhardt said. 'But even so, fighting is never the right thing.'

'It wasn't a fight,' Roy insisted. 'I only punched him to make him let go. Then I got off the bus and ran.'

'And that's when you were struck by the golf ball?' his father asked, wincing at the thought.

'He ran a long, long way,' his mother said.

Roy sighed. 'I was scared.' He didn't like lying to his parents but he was too worn out to explain the real reason that he had run so far.

Mr Eberhardt examined the bruise over his son's ear. 'You took a nasty shot here. Maybe Dr Shulman ought to have a look.'

'No, Dad, I'm OK.' The paramedics had checked him out on the golf course, and the school nurse at Trace Middle had spent forty-five minutes 'observing' him for signs of a possible concussion.

'He seems to be fine,' agreed Roy's mother. 'The other young man, however, has a broken nose.'

'Oh?' Mr Eberhardt's eyebrows arched.

To Roy's surprise, his father didn't seem angry. And

while he wasn't exactly beaming at Roy, there was unmistakable affection – and possibly even pride – in his gaze. Roy thought it was a good opportunity to renew his plea for leniency.

'Dad, he was strangling me. What else could I do? What would *you* have done?' He pulled down his collar to display the bluish finger marks on his neck.

Mr Eberhardt's expression darkened. 'Liz, did you see this?' he asked Roy's mother, who nodded fretfully. 'Does the school know what that thug did to our son?'

'The vice-principal does,' Roy piped up. 'I showed her.'

'What did she do?'

'Suspended me from the bus for two weeks. Plus I have to write an apology—'

'What happened to the other boy? Wasn't he disciplined, too?'

'I don't know, Dad.'

'Because this is assault,' Mr Eberhardt said. 'You can't choke another person. It's against the law.'

'You mean, they could arrest him?' Roy didn't want to get Dana Matherson thrown in jail, because then Dana's mean and equally large friends might come after him. Being the new kid in school, Roy didn't need to be making those types of enemies.

His mother said, 'Roy, honey, they're not going to arrest him. But he needs to be taught a lesson. He could seriously hurt somebody, picking on smaller kids the way he does.'

Mr Eberhardt sat forward intently. 'What's the boy's name?'

Roy hesitated. He wasn't sure exactly what his father did for a living, but he was aware it had something to do with law enforcement. Occasionally, when talking to Roy's mother, Mr Eberhardt would refer to his working for the 'D.O.J.,' which Roy had deciphered as the United States Department of Justice.

As much as Roy disliked Dana Matherson, he didn't believe the kid was worthy of the US government's attention. Dana was just a big stupid bully; the world was full of them.

'Roy, please tell me,' his father pressed.

'The boy's name is Matherson,' Mrs Eberhardt chimed in. 'Dana Matherson.'

At first Roy was relieved that his father didn't write the name down, hoping it meant that he wasn't going to pursue the incident. Then Roy remembered that his father seemed to have a supernatural memory – for instance, he could still recite the batting averages of the entire starting line-up for the 1978 New York Yankees.

'Liz, you should call the school tomorrow,' Mr Eberhardt said to Mrs Eberhardt, 'and find out if – and how – this boy will be disciplined for attacking Roy.'

'First thing in the morning,' Mrs Eberhardt promised.

Roy groaned inwardly. It was his own fault that his parents were reacting so strongly. He should never have shown them the marks on his neck.

'Mom, Dad, I'll be fine. Honest I will. Can't we just let the whole thing drop?'

'Absolutely not,' his father said firmly.

'Your dad's right,' said Roy's mother. 'This is a serious matter. Now come to the kitchen and let's put some ice on your bump. Afterwards you can work on that apology letter.'

On one wall of Roy's bedroom was a poster from the Livingston rodeo that showed a cowboy riding a ferocious humpbacked bull. The cowboy held one hand high in the air, and his hat was flying off his head. Every night before turning off the lights, Roy would lie on his pillow and stare at the poster, imagining that he was the sinewy young bull rider in the picture. Eight or nine seconds was an eternity on top of an angry bull, but Roy imagined himself hanging on so tightly that the animal couldn't shake him no matter how furiously it tried. The seconds would tick by until finally the bull would sink to its knees in exhaustion. Then Roy would calmly climb off, waving to the roaring crowd. That's how he played the scene in his mind.

Maybe someday, Roy thought hopefully, his father would be transferred back to Montana. Then Roy could learn to ride bulls like a cowboy.

On the same wall of his bedroom was a yellow flyer handed out to drivers entering Yellowstone National Park. The flyer said:

```
┌ ━ ━ ━ ━ ━ ━ ━ ━ ━ ━ ━ ━ ┐

      WARNING!

   MANY VISITORS HAVE BEEN
      GORED BY BUFFALO.
  BUFFALO CAN WEIGH 2,000 POUNDS
    AND CAN SPRINT AT 30 MPH,
  THREE TIMES FASTER THAN YOU CAN RUN.


  THESE ANIMALS MAY APPEAR TAME BUT ARE
  WILD, UNPREDICTABLE AND DANGEROUS.

  DO NOT APPROACH BUFFALO!

└ ━ ━ ━ ━ ━ ━ ━ ━ ━ ━ ━ ━ ┘
```

At the bottom of the handout was a drawing of a tourist being tossed on the horns of a fuming bison. The tourist's camera was flying one way and his cap was flying another, just like the cowboy's hat in the rodeo poster.

Roy had saved the Yellowstone flyer because he was so amazed that anybody would be dumb enough to stroll up to a full-grown buffalo and snap its picture. Yet it happened every summer, and every summer some nitwit tourist got gored.

It was exactly the sort of idiotic stunt that Dana Matherson would try, Roy thought as he contemplated his apology letter. He could easily envision the big goon trying to hop on a bison, like it was a carousel pony.

Roy took a piece of lined notebook paper out of his English folder and wrote:

Dear Dana,

  I'm sorry I busted your nose. I hope the bleeding has stopped.

  I promise not to hit you ever again as long as you don't bother me on the school bus. I think that's a fair arangement.

                              Most sincerely,

                              Roy A. Eberhardt

He took the page downstairs and showed his mother, who frowned slightly. 'Honey, it seems a little too...well, forceful.'

'What do you mean, Mom?'

'It's not the content of the letter so much as the tone.'

She handed it to Roy's father, who read it and said, 'I think the tone is exactly right. But you'd better look up "arrangement" in the dictionary.'

The police captain slumped at his desk. This wasn't how he had planned to end his career. After twenty-two winters pounding the streets of Boston, he'd moved to Florida with the hope of five or six warm and uneventful years before retirement. Coconut Cove had sounded ideal. Yet it had turned out not to be the sleepy little village that the captain had envisioned. The place was growing like a weed – too much traffic, too many tourists, and, yes, even crime.

Not nasty big-city crime, but flaky Florida-style crime.

'How many?' he asked the sergeant.

The sergeant looked at Officer Delinko, who said, 'Total of six.'

'Two in each toilet?'

'Yes, sir.'

'How big?'

'The largest was four feet even. The smallest was thirty-one inches,' replied Officer Delinko, reading matter-of-factly from his report.

'Real alligators,' the captain said.

'That's right, sir.'

Officer Delinko's sergeant spoke up: 'They're gone now, Captain, don't worry. A reptile wrangler came and got 'em out of the johns.' With a chuckle he added, 'The little one almost took the guy's thumb off.'

The captain said, 'What's a "reptile wrangler"? Aw, never mind.'

'Believe it or not, we found him in the Yellow Pages.'

'Figures,' the captain muttered.

Normally an officer of his rank wouldn't get involved in such a silly case, but the company building the pancake franchise had some clout with local politicians. One of Mother Paula's big shots had called Councilman Grandy, who immediately chewed out the police chief, who quickly sent word down the ranks to the captain, who swiftly called for the sergeant, who instantly summoned (last and least) Officer Delinko.

'What the heck's going on out there?' the captain demanded. 'Why would kids single out this one construction site to vandalize?'

'Two reasons,' said the sergeant, 'boredom and convenience. I'll bet you five bucks it's juvies who live in the neighbourhood.'

The captain eyed Officer Delinko. 'What do you think?'

'It seems too organized to be kids – pulling out every stake, not just once but twice. Think about what happened today. How many kids do you know who could handle a four-foot 'gator?' Officer Delinko said. 'Seems awful risky, for a practical joke.'

Delinko is no Sherlock Holmes, thought the police captain, but he's got a point. 'Well, then, let's hear your theory,' he said to the patrolman.

'Yes, sir. Here's what I think,' Officer Delinko said. 'I think somebody's got it in for Mother Paula. I think it's some kind of revenge deal.'

'Revenge,' repeated the captain, somewhat sceptically.

'That's right,' the patrolman said. 'Maybe it's a rival pancake house.'

The sergeant shifted uncomfortably in his chair. 'There is no other pancake house in Coconut Cove.'

'OK,' said Officer Delinko, rubbing his chin, 'so then, how about a disgruntled customer? Maybe someone who once had a bad breakfast at a Mother Paula's!'

The sergeant laughed. 'How can you mess up a flapjack?'

'I agree,' the captain said. He'd heard enough. 'Sergeant, I want you to send a patrol car by the construction site every hour.'

'Yes, sir.'

'Either you catch these vandals or you scare 'em away. It doesn't matter to me as long as the chief isn't getting any more phone calls from Councilman Bruce Grandy. Clear?'

As soon as they left the captain's office, Officer Delinko asked his sergeant if he could come in early to work the Mother Paula patrol.

'No way, David. The overtime budget's tapped out.'

'Oh, I don't want any overtime,' the patrolman said. All he wanted was to solve the mystery.

FOUR

Roy's mother made him stay home all weekend to make sure there was no delayed reaction to the golf-ball bonking. Though his head felt fine, he didn't sleep well either Saturday night or Sunday night.

On the way to school Monday morning, his mother asked what was bothering him. Roy said it was nothing, which wasn't true. He was worried about what would happen when Dana Matherson caught up with him.

But Dana was nowhere to be seen at Trace Middle.

'Called in sick,' Garrett reported. He claimed to have inside information, owing to his mother's high-ranking position as a guidance counsellor. 'Dude, what'd you do to that poor guy? I heard there was guts all over the bus.'

'That's not true.'

'I heard you pounded him so hard, his nose got knocked up to his forehead. I heard he'll need plastic surgery to put it back where it belongs.'

Roy rolled his eyes. 'Yeah, right.'

Garrett made a fart noise through his teeth. 'Hey, everybody in school is talkin' about this – talkin' about *you*, Eberhardt.'

'Great.'

They were standing in the hall after homeroom, waiting for the first-period bell.

Garrett said, 'Now they think you're a tough guy.'

'Who does? Why?' Roy didn't want to be thought of as tough. He didn't particularly want to be thought of at all. He just wanted to blend in quietly and not be noticed, like a bug on a riverbank.

'They think you're tough,' Garrett went on. 'Nobody's ever slugged a Matherson before.'

Apparently Dana had three older brothers, none of whom was remembered fondly at Trace Middle.

'What'd you put in your apology letter? "Dear Dana, I'm sorry I thumped you. Please don't break every bone in my body. Leave me one good arm so at least I can feed myself."'

'You're so funny,' Roy said dryly. The truth was, Garrett *was* pretty funny.

'What do you think that gorilla's gonna do next time he sees you?' he said to Roy. 'I was you, I'd start thinkin' about plastic surgery myself so that Dana wouldn't recognize me. Seriously, man.'

'Garrett, I need a favour.'

'What – a place to hide? Try the South Pole.'

The bell rang and streams of students filled the hall. Roy pulled Garrett aside. 'There's a tall girl with curly blonde hair, she wears red glasses—'

Garrett looked alarmed. 'Don't tell me.'

'Tell you what?'

'You got the hots for Beatrice Leep?'

'That's her name?' Roy figured it had been at least a hundred years since anyone had named their daughter Beatrice. No wonder she was such a sorehead.

'What do you know about her?' he asked Garrett.

'I know enough to stay out of her way. She's a major soc-cer jock,' Garrett said, 'with a major attitude. I can't believe you got the hots for her—'

'I don't even know her!' Roy protested. 'She's hacked off at me for some crazy reason, and I'm just trying to figure out why.'

Garrett groaned. 'First Dana Matherson, now Beatrice the Bear. You got a death wish, Tex?'

'Tell me about her. What's her story?'

'Not now. We're gonna be late for class.'

'Come on,' Roy said. 'Please.'

Garrett stepped closer, checking nervously over his shoulder. 'Here's all you need to know about Beatrice Leep,' he said in a whisper. 'Last year one of the star line-backers for Graham High snuck up from behind and slapped her on the bottom. This was at the Big Cypress Mall, broad daylight. Beatrice chased the guy down and heaved him into the fountain. Broke his collarbone in three places. Out for the season.'

'No way,' said Roy.

'Maybe you ought to think about Catholic school.'

Roy gave a hollow laugh. 'Too bad we're Methodists.'

'Then convert, dude,' Garrett said. 'Seriously.'

Officer David Delinko looked forward to getting up early to scout the construction site. It was a welcome break from his daily routine, which offered few opportunities for real surveillance. Usually that was left to the detectives.

Although Officer Delinko liked the town of Coconut Cove, he had become bored with his job, which mostly involved traffic enforcement. He had joined the police force because he wanted to solve crimes and arrest criminals. Yet, except for the occasional drunk driver, Officer Delinko rarely got to lock up anybody. The handcuffs clipped to his belt were as shiny and unscratched as the day he joined the force, almost two years earlier.

Vandalism and trespassing weren't big-time crimes, but Officer Delinko was intrigued by the continuing pattern of mischief at the future site of Mother Paula's All-American Pancake House. He had a hunch that the culprit (or culprits) intended something more serious than juvenile pranks.

Since the police chief was getting pressure to stop the incidents, Officer Delinko knew that catching the vandals would be a feather in his cap – and possibly the first step toward a promotion. His long-term career goal was to become a detective, and the Mother Paula case was a chance to show he had the right stuff.

On the first Monday after the alligator episode, Officer Delinko set his alarm clock for five a.m. He rolled out of bed, took a quick shower, toasted himself a bagel and headed out for the construction site.

It was still dark when he arrived. Three times he circled the block and saw nothing unusual. Except for a garbage truck, the streets were empty. The police radio was quiet as well; not much happened in Coconut Cove before dawn.

Or *after* dawn, for that matter, Officer Delinko mused.

He parked the squad car next to Leroy Branitt's work trailer and waited for the sun to rise. It promised to be a pretty morning; the sky looked clear, with a rim of pink in the east.

Officer Delinko wished he'd brought a thermos of coffee, because he wasn't accustomed to getting up so early. Once he caught himself sagging behind the steering wheel, so he slapped briskly at his cheeks in order to stay awake.

Peering through the fuzzy early-morning grey, Officer Delinko thought he saw movement in the open field ahead of him. He flicked on the squad car's headlights and there, on a grassy mound marked by a freshly planted survey stake, stood a pair of burrowing owls.

Curly hadn't been kidding. These were the dinkiest owls that Officer Delinko had ever seen – only eight or nine inches tall. They were dark brown with spotted wings, whitish throats, and piercing amber eyes. Officer Delinko wasn't a bird-watcher, but he was intrigued by the toy-sized owls. For several moments they stared at the car, their big eyes blinking uncertainly. Then they took off, chattering to each other as they swooped low over the scrub.

Hoping he hadn't scared the birds away from their nest, Officer Delinko turned off his headlights. He rubbed his heavy eyelids and propped his head against the inside of the car window. The glass felt cool against his skin. A mosquito buzzed around his nose, but he was too sleepy to swipe at it.

Soon he nodded off, and the next thing he heard was the radio crackle of the dispatcher's voice, routinely asking for his location. Officer Delinko fumbled for the microphone and recited the address of the construction site.

'Ten-four,' the dispatcher said, signing off.

Officer Delinko gradually roused himself. The squad car was hot but, oddly, it looked darker outside now than when he'd first arrived – so dark, in fact, that he couldn't see anything, not even the construction trailer.

In a fleeting moment of dread, Officer Delinko wondered if it was already the next night. Was it possible he'd accidentally slept through the whole day?

Just then, something smacked against the squad car – *pow!* Then came another smack, and another after that . . . a steady invisible pounding. Officer Delinko grabbed for his gun but it wouldn't come out of his holster – the seat belt was in the way.

As he struggled to unstrap himself, the car door flew open and a white blast of sunlight hit him in the face. He shielded his eyes and, remembering what they'd taught him at the academy, shouted, 'Police officer! Police officer!'

'Yeah? Could've fooled me.' It was Curly, the sullen construction foreman. 'Whatsa matter, didn't you hear me knockin'?'

Officer Delinko tried to gather his senses. 'Guess I fell asleep. Did something happen?'

Curly sighed. 'Get out and see for yourself.'

The patrolman emerged into the glaring daylight. 'Oh no,' he muttered.

'Oh yeah,' Curly said.

While Officer Delinko had been dozing, somebody had

sprayed all the windows of his squad car with black paint.

'What time is it?' he asked Curly.

'Nine-thirty.'

Officer Delinko let out an involuntary whimper. Nine-thirty! He touched his finger to the windshield – the paint was dry.

'My car,' he said despondently.

'Your car?' Curly bent down and scooped up an armful of dug-up survey stakes. 'Who cares about your stupid car?' he said.

Roy spent the morning with a knot in his stomach. Something had to be done, something decisive – he couldn't spend the rest of the school year hiding from Dana Matherson and Beatrice Leep.

Dana could be dealt with later, but Beatrice the Bear couldn't wait. At lunchtime Roy spotted her across the cafeteria. She was sitting with three other girls from the soccer team. They looked lanky and tough, though not as formidable as Beatrice.

Taking a deep breath, Roy walked over and sat at the same table. Beatrice glared in seething disbelief while her friends regarded him with amusement and kept eating.

'What is your problem?' Beatrice demanded. In one hand was a barbecued pork sandwich, suspended between the tray and her sneering mouth.

'I think *you're* the one with the problem.' Roy smiled, even though he was nervous. Beatrice's soccer friends were impressed. They set down their forks and waited to see what was coming next.

Roy ploughed ahead. 'Beatrice,' he began, 'I've got no idea why you're mad about what happened on the bus. You're not the one who got choked, and you're not the one who got punched in the nose. So I'm only going to say this once: If I did something to upset you, I'm sorry. It wasn't on purpose.'

Evidently no one had ever spoken to Beatrice so forthrightly, for she appeared to be in a state of shock. Her sandwich remained fixed in mid air, the barbecue sauce trickling down her fingers.

'How much do you weigh?' Roy asked, not unpleasantly.

'Wha-uh?' Beatrice stammered.

'Well, I weigh exactly ninety-four pounds,' Roy said, 'and I'll bet you're at least a hundred and five . . .'

One of Beatrice's friends giggled, and Beatrice shot her a scowl.

' . . . which means you could probably knock me around the cafeteria all day long. But it wouldn't prove a darn thing,' Roy said. 'Next time you've got a problem just tell me, and then we'll sit down and talk about it like civilized human beings. OK?'

'Civilized,' Beatrice repeated, gazing at Roy over the rims of her glasses. Roy's eyes flickered to her hand, which was now dripping fat glops of barbecue sauce. Soggy chunks of bun and meat were visible between clenched fingers – she had squeezed the sandwich so ferociously that it had disintegrated.

One of the soccer girls leaned close to Roy. 'Listen,

Mouth, you best get outta here while you can. This is *so* not cool.'

Roy stood up calmly. 'Beatrice, are we straight on this? If anything's bothering you, now's the time to tell me.'

Beatrice the Bear dropped the remains of her sandwich on the plate and wiped her hands with a wad of paper napkins. She didn't say a word.

'Whatever.' Roy made a point of smiling again. 'I'm glad we had this chance to get to know each other a little better.'

Then he walked to the other side of the cafeteria and sat down, alone, to eat his lunch.

Garrett snuck into his mother's office and copied the address off the master enrolment sheet. It cost Roy a buck.

Roy handed the piece of paper to his mother as they were riding home in the car. 'I need to stop here,' he told her.

Mrs Eberhardt glanced at the paper and said, 'All right, Roy. It's on our way.' She assumed the address belonged to one of Roy's friends, and that he was picking up a textbook or a homework assignment.

As they pulled into the driveway of the house, Roy said, 'This'll only take a minute. I'll be right back.'

Dana Matherson's mother answered the door. She looked a lot like her son, which was unfortunate.

'Dana home?' Roy asked.

'Who're you?'

'I go to school with him.'

Mrs Matherson grunted, turned around, and yelled Dana's name. Roy was glad that she didn't invite him inside. Soon he heard heavy footsteps, and Dana himself filled the doorway. He wore long blue pyjamas that would have fit a polar bear. A mound of thick gauze, crosshatched by shiny white tape, occupied the centre of his piggish face. Both eyes were badly swollen and ringed with purple bruising.

Roy stood speechless. It was hard to believe that one punch had done so much damage.

Dana glared down at him and, in a pinched nasal voice, said: 'I am *not* believin' this.'

'Don't worry. I just came to give you something.' Roy handed him the envelope containing the apology letter.

'What is it?' Dana asked suspiciously.

'Go ahead and open it.'

Dana's mother appeared behind him. 'Who is he?' she asked Dana. 'What's he want?'

'Never mind,' Dana mumbled.

Roy piped up: 'I'm the one your son tried to strangle the other day. I'm the one who slugged him.'

Dana's shoulders stiffened. His mother clucked in amusement. 'You gotta be kiddin'! This little twerp is the one who messed up your face?'

'I came to apologize. It's all in the letter.' Roy pointed at the envelope clutched in Dana's right hand.

'Lemme see.' Mrs Matherson reached over her son's shoulder, but he pulled away and crumpled the envelope in his fist.

'Get lost, cowgirl,' he snarled at Roy. 'Me and you will settle up when I get back to school.'

When Roy returned to the car, his mother asked: 'Why are those two people wrestling on the porch?'

'The one in the pyjamas is the kid who tried to choke me on the bus. The other one, that's his mother. They're fighting over my apology letter.'

'Oh.' Mrs Eberhardt thoughtfully watched the strange scene through the car window. 'I hope they don't hurt each other. They're both rather husky, aren't they?'

'Yes, they are. Can we go home now, Mom?'

FIVE

Roy zipped through his homework in an hour. When he came out of his room, he heard his mother talking to his father on the phone. She was saying that Trace Middle had decided not to take disciplinary action against Dana Matherson because of his injuries. Apparently the school didn't want to provoke Dana's parents, in case they were considering a lawsuit.

When Mrs Eberhardt began telling Mr Eberhardt about the wild tussle between Dana and his mother, Roy slipped out the back door. He wheeled his bicycle from the garage and rode off. Twenty minutes later, he arrived at Beatrice Leep's bus stop, and from there he easily retraced Friday's ill-fated foot chase.

When Roy got to the golf course, he locked his bike to the pipes of a water fountain and set off jogging down the same fairway where he'd gotten clobbered. It was late in the afternoon, steamy hot, and few golfers were out. Nonetheless, Roy ran with his head down and one arm upraised for deflection in case another errant ball came flying in his direction. He slowed only when he reached the stand of Australian pines into which the running boy had vanished.

The pine trees gave way to a tangled thicket of Brazilian peppers and dense ground scrub, which looked impenetrable. Roy scoured the fringes, looking for a trail or some human sign. He didn't have much time before it would get dark. Soon he gave up trying to locate an entry point and elbowed his way into the pepper trees, which scraped his arms and poked his cheeks. He shut his eyes and thrashed onward.

Gradually the branches thinned and the ground beneath him began to slope. He lost his balance and went sliding down a ditch that ran like a tunnel through the thicket.

There, in the shadows, the air was cool and earthy. Roy spotted a series of charred rocks encircling a layer of ashes: a campfire. He knelt by the small pit and studied the packed dirt around it. He counted half a dozen identical impressions, all made by the same set of bare feet. Roy placed his own shoe beside one of the prints and wasn't surprised to see they were about the same size.

On a whim he called out, 'Hello? You there?'

No answer.

Slowly Roy worked his way along the ditch, hunting for more clues. Concealed beneath a mat of vines he found three plastic garbage bags, each tied at the neck. Inside the first bag was common everyday trash – soda bottles, soup cans, potato chip wrappers, apple cores. The second bag held a stack of boys' clothing, neatly folded T-shirts, blue jeans, and underpants.

But no socks or shoes, Roy observed.

Unlike the other bags, the third one wasn't full. Roy loosened the knot and peeked, but he couldn't see what was inside. Whatever it was felt bulky.

Without thinking, he turned the bag over and dumped the contents on the ground. A pile of thick brown ropes fell out.

Then the ropes began to move.

'Uh-oh,' Roy said.

Snakes – and not just any old snakes.

They had broad triangular heads, like the prairie rattlers back in Montana, but their bodies were muck-coloured and ominously plump. Roy recognized the snakes as cottonmouth moccasins, highly poisonous. They carried no rattles to warn in advance of a strike, but Roy saw that the tips of their stubby tails had been dipped in blue and silver sparkles, the kind used in art projects. It was a most peculiar touch.

Roy struggled to remain motionless while the fat reptiles untangled themselves at his feet. Tongues flicking, some of the moccasins extended to their full lengths while others coiled sluggishly. Roy counted nine in all.

This isn't good, he thought.

He almost leaped out of his sneakers when a voice spoke out from the thicket behind him.

'Don't move!' the voice commanded.

'I wasn't planning to,' Roy said. 'Honest.'

When he lived in Montana, Roy once hiked up Pine Creek Trail into the Absaroka Range, which overlooks Paradise Valley and the Yellowstone River.

It was a school field trip, with four teachers and about thirty kids. Roy had purposely dropped to the rear of the line, and when the others weren't looking, he peeled away from the group. Abandoning the well-worn path, he angled back and forth up the side of a wooded ridge. His plan was to cross over the top and quietly sneak down ahead of the school hikers. He thought it would be funny if they trudged into the campsite and found him napping by the creek.

Hurriedly Roy made his way through a forest of towering lodgepole pines. The slope was littered with brittle dead logs and broken branches, the debris of many cold, windy winters. Roy stepped gingerly to avoid making noise, for he didn't want the hikers down below to hear him climbing.

As it turned out, Roy was too quiet. He walked into a clearing and found himself facing a large grizzly bear with two cubs. It was impossible to say who was more startled.

Roy had always wanted to see a grizzly in the wild, but his buddies at school told him to dream on. Maybe in Yellowstone Park, they said, but not up here. Most grownups spent their whole lives out west without ever laying eyes on one.

Yet there was Roy, and a hundred feet across the glade were three serious bears – snorting, huffing, rising on their hind legs to scope him out.

Roy remembered that his mother had packed a canister of pepper spray in his backpack, but he also remembered what he'd read about bear encounters. The animals had poor eyesight, and the best thing for a human to do was remain perfectly still and silent.

So that's what Roy did.

The sow bear squinted and growled and sniffed for his scent on the wind. Then she made a sharp coughing noise, and her cubs obediently dashed off into the woods.

Roy swallowed hard, but he didn't move.

The mother bear rose to her full height, bared her yellow teeth, and faked a lunge toward him.

Inside, Roy was quaking with terror but on the outside he remained calm and motionless. The bear studied him closely. Her changing expression suggested to Roy that she'd figured out he was too meek and puny to pose a threat. After a few tense moments, she dropped to all fours and, with a final defiant snort, lumbered off to collect her cubs.

Still, Roy didn't move a muscle.

He didn't know how far the bears had gone, or whether they might come back to stalk him. For two hours and twenty-two minutes Roy remained as stationary as a plaster statue on that mountainside, until one of his teachers found him and led him safely back to the group.

So Roy was extremely good at not moving, especially when he was scared. He was plenty scared now, with nine venomous snakes crawling around his feet.

'Take a deep breath,' advised the voice behind him.

'I'm trying,' Roy said.

'OK, now step backwards real slow on the count of three.'

'Oh, I don't think so,' said Roy.

'One...'

'Now wait a second.'

'Two . . .'

'Please!' Roy begged.

'Three.'

'I can't!'

'Three,' the voice said again.

Roy's legs felt like rubber as he teetered backward. A hand seized his shirt and yanked him into the thicket of pepper trees. As Roy's butt landed in the dirt, a hood came down over his face and his arms were jerked behind his back. Before he could react, a rope was looped twice around his wrists and secured to the trunk of a tree. Roy could feel the smooth sticky bark when he wiggled his fingers.

'What's going on!' he demanded.

'You tell me.' The voice had moved in front of him. 'Who are you? Why're you here?'

'My name is Roy Eberhardt. I saw you run by the school bus the other day.'

'I don't know what you're talkin' about.'

'On two different days, actually,' Roy said. 'I saw you running and I got curious. You looked kind of . . . I don't know, wired.'

'Wasn't me.'

'Yeah, it was.' The snake wrangler was using a false husky tone – the voice of a boy trying to sound like a grown-up.

Roy said, 'Honest, I didn't come out here to hassle you. Take off this hood so we can see each other, OK?'

He could hear the boy's breathing. Then: 'You're gonna have to get outta here. Like right now.'

'But what about the snakes?'

'They're mine.'

'Yeah, but—'

'They won't go far. I'll catch 'em again later.'

Roy said, 'That's not what I meant.'

The boy laughed. 'Don't worry, I'll take you out the back way. Just do as I say and you won't get bit.'

'What a guy,' muttered Roy.

The boy untied him from the Brazilian pepper and boosted him to his feet. 'I gotta admit, you did pretty good,' the boy said. 'Most kids woulda peed their pants.'

'Are those cottonmouths?' Roy asked.

'Yep.' The boy sounded pleased that Roy knew what kind of snakes they were.

'Where I used to live, we had lots of rattlers,' Roy volunteered. He thought that if he could start a friendly conversation, the kid might change his mind and take the hood off Roy's face. 'I never heard of a cottonmouth with sparkles on its tail.'

'They're goin' to a party. Now start walkin'.' The boy grabbed Roy from behind and guided him forward. He had a strong grip. 'I'll tell you when to duck for branches,' he said.

The hood was either black or dark blue, and Roy couldn't see a speck of light through the heavy fabric. Blindly he stumbled and swayed through the thicket, but the barefoot boy kept him from falling. Roy knew they were out of the trees when the air got warmer and the ground beneath his feet got flat. He could smell the fertilized sod of the golf course.

Soon they stopped marching, and the kid began to loosen the knots on Roy's wrists. 'Don't turn around,' he said.

'What's your name?' Roy asked.

'I don't have a name no more.'

'Sure you do. Everybody's got a name.'

The kid grunted. 'I been called Mullet Fingers. And I been called worse.'

'You don't really live out here, do you?'

'None a your business. What'f I do?'

'All by yourself? What about your family?' Roy asked.

The boy rapped him lightly on the back of the head. 'You ask too many nosy questions.'

'Sorry.' Roy noticed his hands were free, but he continued to hold them behind his back.

'Don't turn around until you count to fifty,' the kid instructed him. 'Otherwise, you're gonna wake up one morning with one of those big ole cottonmouths in your bed. Got it?'

Roy nodded.

'Good. Now start countin'.'

'One, two, three, four...' Roy said aloud. When he reached fifty, he whipped the hood off his head and wheeled around. He was alone in the middle of the driving range, surrounded by acres of golf balls.

The barefoot boy was gone, again.

Roy ran all the way back to his bicycle and rode home as fast as he could. He wasn't frightened and he wasn't discouraged. He was more excited than ever.

SIX

At breakfast the next morning, Roy asked if it was against the law for a kid his age not to go to school.

His mother said, 'Well, I'm not sure if it's an actual *law* but—'

'Oh yes, it is,' his father cut in. 'Truancy is what it's called.'

'Can they put you in jail?' Roy asked.

'Usually they just put you back in school,' Mr Eberhardt said. Half-jokingly he added, 'You weren't thinking of dropping out, were you?'

Roy said no, school was all right.

'I bet I know what this is about,' Mrs Eberhardt said. 'You're worried about bumping into that Matherson boy again. See, didn't I tell you the apology letter was too assertive?'

'The letter was just fine,' Roy's father said, spreading open the newspaper.

'If it was "just fine", then why is Roy so scared? Why's he talking about dropping out of school?'

'I'm not scared,' Roy said, 'and I don't want to drop out of Trace Middle. It's just...'

His mother eyed him. 'What?'

'Nothing, Mom.'

Roy decided not to tell his parents about his encounter

with Mullet Fingers, the running boy. Being in law enforcement, Roy's father probably was required to report all crimes, even truancy. Roy didn't want to get the kid in trouble.

'Listen to this,' Mr Eberhardt said, and began reading aloud from the newspaper: ' "A Coconut Cove police cruiser was vandalized early Monday morning while parked at a construction site on East Oriole Avenue. The officer had fallen asleep inside the car at the time, according to a police spokesperson." Can you believe that?'

Roy's mother clucked. 'Sleeping on duty? That's disgraceful. They should fire that fellow.'

Roy thought the story was pretty amusing.

'It gets better,' his father said. 'Listen: "The incident happened shortly before sunrise, when an unknown prankster sneaked up to the patrol car, a 2001 Crown Victoria, and spray-painted the windows with black paint." '

Roy, who had a mouthful of raisin bran, burst out laughing. Milk dribbled down his chin.

Mr Eberhardt was also smiling as he continued: ' "Coconut Cove Police Chief Merle Deacon declined to release the name of the officer who fell asleep, saying that he is part of a special surveillance team investigating property crimes on the east side of town. Deacon said the officer has recently been ill with the flu and had been given medication that made him drowsy." '

Roy's father looked up from the article. 'Medication, ha!'

'What else does the story say?' Mrs Eberhardt asked.

'Let's see . . . It says this was the third suspicious

incident within a week at this location, which is the future home of a Mother Paula's All-American Pancake House.'

Roy's mother brightened. 'We're getting a Mother Paula's here in Coconut Cove? That'll be nice.'

Roy swabbed a napkin across his chin. 'Dad, what else happened out there?'

'I was wondering the same thing.' Mr Eberhardt skimmed the rest of the article. 'Here it is: "Last Monday, unknown intruders uprooted survey stakes from the property. Four days later, vandals entered the site and placed live alligators in three portable toilets. According to police, the reptiles were captured unharmed and later released into a nearby canal. No arrests have been made." '

Mrs Eberhardt rose and started clearing the breakfast dishes. 'Alligators!' she said. 'Good heavens, what next?'

Mr Eberhardt folded the paper and tossed it on the kitchen counter. 'This is turning out to be an interesting little town after all, isn't it, Roy?'

Roy picked up the newspaper to see for himself. East Oriole Avenue sounded familiar. As he read the story, Roy remembered where he'd seen that street sign. Beatrice Leep's bus stop, the place he had first spotted the running boy, was on *West* Oriole Avenue, just the other side of the main highway.

'The article doesn't say how big those 'gators were,' Roy remarked.

His father chuckled. 'I don't think it's important, son. I think it's the thought that counts.'

*

The police captain said, 'I've read your report, David. Is there anything else you'd like to add?'

Officer Delinko shook his head. His hands were folded on his lap. What could he say?

His sergeant spoke up: 'David understands how serious this is.'

' "Embarrassing" is the word,' the captain said. 'The chief has been sharing some of the emails and phone messages with me. It's not pretty. Did you see the newspaper?'

Officer Delinko nodded. He had read and reread the article a dozen times. Each time it made his stomach churn.

'You probably noticed that your name wasn't mentioned,' the captain said. 'That's because we refused to release it to the media.'

'Yes. Thank you,' Officer Delinko said. 'I'm very sorry about all this, sir.'

'And you read Chief Deacon's explanation for what happened? I assume you're comfortable with that.'

'To be honest, sir, I haven't had the flu. And I wasn't taking any medication yesterday—'

'David,' the sergeant cut in, 'if the chief says you were taking flu medicine, you were *definitely* taking flu medicine. And if the chief says that's why you fell asleep in your patrol car, then that's *exactly* what happened. Understand?'

'Oh. Yes, sir.'

The captain held up a yellow slip of paper. 'This is a bill from the Ford dealership for four hundred and ten bucks.

They got that black paint off your windows, that's the good news. Took 'em all day, but they did it.'

Officer Delinko was sure that the captain was going to hand him the repair bill, but he didn't. Instead he placed it inside the patrolman's personnel file, which lay open on his desk.

'Officer, I don't know what to do with you. I just don't.' The captain's tone was one of paternal disappointment.

'I'm very sorry. It won't happen again, sir.'

Officer Delinko's sergeant said, 'Captain, I ought to tell you that David volunteered for this surveillance duty at the construction site. And he went out early in the morning, on his own off-duty time.'

'His own time?' The captain folded his arms. 'Well, that's commendable. David, can I ask why you did that?'

'Because I wanted to catch the perpetrators,' Officer Delinko replied. 'I knew it was a priority with you and the chief.'

'That's the only reason? You didn't have some sort of personal stake in this case?'

I do now, thought Officer Delinko. Now that they've made a fool of me.

'No, sir,' he said.

The captain turned his attention toward the sergeant. 'Well, there's got to be some type of punishment, whether we like it or not. The chief's taking too much grief over this.'

'I agree,' the sergeant said.

Officer Delinko's heart sank. Any disciplinary action would automatically become part of his permanent record.

It might be an issue when it came time for a promotion.

'Sir, I'll pay that bill myself,' Officer Delinko offered. Four hundred and ten dollars was a serious chunk out of his pay-cheque, but keeping his record spotless was worth every penny.

The captain said it wasn't necessary for Officer Delinko to cover the bill – and that wouldn't satisfy the chief, anyway. 'So I'm putting you on desk duty,' he said, 'for a month.'

'David can live with that,' said the sergeant.

'But what about the Mother Paula's surveillance?' Officer Delinko asked.

'Don't worry, we'll get it covered. We'll pull somebody off the midnight shift.'

'Yes, sir.' Officer Delinko was depressed at the idea of being stuck behind a desk, doing nothing for a whole boring month. Still, it was better than being suspended. The only thing worse than sitting at headquarters would be sitting at home.

The captain stood up, which meant the meeting was over. He said, 'David, if anything like this ever happen again...'

'It won't. I promise.'

'Next time you're definitely going to see your name in the newspaper.'

'Yes, sir.'

'Under a headline that says: OFFICER TERMINATED. Is that clear?'

Officer Delinko cringed inwardly. 'I understand, sir,' he said quietly to the captain.

He wondered if the little jerks who'd sprayed his Crown Victoria realized how much trouble they were getting him into. My whole career is in jeopardy, Officer Delinko thought angrily, all because of some smart-ass juvenile delinquents. He was more determined than ever to catch them in the act.

In the hallway outside the captain's office, the sergeant told him, 'You can pick up your car at the motor pool. But remember, David, you're off road patrol. That means you're allowed to drive the unit home and back, but that's all.'

'Right,' said Officer Delinko. 'Home and back.'

He had already thought of a route that would take him directly past the corner of East Oriole and Woodbury, the future location of Mother Paula's All-American Pancake House.

Nobody said he couldn't leave his house extra early in the morning. Nobody said he couldn't take his sweet time getting to work.

Dana Matherson was absent from school again. Roy felt somewhat relieved, though not enough to relax. The longer Dana had to stay away so his nose could recover from Roy's punch, the nastier he would be when he finally returned to Trace Middle.

'You've still got time to blow town,' Garrett suggested helpfully.

'I'm not running away. Whatever happens just happens.'

Roy wasn't trying to act cool. He'd thought a lot about

the Dana situation. Another confrontation seemed inevitable, and part of him simply wanted to get it over with. He wasn't cocky, but he had a stubborn streak of pride. He had no intention of spending the rest of the year cowering in the restroom or sneaking through the halls just to avoid some dumb bully.

'I probably shouldn't tell you this,' said Garrett, 'but some of the kids are taking bets.'

'Great. They're betting on whether Dana's going to beat me up?'

'No, on how many *times* he's going to beat you up.'

'Nice,' Roy said.

Actually, two good things had come out of the altercation with Dana Matherson. The first was Roy successfully tailing the barefoot boy to the golf course. The second was Roy being booted off the bus for two weeks by the vice-principal.

It was nice having his mother pick him up at school. They got to chat in the car, and Roy arrived home twenty minutes earlier than usual.

The phone was ringing when they walked in the door. It was his mother's sister calling from California to chat. Roy seized the opportunity to retrieve a cardboard shoe box from his room and slip quietly out the back door of the house.

He was heading for the golf course again, with a slight detour. Instead of making a left on West Oriole, toward the bus stop, Roy rode his bicycle across the highway to East Oriole. He'd gone less than two blocks when he came upon a scrub-covered lot with a dented work trailer in one corner.

Parked beside the trailer was a blue pickup truck. Not far away sat three bulldozer-type vehicles and a row of portable toilets. Roy figured this had to be the same place where the police car got spray-painted and the alligators were hidden inside the latrines.

As soon as Roy stopped his bicycle, the door of the trailer flew open and a stocky bald man charged out. He wore stiff tan work pants and a tan shirt that had a name stitched to the breast. Roy was too far away to read it.

'What do you want?' the man snapped, his face flushed with anger. 'Hey, kid, I'm talking to you!'

Roy thought: What's *his* problem?

The man came toward him, pointing. 'What's in that box?' he yelled. 'What've you and your little buddies got planned for tonight, huh?'

Roy spun his bike around and started pedalling away. The guy was acting like a total psycho.

'That's right, and don't you come back!' the bald man hollered, shaking a fist. 'Next time there'll be guard dogs waiting for you. The meanest damn dogs you ever saw!'

Roy pedalled faster. He didn't turn around. The clouds were darkening, and he thought he felt a raindrop on one cheek. From the distance came a rumble of thunder.

Even after crossing the highway to West Oriole, Roy didn't slow his pace. By the time he made it to the golf course, a steady drizzle was coming down. He hopped off his bicycle and, shielding the shoe box with both arms, began to jog across the deserted greens and fairways.

Soon he reached the thicket of pepper trees where he'd encountered the boy called Mullet Fingers. Roy had mentally prepared himself to be blindfolded and tied up again – he'd even composed a short speech for the occasion. He was determined to persuade Mullet Fingers that he was someone to be trusted, that he hadn't come to interfere but rather to help, if Mullet Fingers needed it.

While working his way through the thicket, Roy grabbed a dead branch off the ground. It was heavy enough to make an impression on a cottonmouth moccasin, though he hoped that wouldn't be necessary.

When he got to the ditch, he saw no signs of the deadly sparkle-tailed snakes. The running boy's camp was gone – cleaned out. All the plastic bags had been removed, and the fire pit had been buried. Roy poked the tip of the dead branch through the loose dirt, but it yielded no clues. Glumly he checked for footprints and found not one.

Mullet Fingers had fled without a trace.

As Roy emerged on to the fairway, the purple sky opened up. Rain slashed down in wind-driven sheets that stung his face, and lightning crashed ominously nearby. Roy shivered and took off running. In an electrical storm, the worst place to be was on a golf course, standing near trees.

As he ran, flinching at every thunderclap, he began to feel guilty about sneaking away from the house. His mother would be worried sick once she realized he was out in this weather. She might even get in the car and come searching for him, a prospect that troubled Roy. He didn't want his mom driving around in such dangerous conditions; the rain was so heavy that she wouldn't be able to see the road very well.

As wet and weary as he was, Roy forced himself to run faster. Squinting through the downpour, he kept thinking: It can't be much farther.

He was looking for the water fountain where he'd left his bicycle. Finally, as another wild burst of lightning illuminated the fairway, he spotted it twenty yards ahead of him.

But his bicycle wasn't there.

At first Roy thought it was the wrong fountain. He thought he must have lost his direction in the storm. Then he recognized a nearby utility shed and a wooden kiosk with a soda machine.

This was the place, all right. Roy stood in the rain and stared miserably at the spot where he'd left his bike. Usually he was careful about locking it, but today he'd been in too much of a hurry.

Now it was missing. Stolen, undoubtedly.

To get away from the rain, Roy dashed into the wooden kiosk. The soggy cardboard box was coming apart in his hands. It would be a very long walk home, and Roy knew he couldn't get there before nightfall. His parents would be going bananas.

For ten minutes Roy stood in the kiosk, dripping on the floor, waiting for the downpour to slacken. The lightning and thunder seemed to be rolling eastward but the rain just wouldn't quit. Finally Roy stepped outside, lowered his head, and started trudging in the direction of his neighbourhood. Every step made a splash. Raindrops streaked down his forehead and clung to his eyelashes. He wished he'd worn a cap.

When he got to the sidewalk he tried to run but it was like sloshing through the shallows of an endless lake. Roy had noticed this about Florida: It was so low and flat that puddles took for ever to drain. He plodded onward and soon he reached the bus stop where he'd first spotted the running boy. Roy didn't pause to look around. It was growing darker by the minute.

Just as he made it to the corner of West Oriole and the highway, the streetlights flickered on.

Oh brother, he thought. I'm really late.

Traffic was steady in both directions, creeping through the standing water. Roy waited impatiently. Every car pushed a wake that splashed against his shins. He didn't care. He was already soaked to the bone.

Spying a gap in the traffic, Roy ventured into the road.

'Watch it!' shouted a voice behind him.

Roy jumped back on the curb and spun around. There was Beatrice Leep, sitting on his bicycle.

She said, 'What's in the shoe box, cowgirl?'

SEVEN

How it happened was no big mystery.

Like all students, Beatrice the Bear lived in the vicinity of her school bus stop. Roy likely had ridden right past her front door, and when Beatrice had spotted him, she'd simply tailed him to the golf course.

'That's my bike,' he said to her.

'Yeah, it is.'

'Can I have it back?'

'Maybe later,' she said. 'Hop on.'

'What?'

'The handlebars, you dork. Get on the handlebars. We're goin' for a ride.'

Roy did what he was told. He wanted to retrieve his bicycle and go home.

Two years of pushing up and down high hills in Montana's thin air had made Roy a powerful rider, but Beatrice Leep was stronger. Even through deep puddles she pedalled swiftly and effortlessly, as if Roy were weightless. Perched uncomfortably on the handlebars, he clutched the sodden cardboard box.

'Where are we going?' he shouted.

'Hush up,' Beatrice said.

She steamed past the fancy brick entrance to the golf course and soon the paved road gave way to a dirt rut, with no curbs or streetlights. Roy braced himself as the bike jounced through muddy potholes. The rain had softened to a mist, and his wet shirt felt cool against his skin.

Beatrice stopped when they came to a tall chain-link fence. Roy observed that a small section had been cut with wire clippers so that it could be pulled back. He got off the handlebars and tugged at his jeans, which had ridden up the crack of his butt.

Beatrice parked the bicycle and motioned for Roy to follow her through the hole in the fence. They entered a junkyard full of wrecked automobiles, acres of them. In the twilight Roy and Beatrice crept along, darting from one rusted hulk to the next. From the way Beatrice was acting, Roy assumed they weren't alone on the property.

Soon they came to an old panel truck propped up on cinderblocks. Roy could barely make out the faded red lettering on its battered awning: Jo-Jo's Ice Cream and Sno-Cones.

Beatrice Leep stepped up into the cab, pulling Roy behind her. She led him through a narrow doorway into the back, which was cluttered with crates, boxes, and heaps of clothes. Roy noticed a sleeping bag rolled up in a corner.

When Beatrice closed the door, they were in total darkness; Roy couldn't see his own fingers in front of his face.

He heard Beatrice's voice: 'Lemme have your box.'

'No,' Roy said.

'Eberhardt, are you fond of your front teeth?'

'I'm not afraid of you,' Roy lied.

It was stuffy and humid inside the old ice-cream truck. Mosquitoes hummed in Roy's ears and he slapped at them blindly. He smelled something that seemed out of place, something oddly familiar – cookies? The truck smelled like freshly baked peanut-butter cookies, the kind Roy's mother made.

The piercing beam of a flashlight caught him squarely in the eyes, and he turned away.

'For the last time,' Beatrice said menacingly, 'what's in that shoe box?'

'Shoes,' said Roy.

'I'm so sure.'

'Honest.'

She snatched the box from his hands and flipped it open, aiming the flashlight at the contents.

'I told you,' Roy said.

Beatrice huffed. 'Why are you carryin' around an extra pair of sneakers? That's really weird, cowgirl.'

'The shoes aren't for me,' Roy said. They were almost brand-new; he'd only worn them a couple of times.

'Then who're they for?'

'Just a kid I met.'

'What kid?'

'The one I told you about at school. The one who went running by your bus stop that day.'

'Oh,' Beatrice said caustically, 'the one you went chasing when you shoulda been minding your own business.' She turned the flashlight off and everything went black again.

'Well, I finally met him. Sort of,' Roy said.

'You don't give up, do you?'

'Look, the kid needs shoes. He could step on broken glass or rusty nails...or even a cottonmouth.'

'How do you know he *wants* to wear shoes, Eberhardt? Maybe he can run faster without 'em.'

Roy wasn't sure what Beatrice Leep's problem was, but he knew he was seriously late for dinner and his parents were probably frantic. He planned to make a break as soon as Beatrice turned on the flashlight again. If he could somehow beat her to the bicycle, he might be able to get away.

'Whatever,' Roy said. 'If he doesn't want the shoes, I'll keep 'em myself. If he does, well, they ought to fit him. He looked about as tall as me.'

From the darkness, only silence.

'Beatrice, if you're going to beat me up, could you please hurry up and get it over with? My mom and dad are probably calling the National Guard right now.'

More heavy silence.

'Beatrice, you awake?'

'Eberhardt, why do you care about this kid?'

It was a good question, and Roy wasn't certain he could put the answer into words. There was something about the look on the boy's face when he went running past the school bus those days; something urgent and determined and unforgettable.

'I don't know,' Roy said to Beatrice Leep. 'I don't know why.'

The flashlight blinked on. Roy clambered for the door, but Beatrice calmly snatched him by the seat of his jeans and yanked him to the floor beside her.

Roy sat there panting, waiting to get clobbered.

Yet she didn't seem mad. 'What size are these?' she asked, holding up the sneakers.

'Nines,' said Roy.

'Hmm.'

In the cupped glow of light, Beatrice put a finger to her lips and pointed over her shoulder. Then Roy heard the footsteps outside.

Beatrice clicked off the light and they waited. The steps in the gravel sounded heavy and ponderous, like those of a large man. Something jangled as he moved; a set of keys, maybe, or loose coins in a pocket. Roy held his breath.

As the watchman approached the ice-cream truck, he whacked one of the fenders with what sounded like a lead pipe. Roy jumped but made no noise. Luckily, the man kept walking. Every so often he'd bang the pipe loudly on another junker, as if he were trying to scare something out of the shadows.

After the man was gone, Beatrice whispered: 'Rent-a-cop.'

'What are we doing here?' Roy asked weakly.

In the darkness of the compartment, he could hear Beatrice the Bear standing up. 'Tell you what I'm gonna do, cowgirl,' she said. 'I'll make you a little deal.'

'Go on,' said Roy.

'I'll see that the barefoot kid gets these shoes, but only

if you promise to leave him alone. No more spying.'

'So you *do* know him!'

Beatrice hoisted Roy to his feet.

'Yeah, I know him,' she said. 'He's my brother.'

At four-thirty in the afternoon, when Officer David Delinko normally got off work, his desk was still piled high with paperwork. He had lots of forms to fill out and reports to complete about what had happened to his patrol car. He kept writing until his wrist began to ache, and at six he finally called it quits.

The motor pool was only a few blocks away, but the rain was pouring down when Officer Delinko wearily came out of the headquarters building. He didn't want his uniform to get drenched, so he waited under the eaves, directly beneath the capital P in COCONUT COVE PUBLIC SAFETY DEPARTMENT.

Lots of cities had started referring to their police forces as 'public safety' departments, a phrase intended to promote a softer, friendlier image. Like most officers, David Delinko thought the name change was pointless. A cop was a cop, period. In an emergency, nobody ever yelled, 'Quick! Call the public safety department!'

'Call the police' is what they always shouted – and always would.

David Delinko was proud to be a policeman. His father had been a robbery detective in Cleveland, Ohio, and his older brother was a homicide detective in Fort Lauderdale – and a detective is what David Delinko fervidly wanted to be, someday.

That day, he realized sadly, was probably further in the future than ever, thanks to the vandals at the pancake-house construction site.

Officer Delinko was mulling his situation, watching the rain stream down, when a lightning bolt zapped a utility pole at the end of the street. Briskly he retreated into the lobby of the headquarters building, where the ceiling lights flickered twice and faded out.

'Aw, shoot,' Officer Delinko grumbled to himself. There was nothing to do but wait for the storm to pass.

He couldn't stop thinking about the bizarre incidents at the Mother Paula's property. First, somebody pulling the survey stakes; then dumping the alligators in the latrines; then spray-painting his squad car while he was asleep inside – this was the work of bold and defiant perpetrators.

Immature, certainly, but still bold.

In Officer Delinko's experience, kids weren't usually so persistent, or so daring. In typical cases of juvenile vandalism, the crimes could be traced to a group of youngsters, each trying to outdo the other for thrills.

But this wasn't a typical case, Officer Delinko thought. Possibly it was the work of just one person with a grudge – or a mission.

After a while, the squall began to subside and the thunderclouds scudded away from the centre of town. Officer Delinko covered his head with a newspaper and made a dash for the motor-pool yard. His hand-shined shoes were squirting water by the time he got there.

The Crown Victoria, looking as good as new, sat outside the locked gate. Officer Delinko had asked the garage chief to hide the car keys in the gas cap, but instead they were inserted into the ignition, visible to anyone strolling by. The garage chief believed nobody was loony enough to steal a marked police car.

Officer Delinko started up the car and headed for his apartment. Along the way he made a slow loop around the pancake-house property, but there wasn't a soul to be seen. He wasn't surprised. Criminals disliked lousy weather as much as law-abiding citizens did.

Even when off-duty, Officer Delinko always kept the radio in his police cruiser turned on. That was one of the strict rules for those who were allowed to take their patrol vehicles home with them – you must keep your ears on, just in case a fellow officer needs help.

Tonight the dispatcher was reporting a couple of minor fender benders and a local boy who went missing on his bicycle during the electrical storm. Roy something-or-other. A burp of static on the radio made it hard to hear the boy's last name.

His parents must be pulling their hair out, Officer Delinko thought, but the kid's bound to turn up safe. He's probably just hanging out at one of the shopping malls, waiting for the thunder to stop.

Ten minutes later, Officer Delinko was still half-thinking about the missing boy when he spotted a slender, rain-soaked figure standing at the corner of West Oriole and the highway. It was a boy matching the description given out by the dispatcher: approximately five feet tall, ninety pounds, sandy brown hair.

Officer Delinko steered his car to the curb. He rolled down the window and called out across the intersection, 'Hey, young man!'

The boy waved and moved closer to the edge of the road. Officer Delinko noticed that he was walking a bicycle, and that the rear tyre appeared to be flat.

'Is your name Roy?' the policeman asked.

'That's me.'

'How about if I give you a lift?'

The kid crossed the street with his bike, which fit easily inside the spacious trunk of the Crown Victoria. Officer Delinko radioed the dispatcher to report that he'd located the missing youth and that everything was fine.

'Roy, your parents are going to be mighty happy to see you,' the patrolman said.

The boy smiled nervously. 'I sure hope you're right.'

Silently Officer Delinko congratulated himself. Not a bad way to end the shift for a guy stuck on desk duty! Maybe this would help get him out of the captain's doghouse.

Roy had never been in a police car before. He rode in the front seat next to the young officer, who did most of the talking. Roy tried to be polite and keep up his end of the conversation, but his mind was swirling with what Beatrice Leep had told him about the running boy.

'My stepbrother, actually,' she'd said.

'What's his name?'

'He got rid of it.'

'Why do they call him Mullet Fingers? Is he an Indian?' Back in Bozeman, Roy had gone to school with a boy named Charlie Three Crows.

Beatrice Leep had laughed. 'No, he's not an Indian! I call him Mullet Fingers 'cause he can catch mullet with his bare hands. You know how hard that is?'

A mullet was a slippery, free-jumping baitfish that travelled in schools of hundreds. The bay near Coconut Cove was full of them in the spring. Throwing a cast net was the customary method of capture.

'Why doesn't he live at home?' Roy had asked Beatrice.

'Long story. Plus, none of your business.'

'What about school?'

'My brother got shipped off to a "special" school. He lasted two whole days before he ran away. Then he hitchhiked back, all the way from Mobile, Alabama.'

'What about your parents?'

'They don't know he's here, and I'm not gonna tell 'em. *Nobody* is gonna tell. You understand?'

Roy had solemnly given his word.

After they'd sneaked out of the auto junkyard, Beatrice Leep had given Roy a peanut-butter cookie, which he gobbled hungrily. Considering the circumstances, it was the best-tasting cookie he'd ever eaten.

Beatrice had asked how he planned to explain his whereabouts to his mother and father, and Roy had admitted he hadn't figured that part out yet.

Then Beatrice had performed an astounding feat – she'd lifted his bicycle by the sprockets and chomped a hole in the rear tyre, like she was biting into a pizza.

Roy could only gape in amazement. The girl had jaws like a wolverine. 'There! Now you've got a flat,' she'd said, 'and a halfway decent excuse for missing dinner.'

'Thanks. I guess.'

'So what're you waiting for? Get outta here.'

What a weird family, Roy thought. He was replaying the tyre-biting scene in his mind when he heard the policeman say, 'Can I ask you something, young man?'

'Sure.'

'You go to Trace Middle, right? I was wondering if you've heard any talk at school about stuff that's been happening out where the new pancake house is supposed to go up.'

'No,' Roy said, 'but I saw an article in the newspaper.'

The officer shifted uneasily.

'About the alligators,' Roy added, 'and the police car getting spray-painted.'

The officer paused for a brief coughing spell. Then he said, 'You sure nobody's been talking about it? Sometimes the kids who pull these sorts of pranks like to brag on themselves.'

Roy said he hadn't heard a word. 'This is my street,' he said, pointing. 'We're the sixth house on the left.'

The policeman wheeled into the Eberhardts' driveway and braked to a stop. 'Roy, could I ask you a favour? Could you call me if you *do* hear something – anything, even a rumour – about the Mother Paula's situation? It's very important.'

The officer handed Roy a printed card. 'That's the office line, and that's my cellular.'

Above the phone numbers, the card said:

OFFICER DAVID DELINKO
Patrol Division
COCONUT COVE PUBLIC SAFETY DEPARTMENT

'You can call me anytime,' advised Officer Delinko. 'Just keep your eyes and your ears open, OK?'

'Right,' Roy said, not too eagerly. The policeman was asking him to be an informant: a snitch on his own classmates. It seemed like a steep price to pay for a ride home.

Not that Roy wasn't appreciative, but he didn't feel like he owed the officer anything besides a sincere thank you. Wasn't it part of a policeman's job to help people?

Roy got out of the car and waved to his parents, who were standing on the front steps. Officer Delinko removed Roy's bicycle from the trunk and set it upright, on its kickstand. 'There you go,' he said.

'Thanks,' said Roy.

'They'll patch that tyre for you at the Exxon. Was it a nail that got you?'

'Something like that.'

Roy's father came up and thanked the policeman for bringing his son home. Roy overheard the two men exchanging law-enforcement chit-chat, so Roy figured his father had told the officer he worked for the Justice Department.

When Mr Eberhardt went to put Roy's bicycle in the garage, Officer Delinko lowered his voice and said, 'Hey, young man.'

What now? Roy thought.

'Think your dad would mind writing a letter to the police chief? Or even to my sergeant? No biggie, just a nice note about what happened tonight. Something they could put in my permanent file,' Officer Delinko said. 'The little things help, they really do. They add up.'

Roy nodded in a noncommittal way. 'I'll ask him.'

'Terrific. You're a solid young fellow.'

Officer Delinko got back in his car. Mrs Eberhardt, who had gone inside to get a towel, came up and pumped the patrolman's hand. 'We were worried out of our minds. Thank you so much.'

'Oh, it was nothing.' Officer Delinko shot a wink at Roy.

'You've restored my faith in the police,' Roy's mother went on. 'Honestly, I didn't know what to think after reading that outrageous story in the paper. The one about that policeman who had his windows painted black!'

It was Roy's impression that Officer Delinko suddenly looked queasy. 'You all have a good night,' he told the Eberhardts, and turned the key in the ignition.

'Do you happen to know that fellow?' Roy's mother asked innocently. 'The one who fell asleep inside his car. What's going to happen to him? Will he be fired?'

With a screech of rubber, Officer Delinko backed out of the driveway and drove off.

'Maybe there was an emergency,' Mrs Eberhardt said, watching the patrol car's taillights disappear into the night.

'Yeah,' said Roy, smiling. 'Maybe so.'

EIGHT

Roy stuck to his promise. He quit searching for Beatrice Leep's stepbrother, though it required all the willpower he could muster.

One incentive to stay home was the weather. For three straight days it stormed. According to the television news, a tropical wave had stalled over southern Florida. Eight to twelve inches of precipitation was expected.

Even if the sun had been shining gloriously, Roy wasn't going anywhere. The guy at the gas station reported that the punctured bicycle tyre was beyond repair.

'You folks got a pet monkey?' he'd asked Roy's father. 'Because I swear it looks like teeth marks in the sidewall.'

Roy's parents didn't even ask Roy what had happened. Having lived in Montana, they were accustomed to dealing with flats. A new tyre had been ordered, but in the meantime Roy's bike sat idle in the garage. He spent the soggy afternoons working on homework projects and reading a cowboy novel. When he looked out the bedroom window, all he saw were puddles. He missed the mountains more than ever.

When Roy's mother picked him up after class on Thursday, she said she had some good news. 'Your suspension from the school bus has been lifted!'

Roy wasn't exactly ready to turn cartwheels. 'Why?

What happened?'

'I guess Miss Hennepin reconsidered the situation.'

'How come? Did you call her or something?'

'Actually, I've spoken to her a number of times,' his mother acknowledged. 'It was a fairness issue, honey. It wasn't right that you got suspended while nothing happened to the boy who started the fight.'

'It wasn't a fight, Mom.'

'Regardless. It looks like Miss Hennepin came around to our point of view. Starting tomorrow morning, you're back on the bus.'

Yippee, thought Roy. Thanks a bunch, Mom.

He suspected she had another motive for pestering the vice-principal – she was eager to resume her early-morning yoga sessions at the community college, which she couldn't attend as long as she was driving Roy to Trace Middle.

He didn't want to be selfish, though. He couldn't depend on his parents for ever. Maybe the other kids on the bus wouldn't make too big a deal out of his return.

'What's the matter, honey? I thought you'd be glad to get back on your regular routine.'

'I am, Mom.'

Tomorrow is as good a day as any, Roy thought. Might as well get it over with.

Leroy Branitt, the bald man who called himself Curly, was under too much pressure. His eyelids twitched from lack of sleep, and all day long he perspired like an Arkansas hog.

Supervising a construction job was a large responsibility, and every morning brought new obstacles and headaches. Thanks to the mystery intruders, the pancake-house project already was two weeks behind schedule. Delays cost money, and the big shots at the Mother Paula's corporation weren't happy.

Curly expected to be fired if anything else went wrong. He'd been told as much by a top-level executive of Mother Paula's. The man's job title was Vice-President for Corporate Relations, and his name was Chuck Muckle, which Curly thought would be more suitable for a circus clown.

Chuck Muckle wasn't a very jolly fellow, though, especially after seeing the newspaper article about the police car being spray-painted on Mother Paula's property. Among Chuck Muckle's responsibilities was keeping Mother Paula's valuable brand name out of the media, unless the company was opening a new franchise or introducing a new menu item (such as its sensational Key lime flapjacks).

In all his years of supervising construction, Curly had never gotten a phone call like the one he received from Chuck Muckle after the newspaper story appeared. He'd never before been chewed out for fifteen minutes nonstop by a company vice-president.

'Hey, it ain't *my* fault,' Curly had finally interjected. 'I ain't the one fell asleep on the job. It was the cop!'

Chuck Muckle instructed him to quit whining and take it like a man. 'You're the foreman, aren't you, Mr Branitt?'

'Yeah, but—'

'Well, you're going to be an unemployed foreman if anything like this happens again. Mother Paula's is a publicly traded company with a global reputation to protect. This is *not* the sort of attention that's beneficial to our image. Do you understand?'

'I do,' Curly had said, though he hadn't. Serious pancake eaters wouldn't care what happened to the police car, or even about the 'gators in the portable potties. By the time the restaurant opened, all that weird stuff would be forgotten.

However, Chuck Muckle had been in no mood for a reasonable discussion. 'Listen closely, Mr Branitt. This nonsense is going to stop. As soon as we hang up, you're going to go out and rent the biggest, most bloodthirsty attack dogs you can find. Rottweilers are the best, but Dobermanns'll do.'

'Yes, sir.'

'Is the site even cleared yet?'

'It's rainin',' Curly had said. 'It's supposed to keep on rainin' all week.' He figured Chuck Muckle would find a way to blame him for the weather, too.

'Unbelievable,' the vice-president grumbled. 'No more delays, you hear me? No more.'

The plan was to get the site cleared before bringing in the VIPs and the media for the official gala groundbreaking ceremony. The highlight was going to be a special appearance by the woman who portrayed Mother Paula in the advertisements and TV spots.

Her name was Kimberly Lou Dixon, a runner-up in the Miss America contest in either 1987 or 1988. Afterward she became an actress, though Curly couldn't recall seeing her anywhere except in the pancake-house commercials. They dressed her up in a calico apron, a grey wig, and granny glasses to make her look like an old lady.

'Let me explain why you'll be out of a job if this project gets stalled again,' Chuck Muckle said to Curly. 'Miss Dixon's window of availability is extremely limited. She's due to start filming a major motion picture in a couple of weeks.'

'No kiddin'. What's it called?' Curly and his wife were avid movie fans.

'*Mutant Invaders from Jupiter Seven*,' said Chuck Muckle. 'The problem is this, Mr Branitt: If the groundbreaking gets postponed, Miss Kimberly Lou Dixon won't be able to attend. She'll be on her way to Las Cruces, New Mexico, preparing for her role as Queen of the Mutant Grasshoppers.'

Wow, thought Curly. She's playing the queen!

'Without Miss Dixon's presence, we will no longer have a blockbuster event, publicity-wise. She's the company icon, Mr Branitt. She's our Aunt Jemima, our Betty Crocker, our—'

'Tony the Tiger?' said Curly.

'I'm glad you understand what's at stake here.'

'I sure do, Mr Muckle.'

'Excellent. If everything goes smoothly, you and I will

never need to speak to each other again. Won't that be nice?'

'Yes, sir,' Curly agreed.

The first order of business was erecting a chain-link fence around the construction site. Finding somebody to work in the rain wasn't easy, but Curly eventually hooked up with an outfit in Bonita Springs. Now the fence was finished, and it was only a matter of waiting for the guard-dog trainer to arrive.

Curly was somewhat nervous. He wasn't really a dog person. In fact, he and his wife had never owned a pet, unless you counted the stray cat that occasionally slept under the back porch. The cat didn't even have a name, which was fine with Curly. He had enough to worry about with the humans in his life.

At half-past four, a red truck with a camper top drove up to the trailer. Curly pulled a yellow poncho over his glistening head and stepped out into the endless drizzle.

The trainer was a beefy, moustached man who introduced himself as Kalo. He spoke with a foreign accent, the same accent that the German soldiers always had in World War II movies. Curly could hear the dogs barking ferociously in the camper bed, heaving themselves against the truck's tailgate.

Kalo said, 'You go home now, yah?'

Curly glanced at his wristwatch and nodded.

'I lock up za fence. I come back tomorrow early, to get za dogs.'

'Fine by me,' Curly said.

'Somezing happens, you call right vay. No touch za dogs,' Kalo warned. 'No talk to zem. No feed zem. Important, yah?'

'Oh yah.' Curly was more than happy to steer clear of the brutes. He backed his pickup off the lot and got out to close the gate.

Kalo waved amiably; then he turned the attack dogs loose. They were extremely large, all Rottweilers. They took off loping along the fence, crashing through the puddles. When they got to the gate, all four of them leapt upright against the fence, snarling and snapping at Curly on the other side.

Kalo ran up, shouting commands in German. Instantly the Rottweilers ceased barking and dropped to sitting positions, their black ears pricking up intently.

'Maybe best you go now,' Kalo said to Curly.

'They got names?'

'Oh yah. That vun dere is Max. That vun, Klaus. That vun, Karl. And that big vun is Pookie Face.'

'Pookie Face?' Curly said.

'Iss my precious baby. I brought him all za way from Munich.'

'They'll be OK in the rain?'

Kalo grinned. 'They be OK even in hurricane. You go home now, don't vorry. Za dogs, zey take care of your problem.'

As he walked back to his truck, Curly saw that the Rottweilers were watching every move he made. They were panting lightly, and their muzzles were flecked with foamy spittle.

Curly figured he finally might get a decent night's sleep. The vandals didn't stand a chance against five hundred-odd pounds of badass dog flesh.

They'd have to be insane to jump the fence, Curly thought. Totally out of their minds.

The next morning, Roy's mother offered to drop him at the bus on her way to yoga class. Roy said no thanks. The rain had finally let up, and he felt like walking.

A fresh breeze was blowing in off the bay, and the tangy salt air tasted good. Seagulls circled overhead, while two ospreys piped at each other in a nest on top of a concrete utility pole. On the ground at the base of the pole were bleached fragments of mullet skeletons that had been picked clean and discarded by the birds.

Roy paused to study the fish bones. Then he stepped back and peered up at the ospreys, whose heads were barely visible over the scraggle of the nest. He could tell that one was larger than the other; a mother, probably, teaching her fledgling how to hunt.

In Montana, ospreys lived in the cottonwoods all along the big rivers, where they dived on trout and whitefish. Roy had been pleasantly surprised to find that Florida had ospreys, too. It was remarkable that the same species of bird was able to thrive in two places so far apart, and so completely different.

If they can do it, Roy thought, maybe I can, too.

He hung around watching the nest for so long that he

almost missed the school bus. He had to jog the last block to get there before it pulled away, and he was the last to board.

The other kids grew strangely quiet as Roy made his way down the aisle. When he sat down, the girl in the window seat quickly stood up and moved to another row.

Roy got a bad feeling, but he didn't want to turn around to see if he was right. He hunkered down and pretended to read his comic book.

He heard kids whispering in the seat behind him, followed by a hasty gathering of books and backpacks. In a flash they were gone, and Roy sensed a larger presence, skulking.

'Hi, Dana,' he said, twisting slowly in his seat.

'Hey, cowgirl.'

After a week, Dana Matherson's nose was still slightly purple and puffy, though it definitely wasn't protruding from the centre of his forehead, as Garrett had claimed.

The only thing startling about Dana's appearance was a fat, scabrous upper lip that hadn't been that way when Roy dropped off the letter at Dana's front door. Roy wondered if Dana's mother had popped him in the kisser.

The new injury endowed the big oaf with a disconcerting lisp. 'You and me got thome bithneth to thettle, Eberhardt.'

'What "business"?' Roy said. 'I gave you an apology. That makes us even.'

Dana clamped a moist, ham-sized hand over Roy's face. 'We're a long way from even, you and me.'

Roy couldn't speak because his mouth was covered, not that he had much to say. He glared out from between Dana's pudgy fingers, which reeked of cigarettes.

'You're gonna be thorry you ever methed with me,' Dana growled. 'I'm gonna be your wortht nightmare.'

The school bus rolled to a sudden halt. Dana quickly let go of Roy's face and folded his hands primly, in case the driver was looking in the mirror. Three kids from Roy's grade got on the bus and, upon spotting Dana, wisely scrambled for seats up front.

As soon as the bus started moving, Dana again grabbed for Roy, who calmly slapped his arm away. Dana rocked back, staring at him in disbelief.

'Didn't you even read the letter?' Roy asked. 'Everything will be cool as long as you leave me alone.'

'Did you jutht hit me? Did you hit my arm?'

'So sue me,' Roy said.

Dana's eyes widened. 'What did you thay?'

'I thay you need to get your hearing checked, partner, along with your IQ.'

Roy wasn't sure what possessed him to wise off to such a violent kid. He didn't particularly enjoy getting roughed up, but the alternative was to cower and beg, which he couldn't lower himself to do.

Every time the Eberhardts moved from one town to another, Roy encountered a whole new set of bullies and goons. He considered himself an expert on the breed. If he stood his ground, they usually backed down or looked for someone else to hassle. Insulting them, however, could be risky.

Roy noticed a couple of Dana's meathead pals, watching the scene from the back of the bus. That meant Dana would feel obligated to demonstrate what a tough hombre he was.

'Hit me,' said Roy.

'What?'

'Go ahead. Get it out of your system.'

'You're a nut cathe, Eberhardt.'

'And you're as dumb as a bucket of mud, Matherson.'

That one did the trick. Dana lunged across the seat and whacked Roy on the side of the head.

After straightening himself, Roy said, 'There. Feel better now?'

'Damn right I do!' Dana exclaimed.

'Good.' Roy turned around and opened his comic book.

Dana smacked him again. Roy toppled sideways on the seat. Dana laughed cruelly and shouted something to his buddies.

Roy sat up right away. His head really hurt but he didn't want anyone to know. Nonchalantly he picked his comic book off the floor and placed it on his lap.

This time Dana hit him with the other hand, equally fat and damp. As Roy went down, he let out an involuntary cry, which was drowned by the loud, gaseous hissing of bus brakes.

For one hopeful moment, Roy thought the driver had seen what was happening and was pulling off the road to intervene. Unfortunately, that wasn't the case – the driver was as oblivious to Dana's bad behaviour as ever. The school bus had merely arrived at the next stop.

While another line of kids boarded, Dana composed himself as if he were a model citizen. Roy looked down, fixing his eyes on the comic book. He knew the assault would resume as soon as the bus got rolling, and he braced grimly for Dana's next blow.

But it never came.

For blocks and blocks Roy sat as rigid as a fence post, waiting to be knocked down once more. Finally his curiosity got the best of him and he peeked over his left shoulder.

Roy could hardly believe it. Dana was slumped sourly against the window. The dumb goon's fun had been spoiled by one of the kids from the last bus stop, who had been brave enough to sit right next to him.

'What are *you* staring at?' the newcomer snapped at Roy.

Despite his pounding headache, Roy had to smile.

'Hi, Beatrice,' he said.

NINE

School was nerve-wracking. Every time Roy entered one of his classrooms, the other kids stopped what they were doing and stared. It was as if they were surprised to see he was still alive, with all limbs intact.

After leaving algebra class, Roy heard a stupendous phoney farting noise behind him in the hallway – Garrett. He took Roy by the shirtsleeve and led him into a bathroom.

'You look sick. You should go home early,' Garrett advised.

'I feel fine,' Roy said, which wasn't true. He still had a headache from the thumping Dana had given him on the bus ride.

'Dude, listen to me,' Garrett said. 'I don't care how you *think* you feel. You're sick. Really sick, OK? You need to call your mom and go home.'

'What have you heard?'

'He'll be waiting after seventh period.'

'So let him wait,' Roy said.

Garrett tugged Roy into one of the toilet stalls and locked it from the inside.

'This is so lame,' said Roy.

Garrett touched a finger to his lips. 'I know a guy in Dana's PE class,' he whispered excitedly. 'He says Dana's 'gonna snatch you before you get on the bus home.'

'And do what?'

'Duh!'

'Right here at school? How?' Roy asked.

'Bro, I wouldn't hang around to find out. Hey, you never told me you busted him in the chops, too.'

'That wasn't me. Sorry.' Roy unlocked the toilet stall and gently nudged his friend out.

'So what are you going to do?' Garrett called over the top of the door.

'Take a pee.'

'No. I'm talking about you-know-who.'

'I'll think of something.'

But what? Even if Roy managed to elude Dana Matherson this afternoon, the drama would start all over again Monday. Dana would resume the stalking, and Roy would have to dream up another escape plan. And that's how it would be every single day until school let out in June.

Roy had other options, none particularly appealing. If he reported Dana to Miss Hennepin, she'd do nothing more than summon him to her office for a stern lecture, which Dana would laugh off. Who could take seriously a vice-principal with one gnarly hair sprouting out of her lip?

If Roy told his parents about the Dana situation, they might be alarmed enough to withdraw him from Trace Middle. Then he would end up getting bussed to some private school, where he'd be forced to wear the same dorky uniform every day and (according to Garrett) learn Latin.

A third alternative was for Roy to try apologizing to Dana again, this time oozing remorse and sincerity. Not only would that be grovelling, it probably wouldn't achieve the desired effect; Dana would still hassle him without mercy.

His final option was to stand and fight. Roy was a practical boy; he knew the odds were overwhelmingly against him. He had quickness and brains on his side, but Dana was big enough to crush him like a grape.

Roy remembered the time he and his father had a talk about fighting. 'It's important to stand up for what's right,' Mr Eberhardt had said, 'but sometimes there's a fine line between courage and stupidity.'

Roy suspected that fighting Dana Matherson fell into the second category.

While he disliked the prospect of getting beaten to a pulp, what worried him even more was the effect it would have on his mother. He was very conscious of being an only child, and he knew his mom would be devastated if something bad happened to him.

Roy had almost had a little sister, though he wasn't supposed to know about it. His mother carried the baby for five months, and then one night she got terribly sick and an ambulance rushed her to the hospital. When she came home a few days later, the baby wasn't there any more and nobody really explained why. Roy was only four years old at the time, and his parents were so upset that he was afraid to ask questions. A few years later, an older cousin told him what a miscarriage was, and confided that Roy's mother had lost a baby girl.

Ever since then, he'd tried not to give his parents extra reasons to worry about him. Whether on horseback, bike, or snowboard, he refrained from doing some of the wild, daredevil stunts that boys his age usually tried – not because he feared for his safety, but because he felt it was his solemn duty as an only child.

Yet there he was this morning, on the school bus, insulting the same pea-brained thug who already held a mortal grudge against him. Sometimes Roy didn't understand what came over him. Sometimes he was too proud for his own good.

The last class of the day was American history. After the bell, Roy waited for the other students to file out ahead of him. Then, cautiously, he peeked into the hall: No sign of Dana Matherson.

'Roy, is something wrong?'

It was Mr Ryan, the history teacher, standing behind him.

'No, everything's fine,' Roy said breezily, stepping out of the classroom. Mr Ryan closed the door behind them.

'You going home, too?' Roy asked.

'I wish. I've got to grade papers.'

Roy didn't know Mr Ryan very well, but he walked with him all the way to the faculty lounge. Roy made small talk and tried to act casual while constantly checking behind him, to see if Dana was lurking.

Mr Ryan had played football in college and since then

he hadn't gotten any smaller, so Roy felt fairly safe. It was almost as good as walking with his dad.

'You taking the bus home?' Mr Ryan asked.

'Sure,' Roy said.

'But isn't the pickup on the other side of school?'

'Oh, I'm just getting some exercise.'

When they reached the door of the faculty lounge, Mr Ryan said, 'Don't forget the quiz on Monday.'

'Right. War of 1812,' said Roy. 'I'm ready.'

'Yeah? Who won the Battle of Lake Erie?'

'Commodore Perry.'

'Which one, Matthew or Oliver?'

Roy took a guess. 'Matthew?'

Mr Ryan winked. 'Study a little more,' he said, 'but have a good weekend.'

Then Roy was alone in the hall. It was amazing how rapidly schools emptied after the final bell, as if someone pulled the plug under a giant whirlpool. Roy listened closely for footsteps – sneaking footsteps – but heard only the *tick-tick-tick* of the clock mounted above the door to the science lab.

Roy observed that he had exactly four minutes to reach the bus pickup zone. He wasn't worried, though, because he'd already mapped a shortcut through the gym. His plan was to be among the very last to board his bus. That way he could grab one of the empty seats up front and jump off quickly at his stop. Dana and his cronies customarily occupied the back rows and seldom bothered the kids sitting up near the driver.

Not that Mr Kesey would ever notice, Roy thought.

He jogged to the end of the hallway and turned right, heading for the double doors that marked the back entrance of the gymnasium. He almost made it, too.

'Let's be crystal-clear about this, Mr Branitt. You didn't report it to the police?'

'No, sir,' Curly said emphatically into the telephone.

'So there shouldn't be any paperwork, correct? No possible way for this latest travesty to end up in the press.'

'Not that I can figure, Mr Muckle.'

For Curly it had been another long, discouraging day. The sun had finally broken through the clouds, but after that it was all downhill. The construction site remained uncleared, the earthmoving equipment sitting idle.

Curly had stalled as long as possible before phoning Mother Paula's corporate headquarters.

'Is this your idea of a sick joke?' Chuck Muckle had snarled.

'It ain't no joke.'

'Tell me again, Mr Branitt. Every miserable detail.'

So Curly had repeated everything, beginning from when he'd arrived at the site early that morning. The first sign of trouble had been Kalo waving a tattered red umbrella and chasing his four attack dogs along the inside perimeter of the fence. He was shrieking hysterically in German.

Not wishing to be mauled by the dogs (or gored by the umbrella), Curly had remained outside the gate, watching in puzzlement. A Coconut Cove police cruiser had pulled up to investigate – Officer Delinko, the same cop who'd dozed off while 'guarding' the construction site. It was because of him that the spray-painting fiasco had made the newspaper and gotten Curly into hot water with the Mother Paula's company.

'I was on my way to the station when I saw the commotion,' Officer Delinko had said, raising his voice over the barking of the Rottweilers. 'What's wrong with those dogs?'

'Nuthin',' Curly had told him. 'It's just a training exercise.'

The cop had bought it and driven away, much to Curly's relief. Once the Rottweilers were secured on leashes, Kalo had hustled them into the camper truck and locked the tailgate. Furiously he'd turned toward Curly and jabbed the umbrella in mid air. 'You! You try und kill my dogs!'

The foreman had raised his palms. 'What're you talkin' about?'

Kalo had thrown open the gate and stomped up to Curly, who was wondering if he should pick up a rock for self-defence. Kalo was drenched with sweat, the veins in his neck bulging.

'Snakes!' He had spit out the word.

'What snakes?'

'Yah! You know vhat snakes! Za place iss crawling wis zem. Poison vuns!' Here Kalo had wiggled one of his pinky fingers. 'Poison snakes wis shiny tails.'

'No offence, but you're nutty as a fruitcake.' Curly never once had seen a snake on the Mother Paula's site, and he would have remembered if he had. Snakes gave him the willies.

'Nuts, you say?' Kalo had seized him under one arm and led him to the portable trailer that served as Curly's office. There, coiled comfortably on the second step, was a thick mottled specimen that Curly recognized as a cottonmouth water moccasin, common in southern Florida.

Kalo was right: It was seriously poisonous. And its tail was sparkly.

Curly had found himself backing up. 'I think you're gettin' carried away,' he'd said to Kalo.

'Yah? You zink?'

The dog trainer then had hauled him toward the fence to point out another moccasin, then another, and still another – nine in all. Curly had been flabbergasted.

'Vhat you zink now? Zink Kalo iss nutsy fruitbar?'

'I can't explain it,' Curly had admitted shakily. 'Maybe all this rain brought 'em outta the swamp.'

'Yah, shore.'

'Listen, I—'

'No, you lissen. Each of dogs iss vorth three thousand US dollars. Zat iss twelve thousand bucks barking here in za truck. Vhat happens, dog gets bit by snake? Dog dies, yah?'

'I didn't know about no snakes, I swear—'

'Iss miracle za dogs zey all OK. Pookie Face, za snake came after him zis close!' Kalo had indicated a distance of about a yard. 'I take umbrella und push him away.'

It was just about then that Kalo had accidentally

stepped in an owl burrow and twisted his ankle. Rejecting Curly's offer of assistance, the dog trainer had hopped on one leg back to the camper truck.

'I go now. Don't effer call me again,' he had fumed.

'Look, I said I was sorry. How much do I owe you?'

'Two bills I send. Vun for za dogs, vun for my leg.'

'Aw, come on.'

'OK, maybe not. Maybe I talk to lawyer instead.' Kalo's pale eyes had been gleaming. 'Maybe I cannot any longer train dogs, my leg hurt so much. Maybe I go on, vhat you say, disability!'

'For Pete's sake.'

'Mother Paula iss very big company. Has lots of money, yah?'

After Kalo had roared away, Curly carefully made his way to the trailer. The cottonmouth was no longer sunning on the steps, but Curly didn't take any chances. He set up a stepladder and hoisted himself through a window.

Fortunately, he'd saved the phone number of the reptile wrangler who had successfully removed the alligators from the toilets. The guy was tied up on an iguana call, but his secretary promised he'd come to the construction site as soon as possible.

Curly had holed up in the trailer for almost three hours, until the reptile wrangler pulled up to the gate. Armed only with a pillowcase and a modified five-iron, the guy had methodically scoured the pancake-house property in search of sparkle-tailed water moccasins.

Incredibly, he'd found none.

'That ain't possible!' Curly had exclaimed. 'They were all over the place this mornin'.'

The reptile wrangler had shrugged. 'Snakes can be unpredictable. Who knows where they went?'

'That's *not* what I want to hear.'

'You sure they were moccasins? I never saw one with a shiny tail.'

'Thanks for all your help,' Curly had said snidely, and slammed the trailer door.

Now it was he who was on the receiving end of peevish sarcasm. 'Maybe you can train the snakes to guard the property,' Chuck Muckle was saying, 'since the dogs didn't work out.'

'It ain't so funny.'

'You got that right, Mr Branitt. It's not funny at all.'

'Them cottonmouths can kill a person,' Curly said.

'Really. Can they kill a bulldozer, too?'

'Well … probably not.'

'Then what are you waiting for?'

Curly sighed. 'Yes, sir. First thing Monday morning.'

'Music to my ears,' Chuck Muckle said.

The janitorial closet smelled pungently of bleach and cleaning solvents. Inside, it was almost as black as night.

Dana Matherson had reached out and snagged Roy as he ran toward the gym, pulling him into the closet and slamming the door. Nimbly, Roy had squirted out of Dana's moist grasp, and now he huddled on the cluttered floor while Dana stumbled around, punching blindly.

Scooting on the seat of his pants, Roy made his way toward a paper-thin stripe of light that he assumed was shining through a crack beneath the door. From somewhere above came a bang and then a pained yelp – apparently Dana had delivered a ferocious upper cut to an aluminum bucket.

Somehow Roy located the doorknob in the darkness. He flung open the door and lunged for freedom. Only his head made it into the hallway before Dana caught him. Roy's fingertips squeaked across the linoleum as he was pulled backwards, and again the door closed on his shouts for help.

As Dana yanked him off the floor, Roy desperately groped for something with which to defend himself. His right hand found what felt like a wooden broom handle.

'I gotcha now, cowgirl,' Dana whispered hoarsely.

He locked Roy in a fierce bear hug that emptied the air from Roy's lungs like an accordion. His arms were pinned to his sides and his legs dangled as limply as a rag doll's.

'Now, aren't you thorry you methed with me?' Dana gloated.

As Roy grew dizzy, the broom handle dropped from his fingers, and his ears filled with the sound of crashing waves. Dana's clench was smothering, but Roy found he could still move his lower legs. With all his unsapped strength he started thrashing both feet.

For a moment, nothing happened – then Roy felt himself falling. He landed face-up, so that his backpack absorbed the impact. It was still too dark to see, but Roy surmised from Dana's whimpering gasps that he'd been kicked in a very sensitive part of his body.

Roy knew he had to move swiftly. He tried to roll over, but he was weak and breathless from Dana's brutish hug. He lay there helplessly, like a turtle that had been flipped on its back.

When he heard Dana bellow, Roy closed his eyes and girded himself for the worst. Dana fell heavily upon him, clamping his meaty paws around Roy's throat.

This is it, Roy thought. The dumb goon is really going to kill me. Roy felt hot tears rolling down his cheeks.

Sorry, Mom. Maybe you and Dad can try again . . .

Suddenly the door of the utility closet flew open, and the weight on Roy's chest seemed to vaporize. He opened his eyes just as Dana Matherson was being lifted away, arms flailing, a stunned expression on his pug face.

Roy remained on the floor, catching his breath and trying to sort out what had just happened. Maybe Mr Ryan had overheard the sounds of the struggle; he was plenty strong enough to hoist Dana like a bale of alfalfa.

Eventually Roy flopped over and got to his feet. He fumbled for the light switch and rearmed himself with the broom handle, just in case. When he poked his head out of the closet, he saw that the hallway was deserted.

Roy dropped the broom handle and streaked for the nearest exit. He almost made it, too.

TEN

'I missed my bus,' Roy muttered.

'Big deal. I'm missing soccer practice,' said Beatrice.

'What about Dana?'

'He'll live.'

It wasn't Mr Ryan who'd saved Roy from a whupping in the closet; it was Beatrice Leep. She had left Dana Matherson stripped down to his underpants and trussed to the flagpole in front of the administration building at Trace Middle School. There, Beatrice had 'borrowed' a bicycle, forcefully installed Roy on the handlebars, and was now churning at a manic pace towards an unknown destination.

Roy wondered if this was a kidnapping, in the legal sense of the term. Surely there must be a law against one kid snatching another kid from school property.

'Where are we going?' He expected Beatrice to ignore the question, as she had twice before.

But this time she answered: 'Your house.'

'What?'

'Just be quiet, OK? I'm in no mood, cowgirl.'

Roy could tell by her tone of voice that she was upset.

'I need a favour,' she told him. 'Right away.'

'Sure. Anything you want.'

What else could he say? He was hanging on for dear life as Beatrice zigged across busy intersections and zagged through lines of traffic. She was a skilled bicyclist, but Roy was nervous nonetheless.

'Bandages, tape. Goop to stop infections,' Beatrice was saying. 'Your mom got any of that stuff?'

'Of course.' Roy's mother kept enough medical supplies to run a mini-emergency room.

'Good deal. Now all we need is a cover story.'

'What's going on? Why can't you get bandages at your house?'

'Because it's none of your business.' Beatrice set her jaw and pedalled faster. Roy got a queasy feeling that something bad must have happened to Beatrice's stepbrother, the running boy.

Mrs Eberhardt greeted them at the front door. 'I was getting worried, honey. Was the bus late? Oh – who's this?'

'Mom, this is Beatrice. She gave me a lift home.'

'I'm very pleased to meet you, Beatrice!' Roy's mother wasn't just being polite. She was plainly delighted that Roy had brought home a friend, even if it was a tough-looking girl.

'We're going to Beatrice's and finish up some homework. Is that OK?'

'You're welcome to stay here and work. The house is quiet—'

'It's a science experiment,' Beatrice cut in. 'It might get pretty messy.'

Roy suppressed a smile. Beatrice had sized up his mother perfectly: Mrs Eberhardt kept an exceptionally neat house. Her brow furrowed at the thought of glass beakers bubbling with potent chemicals.

'Is it safe?' she asked.

'Oh, we always wear rubber gloves,' Beatrice said reassuringly, 'and eye goggles, too.'

It was obvious to Roy that Beatrice was experienced at fibbing to grown-ups. Mrs Eberhardt fell for the whole yarn.

While she fixed them a snack, Roy slipped out of the kitchen and darted to his parents' bathroom. The first-aid stash was in the cabinet beneath the sink. Roy removed a box of gauze, a roll of white adhesive tape, and a tube of antibiotic ointment that looked like barbecue sauce. These items he concealed in his backpack.

When he returned to the kitchen, Beatrice and his mother were chatting at the table, a plate of peanut-butter cookies between them. Beatrice's cheeks were full, which Roy took as a promising sign. Enticed by the sweet warm smell, he reached across and grabbed two cookies off the top of the pile.

'Let's go,' Beatrice said, jumping up from her chair. 'We've got lots of work to do.'

'I'm ready,' said Roy.

'Oh, wait – you know what we forgot?'

He had no clue what Beatrice was talking about. 'No. What did we forget?'

'The ground beef,' she said.

'Uh?'

'You know. For the experiment.'

'Yeah,' said Roy, playing along. 'That's right.'

Immediately his mother piped up: 'Honey, I've got two

pounds in the fridge. How much do you need?'

Roy looked at Beatrice, who smiled innocently. 'Two pounds would be plenty, Mrs Eberhardt. Thanks.'

Roy's mother bustled to the refrigerator and retrieved the package of meat. 'What kind of science experiment is this, anyway?' she asked.

Before Roy could answer, Beatrice said, 'Cell decay.'

Mrs Eberhardt's nose crinkled, as if she could already smell something rotting. 'You two better run along,' she said, 'while that hamburger's still fresh.'

Beatrice Leep lived with her father, a former professional basketball player with gimpy knees, a beer gut, and not much enthusiasm for steady work. Leon 'Lurch' Leep had been a high-scoring point guard for the Cleveland Cavaliers and later for the Miami Heat, but twelve years after retiring from the NBA he still hadn't decided what to do with the rest of his life.

Beatrice's mother was not an impatient woman, but she had eventually divorced Leon to pursue her own career as a cockatoo trainer at Parrot Jungle, a tourist attraction in Miami. Beatrice had chosen to remain with her father, partly because she was allergic to parrots and partly because she doubted that Leon Leep could survive on his own. He had basically turned into a lump.

Yet less than two years after Mrs Leep left him, Leon surprised everyone by getting engaged to a woman he met at a celebrity pro-am golf tournament. Lonna was one of the waitresses in bathing suits who drove electric carts around the golf course, serving beer and other beverages to the players. Beatrice didn't even learn Lonna's last name until the day of the wedding. It was the same day Beatrice found out she was going to have a stepbrother.

Lonna arrived at the church towing a sombre, bony-shouldered boy with sun-bleached hair and a deep tan. He looked miserable in a coat and necktie, and he didn't hang around for the reception. No sooner had Leon placed the wedding ring on Lonna's finger than the boy kicked off his shiny black shoes and ran away. This was to become a recurring scene in the Leep family chronicles.

Lonna didn't get along with her son and nagged at him constantly. To Beatrice, it appeared as if Lonna was afraid that the boy's quirky behaviour might annoy her new husband, though Leon Leep seemed not to notice. Occasionally he'd make a halfhearted attempt to bond with the kid, but the two had little in common. The boy held no interest in Leon's prime passions – sports, junk food, and cable television – and spent all his free time roaming the woods and swamps. As for Leon, he wasn't much of an outdoorsman, and was leery of any critter that wasn't wearing a collar and a rabies tag.

One night, Lonna's son brought home an orphaned baby raccoon, which promptly crawled into one of Leon's favourite moleskin slippers and relieved itself. Leon seemed more puzzled than upset, but Lonna went totally ballistic. Without consulting her husband, she arranged for her son to be shipped off to a military prep school – the first of several failed attempts to 'normalize' the boy.

He seldom lasted more than two weeks before running away or being expelled. The last time it happened, Lonna purposely didn't tell Leon. Instead she continued to pretend that her son was doing fine, that his grades were good and his conduct was improving.

The truth was, Lonna didn't know where the boy had gone and didn't intend to go looking for him. She was 'fed up with the little monster,' or so Beatrice overheard her say on the telephone. As for Leon Leep, he displayed no curiosity beyond what his wife had told him about her wayward offspring. Leon didn't even notice when the tuition bills from the military school stopped coming.

Long before his mother sent him away for the last time, the boy and his stepsister had forged a quiet alliance. After Lonna's son made his way back to Coconut Cove, the first and only person he contacted was Beatrice. She agreed to keep his whereabouts a secret, knowing that Lonna would call the juvenile authorities if she ever found out.

That concern was what had prompted Beatrice Leep to confront Roy Eberhardt after she saw him chasing her stepbrother that first day. She did what any big sister would have done.

On the bicycle ride, Beatrice shared enough bits and pieces of her family's story with Roy that he understood the difficult situation. And after seeing her stepbrother's wounds, he knew why Beatrice had run for help after she'd found him moaning inside the old Jo-Jo's ice-cream truck.

It was the first time Roy had been permitted to see the running boy up close and face to face. The kid was stretched out, a crumpled cardboard box serving as a pillow. His straw-blond hair was matted from perspiration, and his forehead felt hot to the touch. In the boy's eyes was a restless, darting, animal flicker that Roy had seen before.

'Does it hurt bad?' Roy asked.

'Nope.'

'Liar,' Beatrice said.

The boy's left arm was purple and swollen. At first Roy thought it was from a snakebite, and worriedly glanced around. Fortunately, the bag of cottonmouths was nowhere in sight.

'I stopped by on the way to the bus stop this morning and found him like this,' Beatrice explained to Roy. Then, to her stepbrother: 'Go on. Tell cowgirl what happened.'

'Dog got me.' The boy turned his arm over and pointed to several angry red holes in the skin.

The bites were nasty, but Roy had seen worse. One time his father had taken him to a state fair where a rodeo clown got chomped by a panicky horse. The clown was bleeding so badly that he was rushed to the hospital in a helicopter.

Roy unzipped his backpack and removed the medical supplies. He knew a little about treating puncture wounds from a first-aid course he'd taken at a summer camp in Bozeman. Beatrice had already cleansed her stepbrother's arm with soda water, so Roy lathered antibiotic ointment on a panel of gauze and taped it firmly around the boy's arm.

'You need a tetanus shot,' Roy said.

Mullet Fingers shook his head. 'I'll be OK.'

'Is the dog still running around here?'

The boy turned inquiringly to Beatrice, who said, 'Go ahead and tell him.'

'You sure?'

'Yeah, he's all right.' She shot an appraising glance at Roy. 'Besides, he owes me. He almost got squashed in a closet today – isn't that right, cowgirl?'

Roy's cheeks flushed. 'Never mind that. What about this dog?'

'Actually, there was four of 'em,' Mullet Fingers said, 'behind a chain fence.'

'So how'd you get bit?' Roy asked.

'Arm got stuck.'

'Doing what?'

'It's no big deal,' said the boy. 'Beatrice, did you get some hamburger?'

'Yeah. Roy's mom gave it to us.'

The kid sat up. 'Then we better roll.'

Roy said, 'No, you need to rest.'

'Later. Come on – they'll be gettin' hungry soon.'

Roy looked at Beatrice Leep, who offered no explanation. They followed Mullet Fingers down the steps of the ice-cream truck and out of the junkyard. 'Meet you there,' he said, and broke into a full run. Roy couldn't imagine the strength it must have taken, considering his painful injury.

As Mullet Fingers scampered off, Roy noticed with some satisfaction that he was wearing shoes – the same sneakers Roy had brought for him a few days earlier.

Beatrice mounted the bicycle and pointed at the handlebars. 'Hop aboard.'

'No way,' Roy said.

'Don't be a wuss.'

'Hey, I don't want any part of this. Not if he's going to hurt those dogs.'

'What are you talking about?'

'That's why he wanted the meat, right?'

Roy thought he'd figured it out. He thought the kid meant to take revenge on the dogs by spiking the hamburger with something harmful, maybe even poisonous.

Beatrice laughed and rolled her eyes. 'He's not that kind of crazy. Now let's go.'

Fifteen minutes later, Roy found himself on East Oriole Avenue, at the same trailer where the foreman had hollered at him a few days before. It was nearly five o'clock, and the construction site looked deserted.

Roy noticed that a chain-link fence had been erected to enclose the lot. He recalled that the cranky foreman had threatened to unleash vicious guard dogs, and he assumed they were the ones that bit Mullet Fingers.

Jumping off the bike, Roy said to Beatrice: 'Does this have anything to do with that cop car that got spray-painted?'

Beatrice said nothing.

'Or the 'gators in the portable potties?' Roy asked.

He knew the answer, but Beatrice's expression said it all: *Mind your own business.*

Despite the fever and the raging infection, her stepbrother had beaten them to the pancake-house construction site.

'Lemme have that,' he said, snatching the package of

meat from Roy's hands.

Roy grabbed it back. 'Not till you tell me what for.'

The kid looked to Beatrice for assistance, but she shook her head. 'Get it over with,' she told him. 'Come on, we haven't got all day.'

His injured arm hanging limply, Mullet Fingers clambered up one side of the fence and down the other. Beatrice followed, effortlessly swinging her long legs over the top.

'What're you waiting for?' she barked at Roy, still standing on the other side.

'What about those dogs?'

'The dogs,' said Mullet Fingers, 'are long gone.'

More confused than ever, Roy scaled the fence. He followed Beatrice and her stepbrother to a parked bulldozer. They huddled in the shaded cup of the blade, safely out of sight from the road. Roy sat in the middle position, with Beatrice on his left side and Mullet Fingers on his right.

Roy held the package of meat on his lap, covering it with both arms like a fullback protecting a football.

'Did you paint that cop car?' he bluntly asked the boy.

'No comment.'

'And hide those alligators in the toilets?'

Mullet Fingers stared straight ahead, his eyes narrowing.

'I don't get it,' Roy said. 'Why would you try crazy stuff like that? Who cares if they build a stupid pancake house here?'

The boy's head snapped around and he froze Roy with a cold look.

Beatrice spoke up. 'My stepbrother got bit by the dogs because his arm got stuck when he reached through the fence. Now ask me why he was reaching through the fence.'

'OK. Why?' Roy said.

'He was putting out snakes.'

'The same snakes from the golf course? The cotton-mouths!' Roy exclaimed. 'But why? You trying to kill somebody?'

Mullet Fingers smiled knowingly. 'They couldn't hurt a flea, them snakes. I taped their mouths shut.'

'I'm so sure,' Roy said.

'Plus I glued sparkles on the tails,' the boy added, 'so they'd be easy to spot.'

Beatrice said, 'He's telling the truth, Eberhardt.'

Indeed, Roy had seen the sparkling tails for himself. 'But come on,' he said, 'how do you tape a snake's mouth closed?'

'Real carefully,' said Beatrice, with a dry laugh.

'Aw, it ain't so hard,' Mullet Fingers added, 'if you know what you're doin'. See, I wasn't tryin' to hurt them dogs – just rile 'em up.'

'Dogs do *not* like snakes,' Beatrice explained.

'Makes 'em freak out. Bark and howl and run around in circles,' her stepbrother said. 'I knew the trainer would drag 'em outta here soon as he saw the cottonmouths. Those Rottweilers ain't cheap.'

It was the wildest plan Roy had ever heard.

'The only part I didn't count on,' said Mullet Fingers, eyeing his bandaged arm, 'was gettin' bit.'

Roy said, 'I'm almost afraid to ask, but what happened to your snakes?'

'Oh, they're fine,' the boy reported. 'I came back and got 'em all. Took 'em to a safe place and let 'em go free.'

'But first he had to peel the tape off their mouths,' said Beatrice, chuckling.

'Stop!' Roy was completely exasperated. 'Hold on right there.'

Mullet Fingers and Beatrice looked at him matter-of-factly. Roy's head was spinning with questions. These kids must be from another world.

'Would one of you please tell me,' he begged, 'what's all this got to do with *pancakes*? Maybe I'm dense, but I really don't get it.'

Grimacing, the boy rubbed his bloated arm. 'It's simple, man,' he said to Roy. 'They can't put a Mother Paula's here for the same reason they can't have big ole nasty Rottweilers runnin' loose.'

'Show him why,' Beatrice said to her stepbrother.

'OK. Gimme the hamburger.'

Roy handed over the package. Mullet Fingers peeled off the plastic wrapper and scooped out a handful of ground beef, which he carefully rolled into six perfect little meatballs.

'Follow me,' he said. 'But try and be quiet.'

The boy led Roy to a hole in a grassy patch of ground. At the entrance of the hole, Mullet Fingers placed two hamburger balls.

Next he walked to an identical-looking hole on the

other side of the lot and left two more meatballs there. He followed the same ritual at another hole in a far corner of the property.

Peeking into one of the dark tunnels, Roy asked, 'What's down there?'

In Montana, the only animals that dug holes like that were gophers and badgers, and Roy was positive there weren't many of those in Florida.

'Hush,' the boy said.

Roy trailed him back to the bulldozer, where Beatrice remained perched on the blade, cleaning her eyeglasses.

'Well?' she said to Roy.

'Well, what?'

Mullet Fingers tapped him on the arm. 'Listen.'

Roy heard a short high-pitched *coo-coo*. Then, from across the open lot, came another. Beatrice's stepbrother rose stealthily, tugged off his new sneakers, and crept forward. Roy followed closely.

The boy was grinning through his fever when he signalled for them to stop. 'Look!'

He pointed toward the first burrow.

'Wow,' Roy said, under his breath.

There, standing by the hole and peering curiously at one of the meatballs, was the smallest owl that he had ever seen.

Mullet Fingers chucked him gently on the shoulder. 'OK – *now* do you get it?'

'Yeah,' said Roy. 'I get it.'

ELEVEN

Officer David Delinko had made a habit of driving past the construction site every morning on the way to the police station, and again every afternoon on his way home. Sometimes he even cruised by late at night if he went out for a snack; conveniently, there was a minimart only a few blocks away.

So far, the policeman hadn't seen much out of the ordinary except for the scene earlier that day: a wild-eyed man waving a red umbrella and chasing several giant black dogs around the property. The foreman of the Mother Paula's project had said it was a K-9 training exercise, nothing to be alarmed about. Officer Delinko had no reason to doubt it.

Even though he'd hoped to capture the vandals himself, the policeman agreed it was an excellent idea for the pancake-house company to put up a fence and post some guard dogs – surely that would scare off potential intruders.

That afternoon, after another eight dull hours of desk duty, Officer Delinko decided to swing by the Mother Paula's site once more. Two hours of daylight remained, and he was eager to see those attack dogs in action.

He got there expecting a mad chorus of barking, but the place was strangely silent; no sign of the dogs. Walking the outer perimeter of the fence, the patrolman clapped his hands and shouted, in case the animals were hiding under Curly's trailer or snoozing in the shade of the bulldozing equipment.

'Boo!' yelled Officer Delinko. 'Yo, Fido!'

Nothing.

He picked up a two-by-four and clanged it against a metal fence post. Again, nothing.

Officer Delinko returned to the gate and checked the padlock, which was secure.

He tried whistling, and this time he got an unexpected response: *Coo-coo, coo-coo.*

Definitely not a Rottweiler.

The policeman saw something move inside the enclosure, and he strained to see what it was. At first he thought it was a rabbit, because of its sandy brown colouring, but then it suddenly lifted off the ground and swooped from one corner of the property to another, finally landing on the cowling of a bulldozer.

Officer Delinko smiled – it was one of those stubborn little burrowing owls that Curly had complained about.

But where were the guard dogs?

The patrolman stepped back and scratched his chin. Tomorrow he'd stop by the trailer and ask the foreman what was going on.

As a warm breeze swept in, Officer Delinko noticed something fluttering at the top of the fence. It looked like a streamer from one of the survey stakes, but it wasn't. It was a ragged strip of green cloth.

The policeman wondered if somebody had gotten their

shirt snagged on the wire mesh while climbing over the fence.

Officer Delinko stood on his tiptoes and retrieved the torn piece of fabric, which he carefully placed in one of his pockets. Then he got into his squad car and headed down East Oriole.

'Faster!' shouted Beatrice Leep.

'I can't,' Roy panted as he ran behind her.

Beatrice was pedalling the bicycle she'd taken from the rack at Trace Middle. Mullet Fingers was slumped across the handlebars, barely conscious. He had become dizzy and fallen from the fence as they were hurrying to leave the construction site.

Roy could see that the boy was getting sicker from the infected dog bites. He needed a doctor right away.

'He won't go,' Beatrice had declared.

'Then we've got to tell his mother.'

'No way!' And off she'd ridden.

Now Roy was trying to keep her in sight. He didn't know where Beatrice was taking her stepbrother, and he had a feeling she didn't know, either.

'How's he doing?' Roy called out.

'Not good.'

Roy heard a car and turned his head to look. Coming up behind them, barely two blocks away, was a police cruiser. Automatically Roy stopped in his tracks and began waving his arms. All he could think about was getting Mullet Fingers to the hospital, as soon as possible.

'What're you doing!' Beatrice Leep yelled at him.

Roy heard a clatter as the bicycle hit the pavement. He turned to see Beatrice bolting away, her stepbrother slung like a sack of oats over one shoulder. Without glancing back, she cut between two houses at the end of the block and disappeared.

Roy stood rooted in the centre of the road. He had an important decision to make, and quickly. From one direction came the police car; running in the other direction were his two friends . . .

Well, the closest things to friends that he had in Coconut Cove.

Roy drew a deep breath and dashed after them. He heard a honk, but he kept going, hoping that the police officer wouldn't jump out and chase him on foot. Roy didn't think he'd done anything wrong, but he wondered if he could get in trouble for helping Mullet Fingers, a fugitive from the school system.

The kid was only trying to take care of some owls – how could that possibly be a crime? Roy thought.

Five minutes later, he found Beatrice Leep resting under a shady mahogany tree in a stranger's backyard. Her stepbrother's head was cradled on her lap, his eyelids half-shut and his forehead glistening.

The deep bite wounds on his swollen arm were exposed, for the bandage had been pulled off (along with a sleeve of his green T-shirt) when he'd toppled from the fence.

Beatrice stroked the boy's cheeks and sadly looked up at Roy. 'What are we gonna do now, cowgirl?'

*

Curly was done fooling around with attack dogs. And while he wasn't thrilled about spending nights at the trailer, it was the only surefire way to stop the delinquents – or whoever was sabotaging the construction site – from jumping the fence and going wild.

If something were to happen over the weekend that resulted in another delay of the Mother Paula's project, Curly would be fired as foreman. Chuck Muckle had been crystal-clear about that.

When Curly told his wife of his overnight guard duties, she received the news with no trace of annoyance or concern. Her mother was in town visiting, and the two of them had planned numerous shopping excursions for Saturday and Sunday. Curly's charming presence would not be missed.

Sullenly he packed a travel kit with his toothbrush, dental floss, razor, shaving cream, and a jumbo bottle of aspirin. He folded some clean work clothes and underwear into a carrier bag and grabbed the pillow off his side of the bed. On his way out the door, his wife handed him two fat tuna sandwiches, one for dinner and one for breakfast.

'You be careful out there, Leroy,' she said.

'Yeah, sure.'

Upon returning to the construction site, Curly locked the gate behind him and high-stepped to the safety of the trailer. All afternoon he'd been fretting about those elusive cottonmouth moccasins, wondering why the reptile wrangler hadn't been able to find them.

How could so many snakes disappear all at once?

Curly was afraid that the moccasins were lurking nearby in some secret subterranean den, waiting for darkness before they slithered out to begin their deadly hunt.

'I'll be ready for 'em,' Curly said aloud, in the hope of convincing himself.

Bolting the trailer door, he sat down in front of the portable television and turned on ESPN. The Devil Rays were playing the Orioles later in the evening, and Curly was looking forward to the ball game. For the time being, he was perfectly content to watch a soccer match being played in Quito, Ecuador – wherever *that* was.

He sat back and loosened his belt to accommodate the bulge in his waistband from the .38-calibre revolver he'd brought along for protection. He hadn't actually fired a gun since he had been in the Marines, which was thirty-one years ago, but he kept a pistol hidden at the house and remained confident of his abilities.

Anyway, how hard could it be to hit a big fat snake?

Just as Curly was polishing off his first tuna sandwich, a commercial for Mother Paula's All-American Pancake House came on the television. There, dressed up as kindly old Mother Paula herself, was none other than Kimberly Lou Dixon, the former Miss America runner-up. She was flipping flapjacks over a hot griddle and singing some sort of goofy song.

Although the make-up artists had done a darn good job, Curly could still tell that the old lady in the commercial was actually a much younger woman, and that she was pretty. Remembering what Chuck Muckle had told him about Kimberly Lou Dixon's new movie deal, Curly tried to picture her as the Queen of the Mutant Grasshoppers. Undoubtedly the special-effects department would give her six green legs and a pair of antennae, which Curly found intriguing to contemplate.

He wondered if he would be introduced personally to Kimberly Lou Dixon when she came to Coconut Cove to attend the groundbreaking ceremony for the new pancake house. The possibility wasn't so far-fetched, him being the supervising engineer of the project – the top guy in charge.

Curly had never met a movie star or a television actress or a Miss America or a Miss Anything. Was it OK to ask for an autograph? he wondered. Would she mind posing with him for a picture? And would she speak to him in her phony Mother Paula's voice, or as Kimberly Lou Dixon?

These were the questions knocking around inside Curly's head as the image on the TV screen dissolved to electric fuzz before his disbelieving eyes. Heatedly he banged a mayonnaise-smeared fist on the side of the television console, to no avail.

The cable had gone out in the middle of a Mother Paula's commercial! Not a good omen, Curly thought sourly.

He used many bad words to curse his rotten luck. It had been years since he'd gone a whole night without television, and he wasn't sure how else to amuse himself. There was no radio in the trailer, and the only reading material was a construction industry journal with boring articles about hurricane-resistant roof sheathing and anti-termite treatments for plywood.

Curly considered a quick trip to the minimart to rent some videos, but that would require crossing the property to reach his truck. With dusk approaching, he couldn't get up the nerve to venture outside – not with those deadly cottonmouths skulking around.

He bunched the pillow under his head and tilted his chair back against the thin panelled wall. Alone in the silence, he wondered if it was possible for a snake to worm its way into the trailer. He remembered hearing a story about a boa constrictor that had crawled through the plumbing and popped out of a bathtub drain in a New York City apartment.

Imagining that scene, Curly felt his stomach knot. He got up and padded cautiously to the entrance of the trailer's small bathroom. Placing one ear to the door, he listened . . .

Was it his imagination, or did he hear a rustle on the other side? Curly drew the gun from his belt and cocked the trigger.

Yes, now he was certain. Something was moving!

The instant Curly kicked open the door, he realized there was no poisonous snake in the bathroom, no cause for mortal alarm. Unfortunately, the message didn't travel fast enough from his brain to his trigger finger.

The boom from the gun startled Curly almost as badly as it startled the field mouse that was sitting on the tile floor, minding its own business. As the bullet whizzed over its tiny whiskered head, shattering the toilet seat, the mouse took off – a squeaking grey blur that scooted out the doorway, between Curly's feet.

His hand trembling, Curly lowered the pistol and stared ruefully at what he'd done. He'd accidentally shot the commode.

It was going to be a long weekend.

Mr Eberhardt was in the den, reading at his desk, when Mrs Eberhardt came to the door with a worried expression.

'That policeman's here,' she said.

'What policeman?'

'The one who brought Roy home the other night. You'd better come talk to him.'

Officer Delinko stood in the living room, holding his hat in his hands. 'Nice to see you again,' he said to Roy's father.

'Is something wrong?'

'It's about Roy,' Mrs Eberhardt cut in.

'Possibly,' said Officer Delinko. 'I'm not certain.'

'Let's all sit down,' suggested Mr Eberhardt. He was trained to remain calm while sorting through loose snippets of information. 'Tell us what happened,' he said.

'Where is Roy? Is he home?' the policeman inquired.

'No, he went to a friend's house to work on a science project,' Mrs Eberhardt said.

'The reason I ask,' Officer Delinko said, 'is that I spotted a couple of kids on East Oriole a little bit ago. One of them looked sort of like your son. The weird thing was: First he waved at the police car, and then all of a sudden he ran away.'

Mr Eberhardt frowned. 'Ran away? That doesn't sound like Roy.'

'Certainly not,' Mrs Eberhardt agreed. 'Why would he do that?'

'The kids left a bike lying in the street.'

'Well, it's not Roy's. His bike has a flat,' Roy's mother announced.

'Yes, I remember,' the policeman said.

'We had to order a new tyre,' Mr Eberhardt added.

Officer Delinko nodded patiently. 'I know it's not Roy's bicycle. This one was stolen from Trace Middle School earlier this afternoon, shortly after classes let out.'

'You're sure?' Mr Eberhardt asked.

'Yes, sir. I found out when I radioed in the serial number.'

The room fell silent. Roy's mother looked gravely at Roy's father, then fixed her gaze upon the policeman.

'My son is no thief,' she said firmly.

'I'm not making any accusations,' said Officer Delinko. 'The boy who was running away looked like Roy, but I can't say for sure. I'm only checking with you folks because you're his parents and, well, this is part of my job.' The policeman turned to Roy's father for support. 'Being in law enforcement, Mr Eberhardt, I'm sure you understand.'

'I do,' Roy's father mumbled distractedly. 'How many kids did you see on the road?'

'At least two, possibly three.'

'And they all took off?'

'Yes, sir.' Officer Delinko was trying to be as professional as possible. Perhaps someday he would apply to become an FBI agent, and Mr Eberhardt could put in a good word for him.

'And how many bicycles?' Mr Eberhardt was asking.

'Just one. It's in the car if you want to take a look.'

Roy's parents followed the policeman out to the driveway, where he opened the Crown Victoria's trunk.

'See?' Officer Delinko motioned toward the stolen bicycle, which was a blue beach-cruiser model.

'I don't recognize it,' said Mr Eberhardt. 'How about you, Lizzy?'

Roy's mother swallowed hard. It looked like the same bike ridden by Roy's new friend, Beatrice, when she'd accompanied him home from school.

Before Mrs Eberhardt could collect her thoughts, Officer Delinko said, 'Oh, I almost forgot. How about this?' He reached into a pocket and took out what appeared to be a torn-off shirt sleeve.

'You found that with the bicycle?' Mr Eberhardt asked.

'Nearby.' Officer Delinko was fudging a little bit. The construction site actually was several blocks from where he'd spotted the kids.

'Does it look familiar?' he asked the Eberhardts, holding up the ragged strip of fabric.

'Not to me,' Roy's father replied. 'Lizzy?'

Mrs Eberhardt appeared relieved. 'Well, it's definitely

not Roy's,' she informed Officer Delinko. 'He doesn't own any green clothes.'

'What colour shirt was the boy wearing when he ran off?' Mr Eberhardt asked.

'I couldn't tell,' the patrolman admitted. 'He was too far away.'

They heard the phone ring, and Roy's mother hurried inside to answer it.

Officer Delinko leaned closer to Roy's father and said: 'I apologize for bothering you folks with this.'

'Like you were saying, it's all part of the job.' Mr Eberhardt remained polite, even though he knew the policeman wasn't telling him everything about the green rag.

'Speaking of jobs,' Officer Delinko said, 'you remember the other night when I brought Roy home with his flat tyre?'

'Of course.'

'In all that nasty weather.'

'Yes, I remember,' said Mr Eberhardt impatiently.

'Did he happen to mention anything about you writing up a letter for me?'

'What kind of a letter?'

'To our police chief,' Officer Delinko said. 'No biggie – just a note for the permanent file, saying you folks appreciated me helping out your boy. Something along those lines.'

'And this "note" should be sent to the chief?'

'Or to the captain. Even my sergeant would be OK. Roy didn't ask you?'

'Not that I recall,' said Mr Eberhardt.

'Well, you know how kids are. He probably forgot.'

'What's your sergeant's name? I'll see what I can do.' Roy's father made no effort to conceal his lack of enthusiasm. He was running out of tolerance for the pushy young cop.

'Thanks a million,' Officer Delinko said, pumping Mr Eberhardt's hand. 'Every little bit helps when you're trying to get ahead. And something like this, coming from a federal agent such as yourself—'

But he didn't get the chance to give his sergeant's name to Mr Eberhardt, for at that very moment Mrs Eberhardt burst out the front door carrying a purse in one hand and a jangling set of car keys in the other.

'Lizzy, what's the matter?' Mr Eberhardt called out. 'Who was that on the phone?'

'The emergency room!' she cried breathlessly. 'Roy's been hurt!'

TWELVE

Roy was exhausted. It seemed like a hundred years ago that Dana Matherson had tried to strangle him inside the janitor's closet, but it had happened only that afternoon.

'Thanks. Now we're even,' Beatrice Leep said.

'Maybe,' said Roy.

They were waiting in the emergency room of the Coconut Cove Medical Center, which was more of a large clinic than a hospital. It was here they'd brought Beatrice's stepbrother after carrying him upright for almost a mile, each of them bracing one of his shoulders.

'He's going to be all right,' Roy said.

For a moment, he thought Beatrice was about to cry. He reached over and squeezed her hand, which was noticeably larger than his own.

'He's a tough little cockroach,' Beatrice said with a sniffle. 'He'll be OK.'

A woman dressed in baby-blue scrubs and wearing a stethoscope approached them. She introduced herself as Dr Gonzalez.

'Tell me exactly what happened to Roy,' she said.

Beatrice and the real Roy exchanged anxious glances. Her stepbrother had forbidden them from giving his name to the hospital, for fear that his mother would be notified. The boy got so agitated that Roy hadn't argued. When the emergency room clerk asked Beatrice for her stepbrother's name, address and phone number, Roy impulsively had stepped forward and blurted his own. It had seemed like the quickest way to get Mullet Fingers into a hospital bed.

Roy knew he was also getting himself in trouble. Beatrice Leep knew it, too. That's why she had thanked him.

'My brother got bit by a dog,' she told Dr Gonzalez.

'Several,' Roy added.

'What kind of dogs?' the doctor asked.

'Big ones.'

'How did it happen?'

Here Roy let Beatrice take over the story, as she was more experienced at fibbing to adults.

'They nailed him at soccer practice,' she said. 'He came runnin' home all chewed up, so we brought him here as fast as we could.'

'Hmm,' said Dr Gonzalez with a slight frown.

'What – don't you believe me?' Beatrice's indignation sounded genuine. Roy was impressed.

But the doctor was a cool one, too. 'Oh, I believe your stepbrother was attacked by dogs,' she said. 'I just don't believe it happened today.'

Beatrice stiffened. Roy knew he had to come up with something, fast.

'The wounds on his arm aren't fresh,' Dr Gonzalez explained. 'Judging by how far the infection has progressed, I'd estimate he was bitten eighteen to twenty-four hours ago.'

Beatrice looked flustered. Roy didn't wait for her to recover.

'Yeah, eighteen hours. That sounds about right,' he said to the doctor.

'I don't understand.'

'See, he passed out right after he got bit,' Roy said. 'It wasn't until the next day he finally woke up, and that's when he came running home. Then Beatrice called me and asked if I'd help get him to the hospital.'

Dr Gonzalez fixed Roy with a stern gaze, though there was an edge of amusement in her voice.

'What's your name, son?'

Roy gulped. She'd caught him off guard.

'Tex,' he answered weakly.

Beatrice nudged him with her elbow, as if to say: That's the best you can do?

The doctor crossed her arms. 'So, *Tex*, let's get this straight. Your friend Roy is mauled at the soccer field by several huge dogs. Nobody tries to help him, and he remains unconscious all night and most of the next day. All of a sudden he wakes up and jogs home. Is that right?'

'Yup.' Roy bowed his head. He was a pathetic liar, and he knew it.

Dr Gonzalez turned her steely attention to Beatrice. 'Why was it left for you to bring your stepbrother here? Where are your parents?'

'Working,' Beatrice replied.

'Didn't you call and tell them there was a medical emergency?'

'They crew on a crab boat. No phone.'

Not bad, Roy thought. The doctor, however, wasn't buying it.

'It's hard to understand,' she said to Beatrice, 'how your stepbrother could go missing for so long and nobody in the family got concerned enough to call the police.'

'Sometimes he runs away from home,' Beatrice said quietly, 'and he doesn't come back for a while.'

It was the closest thing to a true answer that she'd given and, ironically, it was the one that made Dr Gonzalez back off.

'I'm going to go check on Roy now,' she told them. 'In the meantime, you two might want to polish up your story.'

'How's he doing, anyway?' Beatrice asked.

'Better. He got a tetanus shot, and now we're loading him with antibiotics and pain medication. It's strong stuff, so he's pretty sleepy.'

'Can we see him?'

'Not right now.'

As soon as the doctor had gone, Roy and Beatrice hurried outside, where it was safer to talk. Roy sat down on the steps of the emergency room; Beatrice remained standing.

'This isn't gonna work, cowgirl. Once they figure out he's not you...'

'It's a problem,' Roy agreed: the understatement of the year.

'And if Lonna hears about this, you know he'll end up

in juvie detention,' Beatrice said gloomily, 'until she finds a new military school. Probably someplace far-off, like Guam, where he can't run away.'

Roy didn't understand how a mother could kick her own child out of her life, but he knew such tragic things occurred. He'd heard of fathers who acted the same way. It was depressing to think about.

'We'll come up with something,' he promised Beatrice.

'Know what, Tex? You're OK.' She pinched his cheek and went bounding down the steps.

'Hey, where you going?' he called after her.

'Fix dinner for my dad. I do it every night.'

'You're kidding, right? You're not really leaving me here alone.'

'Sorry,' Beatrice said. 'Dad'll freak if I don't show up. He can't make toast without burning off his fingertips.'

'Couldn't Lonna cook his dinner this one time?'

'Nope. She tends bar at the Elk's Lodge.' Beatrice gave Roy a brisk little wave. 'I'll be back as soon as I can. Don't let 'em operate or nuthin' on my brother.'

'Wait!' Roy jumped to his feet. 'Tell me his real name. It's the least you can do, after everything that's happened.'

'Sorry, cowgirl, but I can't. I made him a blood promise a long time ago.'

'Please?'

'If he wants you to know,' Beatrice said, 'he'll tell you himself.' Then she ran off, her footsteps fading into the night.

Roy trudged back into the emergency room. He knew his mother would be getting worried, so he asked the desk clerk if he could borrow the phone. It rang a half dozen times on the other end before the Eberhardts' answering machine picked up. Roy left a message saying he'd be home as soon as he and Beatrice finished cleaning up the mess from the science project.

Alone in the waiting area, Roy dug through a stack of magazines until he found an issue of *Outdoor Life* that had an article about fishing for cut-throat trout in the Rocky Mountains. The best thing about the story was the photographs – anglers wading knee-deep in blue Western rivers lined with tall cottonwoods, rows of snowy mountain crags visible in the distance.

Roy was feeling pretty homesick for Montana when he heard the approach of a siren outside. He decided it was an excellent time to go find a Coke machine, even though he only had two dimes in his pocket.

The truth was, Roy didn't want to be in the emergency room to see what the siren was all about. He wasn't prepared to see them wheel in somebody who'd been injured in a serious wreck, somebody who might even be dying.

Other kids could be really curious about that gory stuff, but not Roy. Once, when he was seven years old and his family lived near Milwaukee, a drunken hunter drove a snowmobile full-speed into an old birch tree. The accident happened only a hundred yards from a slope where Roy and his father were sledding.

Mr Eberhardt had run up the hill to try to help, with

Roy huffing close behind. When they'd reached the tree, they realized there was nothing they could do. The dead man was soaked with blood and twisted at odd angles, like a broken GI Joe doll. Roy knew he would never forget what he saw, and he never wanted to see anything like it again.

Consequently, he had no intention of hanging around the emergency room for the arrival of a new emergency. He slipped through a side door and wandered through the hospital for about fifteen minutes until a nurse intercepted him.

'I think I'm lost,' Roy said, doing his best to appear confused.

'You most definitely are.'

The nurse steered him down a back corridor to the emergency room, where Roy was relieved to find no chaos or carnage. The place was as quiet as he'd left it.

Puzzled, Roy went to the window and checked outside. There was no ambulance in the delivery zone, only a Coconut Cove police cruiser. Maybe it was nothing, he thought, and returned to his magazine.

Soon afterward, Roy heard voices from behind the double doors that led to the area where Mullet Fingers was being treated. A loud discussion was taking place in the patient ward, and Roy strained to make out what was being said.

One voice in particular rose above the rest, and Roy was distressed to recognize it. He sat there in nervous misery, trying to decide what to do next. Then he heard another familiar voice, and he knew there was only one choice.

He walked to the double doors and pushed them open. 'Hey, Mom! Dad!' he shouted. 'I'm right here!'

Officer Delinko had insisted on giving the Eberhardts a ride to the hospital. It was the decent thing to do – and also a prime opportunity to score points with Roy's father.

The patrolman hoped that Mr Eberhardt's son wasn't involved in the continuing mischief at the pancake-house construction site. What a sticky situation that would be!

On the drive to the hospital, Roy's parents sat in the backseat and spoke quietly between themselves. His mother said she couldn't imagine how Roy had got bitten by a dog while he was working on a science project. 'Maybe it had something to do with all that hamburger meat,' she speculated.

'Hamburger?' said Roy's father. 'What kind of school project uses hamburger?'

In the rearview mirror, Officer Delinko could see Mr Eberhardt put an arm around his wife's shoulders. Her eyes were moist and she was biting her lower lip. Mr Eberhardt appeared as tightly wound as a clock spring.

When they got to the emergency room, the desk clerk declared that Roy was sleeping and couldn't be disturbed. The Eberhardts tried to reason with him but the clerk wouldn't budge.

'We're his parents,' Mr Eberhardt said evenly, 'and we intend to see him right away.'

'Sir, don't make me call a supervisor.'

'I don't care if you call the Wizard of Oz,' said Mr Eberhardt. 'We're going in.'

The clerk trailed them through the swinging double doors. 'You can't do this!' he objected, scooting ahead of the Eberhardts and blocking the hallway to the patient ward.

Officer Delinko edged forward, assuming that the sight of a police uniform would soften the fellow's attitude. He was mistaken.

'Absolutely no visitors. It says right here on the doctor's notes.' The clerk solemnly waved a clipboard. 'I'm afraid you'll have to go back to the waiting room. That means you, too, Officer.'

Officer Delinko shrank away. Not the Eberhardts.

'Listen, that's our son lying in there,' Roy's mother reminded the clerk. 'You called us, remember? You told us to come!'

'Yes, and you may see Roy as soon as the doctor says it's allowed.'

'Then page the doctor. Now.' Mr Eberhardt's tone of voice remained level, but the volume had gotten much louder. 'Pick up the phone and dial. If you've forgotten how, we'll be happy to show you.'

'The doctor's on a break. She'll be back in twenty-five minutes,' the clerk said tersely.

'Then she can find us right here,' Mr Eberhardt said,

'visiting our injured son. Now, if you don't move out of the way, I'm going to drop-kick you all the way to Chokoloskee. Understand?'

The clerk went pale. 'I'm r-r-reporting you to my s-s-su-supervisor.'

'That's a dandy idea.' Mr Eberhardt brushed past and started down the hall, guiding his wife by the elbow.

'Hold it right there!' snapped a firm female voice behind them.

The Eberhardts stopped and turned. Emerging from a door marked STAFF ONLY was a woman wearing baby-blue scrubs and a stethoscope.

'I'm Dr Gonzalez. Where do you think you're going?'

'To see our son,' replied Mrs Eberhardt.

'I tried to stop them,' the desk clerk piped up.

'You're Roy's parents?' the doctor asked the Eberhardts.

'We are.' Roy's father noticed Dr Gonzalez eyeing them with an odd curiosity.

'Pardon me if this is out of line,' she said, 'but you sure don't look like you work on a crab boat.'

'What on earth are you talking about?' Roy's mother said. 'Is everybody at this hospital a total wacko?'

'There must be some mistake,' Officer Delinko interjected. 'Mr Eberhardt is a federal law-enforcement agent.'

Dr Gonzalez sighed. 'We'll sort this out later. Come on, let's go peek in on your boy.'

The emergency-patient ward had six beds, five of

which were unoccupied. The sixth bed had a white privacy curtain drawn around it.

'We've got him on IV antibiotics and he's doing pretty well,' Dr Gonzalez said in a low voice, 'but unless we find those dogs, he'll need a series of rabies injections. Those are no fun.'

The Eberhardts locked arms as they approached the enclosed bed. Officer Delinko stood behind them, wondering what colour shirt Roy would be wearing. In the patrolman's pocket was the bright green scrap of clothing that had snagged on the Mother Paula's fence.

'Don't be surprised if he's sleeping,' the doctor whispered, gently pulling the curtain away.

Nobody said a word for several moments. The four grown-ups just stood there, blank-faced, staring at the empty bed.

From a metal rig hung a plastic bag of ginger-coloured fluid, the intravenous tube disconnected and dangling to the floor.

Finally, Mrs Eberhardt gasped, 'Where's Roy!'

Dr Gonzalez's arms flapped helplessly. 'I just ... I really ... I don't know.'

'You don't *know*?' Mr Eberhardt erupted. 'One minute an injured boy is asleep in this bed, and the next minute he's vanished?'

Officer Delinko stepped between Mr Eberhardt and the doctor. The patrolman was afraid that Roy's father was upset enough to do something he might later regret.

'Where is our son?' Mrs Eberhardt demanded again.

The doctor buzzed for a nurse and frantically started searching the emergency ward.

'But he was the only patient here,' Mr Eberhardt said angrily. 'How can you possibly lose the one and only patient you've got? What happened – did aliens beam him up to their spaceship while you were on your coffee break?'

'Roy? Roy, where are you!' cried Mrs Eberhardt.

She and Dr Gonzalez began checking beneath the other five beds in the ward. Officer Delinko whipped out his portable radio and said, 'I'm calling for back-up.'

Just then, the double doors to the waiting room flew open.

'Mom! Dad! I'm right here!'

The Eberhardts practically smothered their son with a tandem hug.

'Little devil,' chuckled Officer Delinko, holstering his radio. He was pleased to see that Roy wasn't wearing a torn green T-shirt.

'Whoa!' Dr Gonzalez clapped her hands sharply. 'Everybody hold on a minute.'

The Eberhardts looked up quizzically. The doctor didn't seem especially overjoyed to have found her lost patient.

'*That's* Roy?' she asked, pointing at their son.

'Of course it is. Who else would it be?' Mrs Eberhardt kissed the top of his head. 'Honey, you get back into that hospital bed right now—'

'Not so fast,' Mr Eberhardt said. 'I'm not sure what's

going on here, but I've got a feeling we owe the doctor an apology. Probably several apologies.' He planted both hands on Roy's shoulders. 'Let's see those dog bites, partner.'

Roy lowered his eyes. 'I didn't get bit, Dad. It wasn't me.'

Mrs Eberhardt groaned. 'OK, now I get it. *I'm* the crazy one, right? *I'm* the raving loony bird . . .'

'Folks? Excuse me, but we've still got a major problem,' Dr Gonzalez said. 'We've still got a patient missing.'

Officer Delinko was thoroughly confused. Once again he reached for his radio in anticipation of calling head-quarters.

'Before my brain explodes,' said Mrs Eberhardt, 'would someone please explain what this is all about?'

'Only one person can do that.' Mr Eberhardt gestured towards Roy, who suddenly wanted to crawl down a hole and hide. His father turned him around to face Dr Gonzalez.

'Tex?' she said, arching an eyebrow.

Roy felt his face redden. 'I'm really sorry.'

'This is a hospital. This is no place for games.'

'I know it's not. I apologize.'

'If you're the real Roy,' the doctor said, 'then who was that young man in the bed, and where did he go? I want the truth.'

Roy stared at the tops of his sneakers. He couldn't remember another day in his life when so many things had gone so wrong.

'Son,' his father said, 'answer the doctor.'

His mother squeezed his arm. 'Come on, honey. It's important.'

'You can be sure we'll find him,' Officer Delinko chimed in, 'sooner or later.'

Bleakly, Roy looked up to address the grown-ups.

'I don't know the boy's name, and I don't know where he is,' he said. 'I'm sorry, but that's the truth.'

And, technically, it was.

THIRTEEN

While Roy took a shower, his mother made a pot of spaghetti. He ate three helpings, though the dinner gathering was as quiet as a chess match.

Setting down his fork, Roy turned to his father.

'I guess it's the den, huh?'

'That's correct.'

It had been years since Roy had gotten a spanking, and he doubted that he was in for one now. The den was where his father summoned him whenever there was serious explaining to be done. Tonight Roy was so tired that he wasn't sure if anything he had to say would make sense.

His father was waiting, seated behind the broad walnut desk.

'What've you got there?' he asked Roy.

'A book.'

'Yes, I can see it's a book. I was hoping for the particulars.'

Roy's father could be sarcastic when he thought he wasn't getting a full answer. Roy figured it came from years of interrogating shifty characters – gangsters or spies, or whoever it was that his father was in the business of investigating.

'I'm assuming,' he said to Roy, 'that the book will cast some light on tonight's strange events.'

Roy handed it across the desk. 'You and Mom got it for me two Christmases ago.'

'I remember,' his father said, scanning the cover. '*The Sibley Guide to Birds.* Sure it wasn't for your birthday?'

'I'm sure, Dad.'

Roy had put the book on his Christmas list after it had settled a friendly wager between him and his father. One afternoon they'd seen a large reddish brown raptor swoop down and snatch a ground squirrel off a cattle range in the Gallatin River valley. Roy's father had bet him a milkshake that the bird was a young bald eagle whose crown feathers hadn't yet turned white, but Roy had said it was a fully grown golden eagle, more common on the dry prairies. Later, after visiting the Bozeman library and consulting *Sibley*, Roy's father conceded that Roy had been right.

Mr Eberhardt held up the book and asked, 'What does this have to do with that nonsense at the hospital?'

'Check out page 278,' Roy said. 'I marked it for you.'

His father flipped the book open to that page.

'Burrowing owl,' he read aloud from the text. '*Athene cunicularia.* Long-legged and short-tailed, with relatively long, narrow wings and flat head. Only small owl likely to be seen perched in the open in daylight.' His father peered quizzically at him over the top of the book. 'Is this connected to that "science project" you were supposedly working on this afternoon?'

'There is no science project,' Roy admitted.

'And the hamburger meat that your mother gave you?'

145

'A snack for the owls.'

'Continue,' Mr Eberhardt said.

'It's a long story, Dad.'

'I've got nothing but time.'

'All right,' Roy said. In some ways, he thought wearily, a spanking might be easier.

'See, there's this boy,' he began, 'about the same age as me . . .'

Roy told his father everything – well, *almost* everything. He didn't mention that the snakes distributed by Beatrice Leep's stepbrother were highly poisonous and that the boy had actually taped their mouths shut. Such details might have alarmed Mr Eberhardt more than the petty acts of vandalism.

Roy also chose not to reveal that Beatrice had nicknamed her stepbrother Mullet Fingers, just in case Roy's father felt legally obligated to report it to the police, or file it away in some government computer bank.

Otherwise, Roy told what he knew about the running boy. His father listened without interruption.

'Dad, he's really not a bad kid,' Roy said when he finished. 'All he's trying to do is save the owls.'

Mr Eberhardt remained silent for a few moments. He reopened the *Sibley Guide* and looked at the colour drawings of the small birds.

'See, if the Mother Paula's people bulldoze that property, they'll bury all the dens,' Roy said.

His father put the book aside and looked at Roy fondly, though with a trace of sadness.

'Roy, they own the property. They can do pretty much whatever they please.'

'But—'

'They've probably got all the necessary paperwork and permits.'

'They've got permits to bury owls?' Roy asked in disbelief.

'The owls will fly away. They'll find new dens somewhere else.'

'What if they've got babies? How will the baby birds fly away?' Roy shot back angrily. 'How, Dad?'

'I don't know,' his father admitted.

'How would you and Mom like it,' Roy pressed on, 'if a bunch of strangers showed up one day with bulldozers to flatten this house? And all they had to say was "Don't worry, Mr and Mrs Eberhardt, it's no big deal. Just pack up and move to another place." How would you feel about that?'

Roy's father stood up slowly, as if the weight of a hundred bricks were on his shoulders.

'Let's go for a walk,' he said.

It was a calm cloudless night, and a pale sliver of moon peeked over the rooftops. Insects as thick as confetti swirled around the cowls of the streetlights. Towards the end of the block, two cats could be heard yowling at each other.

Roy's father walked with his chin slightly downward, his hands stuffed in his pockets.

'You're growing up fast,' he remarked, catching Roy by surprise.

'Dad, I'm the third-shortest kid in my homeroom.'

'That's not what I meant.'

As they went along, Roy hopped from crack to crack on the sidewalk. They talked about comfortable topics – school, sports, sports *in* school – until Roy nudged the conversation back toward the delicate subject of Mullet Fingers. He needed to know where his father stood.

'You remember that day last summer we floated the Madison canyon?'

'Sure,' said his father, 'in inner tubes.'

'Right,' Roy said. 'And remember we counted five great horned owls in one cottonwood? Five!'

'Yes, I remember.'

'And you tried to take a picture but the camera fell in the river?'

'Not exactly. I *dropped* it in the river,' Roy's father recalled sheepishly.

'Hey, it was a cheapo disposable.'

'Yeah, but it would've been a great snapshot. Five in the same tree.'

'Yeah,' said Roy. 'That was pretty amazing.'

The owl story did the trick. His father took the cue.

'This boy you told me about – you really don't know his name?'

'He won't tell me. Neither will Beatrice,' Roy said. 'That's the honest truth.'

'He didn't take his stepfather's last name?'

'Leep? No, not according to Beatrice.'

'And you say he doesn't attend school.'

Roy's spirits fell. It sounded as if his father intended to report Mullet Fingers for truancy.

'What worries me,' Mr Eberhardt said, 'is the family situation. It doesn't sound too good.'

'No, it's not,' Roy conceded. 'That's why he doesn't live at home any more.'

'Aren't there any relatives who can take care of him?'

'He feels safe where he is,' Roy said.

'You're sure about that?'

'Dad, please don't turn him in. Please.'

'How can I, if I don't even know where to find him?' Roy's father gave him a wink. 'But I'll tell you what I am going to do: I'm going to spend some time thinking seriously about all this. You should, too.'

'OK,' said Roy. How could he possibly think of anything else? Even his battle with Dana Matherson seemed like a fuzzy, long-ago dream.

'We'd better head home,' his father said. 'It's getting late and you've had a long day.'

'A real long day,' Roy agreed.

But after he got into bed, he couldn't fall asleep. His body was exhausted but his mind was wide awake, buzzing with the day's turbulence. He decided to do some reading, and reached for a book titled A Land Remembered, which he'd checked out from school. It was the story of a family who lived in Florida back in the 1850s, when it was still a wilderness. Humans were scarce, and the swamps and woods teemed with wildlife – probably a pretty good time to be a burrowing owl, Roy mused.

An hour later, he was half-dozing when he heard a *tap-tap* on the bedroom door. It was his mother, slipping in to say good night. She took the book from his hands and turned off the lamp on the nightstand. Then she sat down on the bed and asked how he was feeling.

'Beat,' Roy said.

Gently she snugged the covers up to his neck. Even though he was way too warm, Roy didn't object. It was a mom thing; she couldn't help herself.

'Honey,' she said, 'you know how much we love you.'

Uh-oh, Roy thought. Here it comes.

'But what you did at the hospital tonight, letting that other boy use your name to get in the emergency ward—'

'It was my idea, Mom, not his.'

'And I'm sure your heart was in the right place,' she said, 'but it was still a lie, technically speaking. Providing false information, or whatever. It's a serious matter, honey—'

'I know.'

'—and it's just, well, your father and I don't want to see you get in trouble. Even for the sake of a friend.'

Roy raised himself up on one elbow. 'He would've run away before he'd give out his real name, and I couldn't let that happen. He was sick. He needed to see a doctor.'

'I understand. Believe me, I do.'

'They were asking him all kinds of nosy questions, Mom, and meanwhile he's about to keel over from the fever,' Roy said. 'Maybe what I did was wrong, but I'd do it all over again if I had to. I mean it.'

Roy expected a mild rebuke, but his mother only smiled. Smoothing the blanket with both hands, she said, 'Honey, sometimes you're going to be faced with situations where the line isn't clear between what's right and what's wrong. Your heart will tell you to do one thing, and your brain will tell you to do something different. In the end, all that's left is to look at both sides and go with your best judgement.'

Well, thought Roy, that's sort of what I did.

'This boy,' his mother said, 'why wouldn't he give out his real name? And why did he run away from the hospital like that?'

Mullet Fingers had escaped through a window in the women's restroom, next door to the X-ray department. He left his torn green shirt dangling from the antenna of Officer David Delinko's patrol car, which was parked outside the emergency room.

'He probably ran,' Roy said, 'because he was afraid somebody would call his mom.'

'So?'

'So, she doesn't want him any more. She'll have him locked up at the juvenile hall.'

'What?'

'His mom sent him off to military school,' Roy explained, 'and now she doesn't want him back. She said so herself, in front of Beatrice.'

Roy's mother cocked her head, as if she wasn't sure

that she'd heard him correctly. 'His mom doesn't want him?'

Roy saw something flash in her eyes. He wasn't certain if it was sorrow or anger – or both.

'She doesn't *want* him?' his mother repeated.

Roy nodded sombrely.

'Oh, my,' she said.

The words came out so softly that Roy was startled. He heard pain in his mother's voice, and he felt bad for telling her that part of Mullet Fingers' story.

'I'm sorry, Mom,' Roy said. 'I love you.'

'I love you, too, honey.'

She kissed his cheek and tucked in the sheets one more time. As she was shutting his door, he saw her hesitate and turn back to look at him.

'We're proud of you, Roy. You need to know that. Your father and I are both extremely proud.'

'Did Dad tell you about the owls?'

'Yes, he told me. It's too bad.'

'What should I do?'

'What do you mean?'

'Nothing,' Roy said, sinking into his pillow. 'G'night, Mom.'

She'd already answered the question, anyway. All he had to do was settle the argument between his heart and his brain.

FOURTEEN

Luckily the next day was Saturday, so Roy didn't have to get up early to catch the school bus.

As he sat down for breakfast, the phone rang. It was Garrett. He'd never before called Roy, but now he wanted him to go skateboarding at the outlet mall.

'I don't have a skateboard, remember?' Roy said.

'That's OK. I got an extra.'

'No thanks. I can't make it today.'

The true reason that Garrett had called was, of course, to find out what had happened to Dana Matherson at Trace Middle.

'Dude, somebody tied him to a flagpole!'

'Wasn't me,' said Roy. On this topic he couldn't talk freely in front of his parents.

'Then who? And how?' Garrett demanded.

'No comment,' said Roy, echoing Mullet Fingers.

'Aw, come on, Eberhardt!'

'See you Monday.'

After breakfast his father drove him to the bicycle shop to pick up his new tyre, and by noon Roy was fully mobile again. An address for 'L. B. Leep' was listed in the phone book, and Roy had no difficulty locating the house. It was on West Oriole Avenue, the same street as the bus stop where he'd first spotted the running boy.

In the Leep driveway sat a dented old Suburban and a shiny new Camaro convertible. Roy leaned his bike against the mailbox post and hurried up the sidewalk. He heard voices bickering inside the house, and he hoped it was only a TV show with the volume turned up.

After three firm knocks, the door swung open and there stood Leon Leep, all six feet nine inches of him. He wore baggy red gym shorts and a sleeveless mesh jersey that exposed a pale kettle-sized belly. Leon looked as if he hadn't spent five minutes in the exercise room since retiring from pro basketball; all that remained of his NBA physique was his height.

Roy tilted back on his heels in order to see Leon's face. His expression was perturbed and preoccupied.

'Beatrice home?' Roy asked.

'Yeah, but she's kinda busy right now.'

'Only take a minute,' Roy said. 'It's about school.'

'Oh. School,' said Leon, as if he'd forgotten where his daughter went five days a week. With a curious grunt, he lumbered off.

A moment later, Beatrice appeared. She looked stressed.

'Can I come in?' Roy asked.

'No,' she whispered. 'It's a bad time.'

'Then can you come out?'

'Nuh-uh.' Beatrice glanced anxiously behind her.

'You heard what happened at the hospital?'

She nodded. 'Sorry I didn't get back in time to help.'

'Is your brother OK?' Roy asked.

'Better than he was,' said Beatrice.

'Who's there? Who *is* that?' demanded a chilly voice from the hallway.

'Just a friend.'

'A boy?'

'Yeah, a boy,' Beatrice said, rolling her eyes for Roy's benefit.

A woman not much taller than Beatrice materialized in the doorway behind her. She had a sharp nose, beady, suspicious eyes, and a wild fountain of curly auburn hair. Blue smoke curled from a cigarette poised in glittering fingertips.

It could only be Lonna, the mother of Mullet Fingers.

'Who're you?' she asked.

'My name's Roy.'

'What do you want, Roy?' Lonna took a noisy drag off the cigarette.

'It's about school,' Beatrice said.

'Yeah, well, it's Saturday,' said Lonna.

Roy gave it a try. 'I'm really sorry to bother you, Mrs Leep. Beatrice and I are doing a science project together—'

'Not today, you're not,' Lonna cut him off. 'Miz Beatrice here will be busy cleanin' the house. And the kitchen. And the bathrooms. And anything else I can think of.'

Roy believed Lonna was skating on thin ice. Beatrice was obviously the stronger of the two, and she was seething mad. Lonna might have softened her tone had she seen what her stepdaughter's teeth had done to Roy's bicycle tyre.

'Maybe tomorrow,' Beatrice said to Roy, her jaw set grimly.

'Sure. Whatever.' He backed down the steps.

'We'll see about "tomorrow".' Lonna's voice was snide and croaky. 'Next time, call first,' she grumped at Roy. 'Ever heard of a telephone?'

As Roy rode away on his bike, he pondered the possibility that Mullet Fingers was better off roaming the woods than living at home with a witch for a mother. Roy wondered what made a grown-up turn out so ill-tempered and obnoxious. It wouldn't have surprised him if one day Beatrice literally chewed Lonna's head off.

His next stop was Dana Matherson's house, where another shaky example of motherhood lived. Roy had a feeling that Dana's father was no prize, either, and it was he who answered the door. Roy had expected another Neanderthal hulk, but Mr Matherson was thin and jittery and unhealthy-looking.

'Hi. My name's Roy.'

'Sorry, we're not interested,' Dana's father said politely, and began to shut the door.

'But I'm not selling anything,' Roy said through the crack. 'I'm here to see Dana.'

'Uh-oh. Not again.' Mr Matherson reopened the door and lowered his voice. 'Let me guess. He's hired you to do his homework for him.'

'No, sir. I'm just a friend from school.'

'A "friend"?'

Dana didn't have many friends, Roy knew, and the few he had were all much larger and meaner-looking than Roy.

'I ride the bus with him,' Roy said, and decided to recycle Beatrice's line one more time: 'We're doing a science project together.'

Mr Matherson's brow furrowed. 'Is this some kind of joke? Who *are* you, really?'

'I told you.'

Dana's father took out his wallet. 'All right, young man, no more kidding around. How much do I owe you?'

'For what?'

'For my son's homework.' Mr Matherson held up a five-dollar bill. 'The usual?'

He looked defeated and ashamed. Roy felt sorry for him. Clearly it was an ordeal, raising a goon like Dana.

'You don't owe me a dime,' Roy said. 'Is he home?'

Mr Matherson asked Roy to wait at the door. Moments later, Dana appeared, wearing droopy boxer shorts and a grimy pair of sweat socks.

'You!' he snarled.

'Yup,' said Roy. 'It's me.'

'What are you starin' at, cowgirl?'

Not much, Roy thought. He noticed that Dana's lisp had disappeared, along with the swelling in his upper lip.

'You must be nuts to ride all the way over here,' Dana said, 'just so you can get stomped to a pulp.'

'Come on outside. I haven't got all day.'

'What did you say?'

Dana stepped on to the porch and shut the door behind him, presumably so that his father wouldn't be a witness to the bloodshed. He wound up and swung fiercely at Roy's head, but Roy saw it coming. He ducked, and Dana's fist connected solidly with a fibreglass bird feeder.

Once Dana stopped howling, Roy said, 'Every time you try to hurt me, something bad happens to you. Haven't you noticed?'

Dana was doubled over, shaking his injured hand. He glared up at Roy.

'Like yesterday,' Roy went on, 'when you tried to kill me in the janitor's closet. Remember? You ended up getting whupped by a girl, stripped naked, and strung to a flagpole.'

'I wasn't naked,' Dana snapped. 'I had my underpants on.'

'When you go back to school Monday, everybody's going to be laughing at you. Everybody, Dana, and it's your own stupid fault. All you had to do was leave me alone. How hard is that?'

'Yeah, well, they'll be laughin' even louder when I kick your skinny ass to kingdom come, cowgirl. They'll be laughin' like hyenas, only you won't be around to hear 'em.'

'In other words,' Roy said irritably, 'you haven't learned a thing.'

'That's right. And you can't make me!'

Roy sighed. 'The only reason I came over here was to talk things out. Put a stop to all this dumb fighting.'

That had been his mission. If only he could make peace with Dana Matherson, even temporarily, then he'd be free to focus his energy on solving the Mullet Fingers dilemma.

But Dana hooted in his face. 'You must be crazy. After all the crap that's happened to me, you're so dead, Eberhardt. You're so dead it ain't even funny.'

Roy realized it was no use. 'Hopeless. That's what you are,' he said. 'By the way, that's a cool shade of purple.' He pointed at Dana's swollen knuckles.

'Get outta here, cowgirl! Now!'

Roy left him there on the porch, pounding the front door and bellowing for his father to let him in. Evidently the lock had clicked behind him when he'd come outside to take a punch at Roy.

It was a funny scene, Dana hopping up and down in his baggy boxer shorts, but Roy wasn't in the mood to enjoy it.

He hid his bicycle and snuck through the hole in the fence. In broad daylight, the junkyard didn't look so spooky; just cluttered. Still, Roy had no difficulty spotting the rusty old panel truck with JO-JO'S ICE CREAM AND SNO-CONES painted on the flimsy awning.

Beatrice's stepbrother was in the back of the truck, zipped into a mouldy sleeping bag. When he heard Roy's footsteps, he stirred and cracked one eye. Roy knelt beside him.

'Brought you some water.'

'Thanks, man.' Mullet Fingers reached for the plastic bottle. 'And thanks for last night. You get in trouble?'

'No big deal,' said Roy. 'How do you feel?'

'Like cow poop.'

'You're looking better than you did,' Roy told him, which was the truth. The shine had returned to the boy's cheeks, and his dog-bitten arm no longer appeared puffy and stiff. A blue button-sized bruise was visible on the other arm, where the boy had yanked out the intravenous tube before fleeing the hospital.

'Fever's gone, but I hurt all over,' he said, squirming out of the sleeping bag. Roy looked the other way while he put on some clothes.

'I came to tell you something. It's about the new pancake house,' Roy said. 'I talked to my dad and he said they can build whatever they want on that land, long as they've got the legal papers. There's nothing we can do.'

Mullet Fingers grinned. ' "We"?'

'All I mean is—'

'You're sayin' it's a lost cause, right? Come on, Tex, you gotta start thinkin' like an outlaw.'

'But I'm *not* an outlaw.'

'Yeah, you are. Last night at the hospital – that was definitely an outlaw move.'

'You were sick. You needed help,' Roy said.

Mullet Fingers finished off the water and tossed the empty bottle. He stood up, stretching like a cat.

'You crossed the line, and why? 'Cause you cared about

what happened to me,' he said to Roy, 'just like I care about what happens to them weird little owls.'

'They're burrowing owls. I've been reading up on them,' Roy said, 'which reminds me – they probably aren't too crazy about hamburger meat. They eat mostly bugs and worms, according to the bird books.'

'So I'll catch 'em some bugs.' The boy spoke with a touch of impatience. 'Point is, it ain't right, what's happening out there. That land belonged to the owls long before it belonged to the pancake house. Where you from, Tex?'

'Montana,' Roy replied automatically. Then he added, 'Well, actually, I was born in Detroit. But we lived in Montana right before we moved down here.'

'Never been out west,' Mullet Fingers said, 'but I know they got mountains.'

'Yeah. Awesome mountains.'

'That's what we need here,' said the boy. 'Florida's so flat, there's nothing to stop 'em from bulldozin' one coast to the other.'

Roy didn't have the heart to tell him that even mountains aren't safe from machines like that.

'Ever since I was little,' Mullet Fingers said, 'I've been watchin' this place disappear – the piney woods, the scrub, the creeks, the glades. Even the beaches, man – they put up all these giant hotels and only goober tourists are allowed. It really sucks.'

Roy said, 'Same thing happens everywhere.'

'Doesn't mean you don't fight back. Here, check it out.' From a pocket of his torn jeans the boy produced a crumpled piece of paper. 'I tried, Tex, see? Had Beatrice write a letter, telling 'em about the owls and all. Here's what they sent back.'

Roy smoothed out the paper, which bore the Mother Paula's company emblem at the top. It said:

```
Dear Ms Leep,

Thank you very much for your letter.
   We here at Mother Paula's All-American Pancake
Houses, Inc., take pride in our strong commitment
to the environment. Every possible effort will be
made to address your concerns.
   You have my personal assurance that Mother
Paula's is working closely with local authorities,
in full compliance with all laws, codes and regu-
lations.

Sincerely,
Chuck E. Muckle
Vice-President for Corporate Relations
```

'Lame,' Roy said, handing the paper back to Beatrice's stepbrother.

'Yeah, it's just a whatcha-call-it . . . a form letter. Didn't even mention the owls.'

They stepped out of the ice-cream truck into the sunlight. Ripples of heat rose from the junked cars, which were lined up in rows as far as Roy could see.

'How long are you going to hide here?' he asked the boy.

'Till they chase me out. Hey, what're you doin' tonight?'

'Homework.'

In truth Roy had only one short chapter to read for Mr Ryan's history class, but he wanted an excuse to stay home. He sensed that Mullet Fingers was planning another illegal visit to the Mother Paula's site.

'Well, you change your mind, meet me you-know-where at sunset,' the boy said, 'and bring a socket wrench.'

Roy felt a strange mixture of apprehension and excitement. Part of him was worried about the tactics used by Beatrice's stepbrother, and part of him was rooting for the kid.

'You've been sick,' Roy said. 'You need to rest up.'

'Ha! No time for that.'

'But the stuff you're doing, it won't work,' Roy persisted. 'It might slow things down but it won't stop 'em. Mother Paula's is a big company. They're not just going to give up and go away.'

'Neither am I, Tex.'

'Sooner or later they'll catch you, and then you'll end up in juvenile hall and—'

'Then I'll run away again. Same as always.'

'But don't you miss, like, a normal life?'

'Can't miss what you never had,' said Beatrice's stepbrother. Roy detected no bitterness in his voice.

'Maybe someday I'll go back to school,' the boy went

on, 'but for now I'm 'bout as smart as I need to be. Maybe I can't do algebra or say "Nice poodle" in French or tell you who discovered Brazil, but I can make a fire with two dry sticks and a rock. I can climb a coconut palm and get me enough fresh milk to last a month—'

They heard a motor start and ducked back into the ice-cream truck.

'Old guy who owns the place,' Mullet Fingers whispered. 'He's got an ATV – it's super cool. Goes flyin' around here like he's Jeff Gordon.'

When the growl of the all-terrain vehicle faded away toward the other side of the junkyard, the boy signalled that it was safe to leave the truck. He led Roy on a short-cut to the opening in the fence, and they slipped out together.

'Where you headed now?' Roy asked.

'I dunno. Maybe do some recon.'

'Recon?'

'You know. Reconnaissance,' Mullet Fingers said. 'Scope out targets for tonight.'

'Oh.'

'Aren't ya gonna ask what I got planned?'

Roy said, 'It's probably better if I don't know.' He considered mentioning that his father was in law enforcement. Maybe it would help the boy understand Roy's reluctance to participate, even though he sympathized with the owl crusade. Roy couldn't bear the thought of facing his parents through jail bars if he and Mullet Fingers got caught.

'My dad works for the government,' Roy said.

'That's swell,' said the boy. 'My dad eats Hot Pockets and stares at ESPN all day long. Come on, Tex, I got somethin' way cool to show you.'

'The name's Roy.'

'OK, *Roy.* Follow me.'

Then he took off running, again.

One summer in the late 1970s, long before Roy Eberhardt was born, a small but powerful tropical storm boiled out of the Gulf of Mexico and came ashore a few miles south of Coconut Cove. No one was injured or killed, though the ten-foot surge caused heavy damage to buildings and roads along the waterfront.

Among the casualties was a stone-crab boat called the *Molly Bell*, which was torn from her anchorage and swept up a swollen tidal creek, where she wallowed and sank from sight.

The storm blew itself out, the surge waters receded, and there, sticking halfway above the surface, was the lost crab boat. And there she stayed, for the creek was so slender and the currents so tricky and the oyster beds so perilous that no salvage captains would risk their own vessels to retrieve the *Molly Bell.*

Each season she grew more shrunken and dilapidated, surrendering her sturdy hull and deck to the ravages of woodworms, barnacles, and weather. After two decades, all of the *Molly Bell* that showed above the surface was the sloping, bleached roof of her pilothouse – just wide enough for two boys to sit side by side, faces upturned toward the sun, legs dangling over the pale green creek.

Roy was dazzled by the wondrous quiet, the bushy old mangroves sealing off the place from the honking and hammering of civilization. Beatrice's stepbrother closed his eyes and gustily inhaled the salty breeze.

A lone osprey hovered overhead, attracted by a glimmer of baitfish in the shallows. Upstream a school of baby tarpon rolled, also with lunch on their minds. Nearby a white heron posed regally on one leg, in the same tree where the boys had hung their shoes before swimming to the derelict boat.

'Two weeks ago I saw a crocodile in here. Nine-footer,' remarked Beatrice's stepbrother.

'Great. *Now* you tell me,' Roy said with a laugh.

The truth was, he felt totally safe. The creek was incredibly beautiful and wild; a hidden sanctuary, only twenty minutes away from his own backyard.

I might have found this place all by myself, Roy thought, if I hadn't spent so much time moping around being homesick for Montana.

The boy said, 'It ain't the crocs ya gotta worry about. It's the mosquitoes.'

'Have you brought Beatrice out here?'

'Just once. A blue crab bit her on the big toe, and that's all she wrote.'

'Poor crab,' said Roy.

'Yeah, it wasn't pretty.'

'Can I ask you something?'

'Anything but my name,' said Mullet Fingers. 'I don't want one and I don't need one. Not out here.'

'What I wanted to ask about,' Roy said, 'is you and your mom. What's the deal?'

'I dunno. We just never connected,' the boy said matter-of-factly. 'I quit sweatin' it a long time ago.'

Roy found that hard to believe.

'What about your real dad?'

'Never knew him.' The boy shrugged. 'Never even saw a picture.'

Roy couldn't think of what to say, so he quietly dropped the subject. Downstream a disturbance shook the water, and a dozen silvery cigar-sized fish jumped in unison, trying to escape some hungry predator.

'Cool! Here they come.' Beatrice's stepbrother pointed at the frantic V-shaped wake. He got flat on his belly and instructed Roy to hold his ankles.

'What for?'

'Hurry up, man, c'mon!'

With Roy anchoring his feet, the boy scooted himself forward over the rim of the pilothouse until his wiry upper torso was suspended out over the creek.

'Don't let go!' he yelled, stretching his tanned arms outwards until his fingertips touched the water.

Roy's hold began to slip, so he pitched forward, exerting his full weight upon the boy's midsection. He expected both of them to go tumbling into the creek, which was all right as long as they didn't scrape any oyster bars.

'Here they come! Get ready!'

'I've gotcha.' Roy managed to hang on as he felt the boy lunge. He heard a grunt, a splash, and then a triumphant 'Whooo-hoooo!!!'

Grabbing the boy's belt loops, Roy pulled him safely back on to the pilothouse. The boy flipped over and sat up beaming, his hands cupped in front of him.

'Take a peek,' he told Roy.

The boy was holding a bright blunt-headed fish that sparkled like liquid chrome. How he had snatched such a slippery little ghost from the water with only his bare hands, Roy didn't know. Even the osprey would have been impressed.

'So that's a mullet,' Roy said.

'Yep.' The boy smiled proudly. 'That's how come I got the nickname.'

'Exactly how'd you do that? What's the trick?'

'Practise,' the boy replied. 'Trust me, it beats home-work.'

The fish glittered blue and green as it wriggled in his palms. Holding it over the creek, the boy let go. The mullet landed with a soft *plop* and vanished in a swirl.

'Bye, little guy,' said Beatrice's stepbrother. 'Swim fast.'

Later, after they paddled to shore, Roy's curiosity got the best of him. He heard himself saying: 'OK, you can tell me now. What's going to happen tonight at Mother Paula's?'

Mullet Fingers, who was shaking a snail off one of his new sneakers, flashed a mischievous glance. 'There's only one way to find out,' he said. 'Be there.'

FIFTEEN

Roy sat cross-legged on the floor, gazing up at the cowboy poster from the Livingston rodeo. He wished he was as brave as a champion bull rider, but he wasn't.

The Mother Paula's mission was simply too risky; somebody, or something, would be waiting. The attack dogs might be gone, but the company wasn't about to leave the new pancake-house location unguarded for long.

In addition to a fear of getting caught, Roy had serious qualms about trying anything illegal – and there was no dodging the fact that vandalism was a crime, however noble the cause.

Yet he couldn't stop thinking ahead to the day when the owl dens would be destroyed by bulldozers. He could picture the mother owls and father owls, helplessly flying in circles while their babies were being smothered under tons of dirt.

It made Roy sad and angry. So what if Mother Paula's had all the proper permits? Just because something was legal didn't automatically make it right.

Roy still hadn't settled the argument between his brain and his heart. Surely there had to be a way for him to help the birds – and Beatrice's stepbrother – without breaking the law. He needed to come up with a plan.

Glancing out the window, Roy was reminded that time was slipping away. The shadows had lengthened, which meant that the sun would be setting soon and that Mullet Fingers would be on the move.

Before leaving the house, Roy poked his head into the kitchen, where his mother stood over the stove.

'Where you going?' she asked.

'Bike ride.'

'Another one? You just got back.'

'When's dinner? It smells great.'

'Pot roast, honey, nothing special. But we won't be eating until seven-thirty or eight – your dad had a late tee time.'

'Perfect,' Roy said. 'Bye, Mom.'

'What are you up to?' she called after him. 'Roy?'

He pedalled at full speed to the block where Dana Matherson lived, and chained his bicycle to a street sign. Approaching the house on foot, he slipped unnoticed through a hedge into the backyard.

Roy wasn't tall enough to see in the windows; he had to jump and hold himself up by his fingers. In the first room he saw a thin rumpled figure lying prone on a sofa: Dana's father, holding what appeared to be an ice pack to his forehead.

In the second room was either Dana's mother or Dana himself, wearing red spandex pants and a ratty wig. Roy decided it was probably Mrs Matherson, since the person was pushing a vacuum cleaner. He lowered himself and resumed creeping along the outside wall until he reached the third window.

And there, sure enough, was Dana.

He lay sprawled on his bed, a lazy blob in dirty cargo pants and unlaced high-top sneakers. He wore a stereo headset, and his head was jerking back and forth to the music.

Standing on tiptoe, Roy tapped his knuckles against the glass. Dana didn't hear him. Roy kept tapping until a dog on the porch next door began to bark.

The next time Roy levered himself up to peek into the room, Dana was glowering at him through the window. He had pulled off the headset and was mouthing some words that even an amateur lipreader could have figured out.

Smiling, Roy dropped to the lawn and took two steps back from the Matherson house. He proceeded to do something that was drastically out of character for a boy who was basically shy.

What he did was salute crisply, spin around, drop his pants, and bend over.

Viewed upside down (which was how Roy saw it), Dana's wide-eyed reaction suggested that he'd never been mooned in such a personal way. He seemed highly insulted.

Calmly Roy pulled up his trousers, then strolled around to the front of the house and waited for Dana to come hurtling out the door in a fury. It didn't take long.

Roy broke into a brisk jog with Dana no more than twenty yards behind him, cursing and spluttering vile names. Roy knew he was a faster runner, so he measured his pace; he didn't want Dana to get discouraged and give up.

Yet after only three blocks it became evident that Dana was in even worse shape than Roy had anticipated. Steadily he ran out of steam, the angry curses dissolving into moans of fatigue, the name calling into sickly wheezes.

When Roy checked behind him, he saw that Dana was gimping along in a lopsided half-trot. It was pathetic. They were still a half-mile from where Roy wanted to be, but he knew Dana wouldn't make it without pausing for a rest. The sorry load was about to keel over.

Roy had no choice but to pretend he was tiring, too. Slower and slower he ran, falling back in the chase until Dana was practically stumbling at his heels. Familiar sweaty hands clamped down on his neck, but Roy realized that Dana was too worn out to throttle him. The kid was simply trying to keep himself from falling down.

It didn't work. They landed in a heap, Roy pinned on the bottom. Dana was panting like a wet plough horse.

'Don't hurt me! I give up!' Roy peeped convincingly.

'Unnnggghhh.' Dana's face was as red as a pepper and his eyeballs were fluttering in their sockets.

'You win!' Roy cried.

'Aaaarrrgghhh.'

Dana's breath was foul, but his body odour was ferocious. Roy turned his head away to gulp some fresh air.

Beneath them the ground was soft and the soil was as

black as coal. Roy guessed that they'd fallen in some-body's garden. They lay there for what seemed like for ever while Dana recovered from the pursuit. Roy felt smushed and uncomfortable, but it was no use trying to squirm loose; Dana was dead weight.

Eventually he stirred, tightened his hold on Roy, and said: 'Now I'm gonna kick your butt, Eberhardt.'

'Please don't do that.'

'You mooned me!'

'It was a joke. I'm really sorry.'

'Hey, you moon somebody and that's it. You get your butt kicked.'

'I don't blame you for being p.o.'ed,' Roy said.

Dana slugged him in the ribs, but there wasn't much muscle in the punch.

'Think it's funny now, cowgirl?'

Roy shook his head no, faking like he was hurt.

Dana grinned malevolently. His teeth were nubby and yellow, like an old barn dog's. Kneeling on Roy's chest, he hauled back to hit him again.

'Wait!' Roy squeaked.

'For what? Beatrice the Bear ain't here to save ya this time.'

'Ciggies,' Roy said in a confidential whisper.

'Uh?' Dana lowered his fist. 'What'd you say?'

'I know where there's a whole case of cigarettes. If you promise not to beat me up, I'll show you.'

'What kinda cigarettes?'

Roy hadn't thought of that detail when he was cooking

up the phoney story. It hadn't occurred to him that Dana would be picky about his brand of smokes.

'Gladiators,' said Roy, remembering the name from a magazine advertisement.

'Gold or Light?'

'Gold.'

'No way!' Dana exclaimed.

'Way,' Roy said.

Dana's expression wasn't hard to read – he was already scheming to keep some of the cigarettes for himself and sell the rest for a tidy profit to his buddies.

'Where are they?' He climbed off of Roy and yanked him upright to a sitting position. 'Tell me!'

'First you gotta promise not to beat me up.'

'Sure, man, I promise.'

'Ever again,' Roy said. 'For all time.'

'Yeah, whatever.'

'I want to hear you say it.'

Dana laughed in a patronizing way. 'All right, little cowgirl. I'll never, ever, *ever* pound on your sorry butt again. OK? Swear on my father's grave. That good enough for ya?'

'Your father's still alive,' Roy pointed out.

'Then I swear on Natalie's grave. Now tell me where those Gladiator Golds are stashed. I ain't kiddin'.'

'Who's Natalie?' Roy asked.

'My mother's parakeet. That's the only dead person I know.'

'I guess that'll do.' Based on what Roy had seen of the

Matherson household, he had an uneasy feeling that poor Natalie hadn't expired of natural causes.

'So, we cool?' Dana asked.

'Yeah,' said Roy.

It was time to turn the big dummy loose. The sun had dropped into the Gulf, and the streetlights were coming on.

Roy said, 'There's an empty lot at the corner of Woodbury and East Oriole.'

'Yeah?'

'In one corner of the lot there's a construction trailer. That's where the cigarettes are stashed.'

'Sweet. A whole case,' Dana said greedily. 'But how come you know 'bout it?'

''Cause me and my friends hid 'em there. We swiped 'em off a truck on the Seminole reservation.'

'You?'

'Yeah, me.'

It was a fairly believable yarn, Roy thought. The Indian tribe sold tax-free tobacco products, and smokers came from miles away to stock up.

'Where'bouts inside the trailer?' Dana demanded.

'You can't miss 'em,' Roy said. 'You want me to, I'll show you.'

Dana snorted. 'No thanks. I'll find 'em.'

He placed two fingers in the centre of Roy's chest and gave a stiff shove. Roy flopped back into the flower bed, his head coming to rest in the same soft indentation. He waited a minute or so before getting up and brushing himself off.

By then Dana Matherson was long gone. Roy would have been disappointed if he wasn't.

Curly made it through Friday night, though not without personal inconvenience. First thing Saturday morning, he drove to the hardware store and bought a sturdy new seat for the toilet in the trailer, plus a dozen jumbo rat-traps. Then he stopped at the Blockbuster and got a movie in case the TV cable went out again.

From there he headed home, where his wife informed him that she would need the pickup truck, since her mother was taking the other car to the bingo hall. Curly didn't like anyone else driving his pickup, so he was sulking when his wife dropped him off at the trailer.

Before settling down in front of the television, Curly took out his gun and made a quick tour of the property. Nothing appeared to have been disturbed, including the survey stakes. He began to believe that his presence was indeed keeping intruders away from the construction site. Tonight would be the true test; without the pickup truck parked near the trailer, the place would appear deserted and inviting.

As he walked the fence line, Curly was pleased not to come across a single cottonmouth moccasin. That meant he could save his five remaining bullets for serious security threats, though he didn't want a repeat of the nerve-rattling fiasco with the field mouse.

Determined to discourage uninvited rodents, Curly carefully baited the rat-traps with peanut butter and placed them at strategic locations along the outside walls of the trailer.

Around five o'clock, he nuked a frozen dinner and popped the movie into the VCR. The turkey potpie wasn't half bad, and the cherry strudel turned out to be surprisingly tasty. Curly didn't leave a crumb.

Unfortunately, the movie was a disappointment. It was called *The Last House on Witch Boulevard III*, and one of the co-stars was none other than Kimberly Lou Dixon.

A clerk at the Blockbuster had helped Curly find the film, which had been released several years earlier, before Kimberly Lou Dixon signed on for the Mother Paula TV commercials. Curly guessed it was her very first Hollywood role after retiring from beauty pageants.

In the movie, Kimberly Lou played a pretty college cheerleader who got hexed into a witch and started boiling the star football players in a basement cauldron. Her hair was dyed fiery red for the part, and she wore a fake nose with a rubber wart on the tip of it.

The acting was pretty lame and the special effects were cheesy, so Curly fast-forwarded to the end of the tape. In the final scene, the hunk college quarterback escaped from the cauldron and threw some sort of magic dust on Kimberly Lou Dixon, who turned from a witch back into a pretty cheerleader before collapsing in his arms. Then, as the quarterback was about to kiss her, she morphed into a dead iguana.

Curly turned off the VCR in disgust. He decided that if he ever got to meet Kimberly Lou Dixon in person, he wouldn't mention *The Last House on Witch Boulevard III*.

He switched to cable and found a golf tournament, which made him drowsy. First prize was a million dollars and a new Buick, but Curly still couldn't keep his eyes open.

When he awoke, it was dark outside. A noise had startled him from his nap, but he wasn't sure what it was. Suddenly he heard it again: SNAP!

Instantly a cry rang out – possibly human, but Curly wasn't sure. He muted the TV and grabbed for his gun.

Something – an arm? a fist? – thumped against the aluminium side of the trailer. Then came another SNAP, punctuated by a muffled profanity.

Curly crept to the door and waited. His heart was thumping so hard, he was afraid the intruder might hear it.

As soon as the doorknob began to jiggle, Curly went into action. He lowered a shoulder, let out a Marine-style roar, and crashed out of the trailer, snapping the door off its hinges.

The intruder let out a cry as he hit the ground in a heap. Curly pinned him there with a heavy boot on the midsection.

'Don't move!'

'I won't! I won't! I won't!'

Curly lowered the gun barrel. By the light from the trailer, he could see that the burglar was just a kid – a large, lumpy kid. He had accidentally stumbled upon the rat-traps, two of which were attached crookedly to his sneakers.

That has to hurt, Curly thought.

'Don't shoot me! Don't shoot me!' the kid cried.

'Aw, shut up.' Curly stuck the .38 in his belt. 'What's your name, son?'

'Roy. Roy Eberhardt.'

'Well, you're in deep doo-doo, Roy.'

'Sorry, man. Please don't call the cops. 'K?'

The boy began to wiggle, so Curly pressed down harder with his boot. Looking across the lot, he noticed that the padlock on the gate had been broken with a heavy chunk of cinderblock.

'You must've thought you was pretty slick,' he said, 'sneakin' in and outta here whenever you pleased. You and your smart-ass sense of humour.'

The boy raised his head. 'What're you talkin' about?'

'Don't play dumb, Roy. You're the one yanked out all the survey stakes, and put them 'gators in the port-o-johnnies—'

'What! You're crazy, man.'

'—and painted the cop car. No wonder you don't want me callin' the police.' Curly leaned closer. 'What's your problem, boy? You got a gripe with Mother Paula's? To be honest, you look like a kid that enjoys a good pancake.'

'I do! I lovepancakes!'

'Then what's the deal?' Curly said. 'Why you doin' all this stuff?'

'But I never even been here before!'

Curly removed his foot from the kid's belly. 'Come on, kid. Get up.'

The boy took his hand, but instead of letting Curly

pull him to his feet, he yanked Curly to the ground. Curly managed to get one arm around the boy's neck, but he twisted free and hurled a handful of dirt into Curly's face.

Just like in that stupid movie, Curly thought as he clawed miserably at his eyes, except I'm not turning into a cheerleader.

He cleared the crud from his vision just in time to see the boy run off, the rat-traps clattering like castanets on the toes of his shoes. Curly attempted to give chase but he made it only about five steps before tripping in an owl hole and falling flat.

'I'll get you, Roy!' he hollered into the darkness. 'You're outta luck, mister!'

Officer David Delinko had Saturday off, which was fine. It had been a hectic week, culminating in that weird scene at the emergency room.

The missing dog-bite victim still had not been found or identified, though Officer Delinko now had a green shirt to match the torn sleeve he'd found on the fence at the Mother Paula's construction site. The boy who'd fled from the hospital must have left the shirt on the antenna of Officer Delinko's squad car, obviously as some sort of joke.

Officer Delinko was tired of being the butt of such jokes, though he was grateful for the fresh clue. It suggested that the emergency-room runaway was one of the Mother Paula's vandals, and that young Roy Eberhardt knew more about the case than he was admitting. Officer Delinko figured that Roy's father would get to the bottom of the mystery, given his special background in interrogations.

The policeman spent the afternoon watching baseball on television, but both Florida teams got creamed – the Devil Rays lost by five, the Marlins by seven. Around dinnertime he opened his refrigerator and discovered there was nothing to eat but three individually wrapped slices of Kraft processed cheese.

Immediately he embarked on a trip to the minimart for a frozen pizza. As was his new routine, Officer Delinko made a detour toward the Mother Paula's property. He still hoped to catch the vandals, whoever they were, in the act. If that happened, the captain and the sergeant would have little choice but to take him off desk duty and put him back on patrol again – with a glowing commendation for his file.

Turning his squad car onto East Oriole, Officer Delinko wondered if the trained Rottweilers were guarding the pancake-house site tonight. In that event, it would be pointless for him to stop; nobody would mess with those crazed dogs.

In the distance, a bulky figure appeared in the middle of the road. It was advancing in an odd halting gait. Officer Delinko braked the Crown Victoria and peered warily through the windshield.

As the figure drew closer, passing through the glow of the streetlights, the policeman could see it was a husky teenaged boy. The boy kept his head down and seemed to be in a hurry, though he wasn't running in a normal way; it was more of a wobbly lurch. Each step made a sharp clacking sound that echoed on the pavement.

When the boy came into range of the squad car's headlights, Officer Delinko noticed a flat rectangular object attached to each of his sneakers. Something very strange was going on.

The police officer flipped on the flashing blue lights and stepped out of the car. The surprised teenager halted and looked up. His pudgy chest was heaving and his face was slick with sweat.

Officer Delinko said, 'Can I talk to you for a second, young man?'

'Nope,' answered the boy, turning to bolt.

With rat-traps on his feet, he didn't get far. Officer Delinko had no difficulty catching the boy and hustling him into the caged backseat of the police cruiser. The patrolman's seldom-used handcuffs worked splendidly.

'Why did you run?' he asked his young prisoner.

'I want a lawyer,' the kid replied, stone-faced.

'Cute.'

Officer Delinko put the squad car into a U-turn so he could take the boy to the police station. Glancing in the rearview mirror, he spotted another figure hurrying up the street, waving frantically.

Now what? thought the policeman, stepping on the brakes.

'Whoa! Wait up!' shouted the approaching figure, his unmistakable bald head glinting under the streetlights.

It was Leroy Branitt, aka Curly, the foreman of the Mother Paula's project. He was huffing and puffing when he reached the police car, and drooped wearily across the hood. His face was florid and smudged with dirt.

Officer Delinko leaned out the window and asked what was the matter.

'You caught him!' the foreman exclaimed breathlessly. 'Way to go!'

'Caught who?' The policeman turned to appraise his prisoner in the backseat.

'Him! The little sneak who's been messin' up our place.' Curly straightened and pointed accusingly at the teenager. 'He tried to bust into my trailer tonight. Lucky I didn't shoot his fool head off.'

Officer Delinko fought to contain his excitement. *He'd actually done it! He'd caught the Mother Paula's vandal!*

'I had him pinned and he got away,' Curly was saying, 'but not before I wrung his name outta him. It's Roy. Roy Eberhardt. Go ahead and ask him!'

'I don't need to,' said Officer Delinko. 'I know Roy Eberhardt, and that's not him.'

'What!' Curly was fuming, as if he'd expected honesty from the young burglar.

Officer Delinko said, 'I assume you want to press charges.'

'You bet your shiny tin badge I do. This creep tried to blind me, too. Threw dirt in my eyes!'

'That's an assault,' Officer Delinko said, 'to go along with the attempted burglary, trespassing, destruction of private property and so forth. Don't worry, I'll put it all in the report.' He motioned to the passenger side and told Curly to hop in. 'You'll need to come down to head-quarters.'

'My pleasure.' Curly scowled at the sullen lump in the backseat. 'You wanna hear how he got those ridiculous rat-traps on his tootsies?'

'Later,' said Officer Delinko. 'I want to hear every-thing.' This was the big break that the policeman had been waiting for. He could hardly wait to get to the sta-tion and pry a full confession out of the teenager.

From training films, Officer Delinko remembered that delicate psychology was necessary when dealing with uncooperative suspects. So in a deliberately mild voice, he said: 'You know, young man, you can make this much easier on yourself.'

'Yeah, right,' the kid muttered from behind the mesh partition.

'You could start by telling us your real name.'

'Gee, I forget.'

Curly chuckled harshly. 'Puttin' this one in jail is gonna be fun.'

Officer Delinko shrugged. 'Have it your way,' he told the teenaged prisoner. 'You got nuthin' to say, that's cool. You're entitled under the law.'

The boy smiled crookedly. 'What if I got a question?'

'Go right ahead and ask it.'

'OK, I will,' said Dana Matherson. 'Either of you dorks got a cigarette I could bum?'

SIXTEEN

The doorbell rang while the Eberhardts were eating lunch.

'On a Sunday, honestly!' Roy's mother said. She believed that Sundays should be reserved for family activities.

'You've got a visitor,' Roy's father said when he returned from answering the door.

Roy's stomach knotted because he wasn't expecting anybody. He suspected that something newsworthy must have happened last night at the pancake-house property.

'One of your buddies,' Mr Eberhardt said. 'He says you guys had plans to go skateboarding.'

'Oh.' It had to be Garrett. Roy was almost dizzy with relief. 'Yeah, I forgot.'

'But, honey, you don't own a skateboard,' Mrs Eberhardt pointed out.

'It's all right. His friend brought an extra,' said Mr Eberhardt.

Roy rose from the table, hurriedly dabbing his mouth with a napkin. 'Is it OK if I go?'

'Oh, Roy, it's Sunday,' his mother objected.

'Please? Just for an hour.'

He knew his parents would say yes. They were happy to think he was making friends at his new school.

Garrett was waiting on the front steps. He started to blurt something, but Roy signalled him to keep quiet until they were away from the house. Wordlessly they skated the sidewalk to the end of the block, where Garrett kicked off of his board and exclaimed: 'You won't believe it – Dana Matherson got busted last night!'

'No way!' Roy was trying to act more surprised than he was. Obviously the Mother Paula's property had been under surveillance, just as he'd anticipated.

'The cops called my mom first this morning,' Garrett reported. 'He tried to break into a trailer to steal some stuff.'

As the guidance counsellor at Trace Middle School, Garrett's mother was notified whenever a student got into trouble with the law.

Garrett said, 'Dude, here's the killer – Dana told 'em he was *you*!'

'Oh, nice.'

'What a butthead, huh?'

'And they probably believed him,' Roy said.

'Not even for a minute.'

'Was he alone?' Roy asked. 'Anybody else get arrested?'

Anybody like Beatrice Leep's stepbrother? he wanted to say.

'Nope. Just him,' Garrett said, 'and guess what – he's got a record!'

'A record?'

'A rap sheet, dude. Dana's been busted before, is what the cops told my mom.'

Again, Roy wasn't exactly shocked by the news. 'Busted for what?'

'Shoplifting, breakin' into Coke machines – stuff like that,' Garrett said. 'One time he even knocked down a lady and swiped her purse. Mom made me promise not to tell. It's supposed to be a secret, since Dana's still a minor.'

'Right,' said Roy sarcastically. 'You wouldn't want to ruin his fine reputation.'

'Whatever. Hey, you oughta be doin' somersaults.'

'Yeah, what for?'

''Cause my mom says they're gonna lock him up this time.'

'Juvie hall?'

'No doubt,' said Dana, 'on account of his rap sheet.'

'Wow,' Roy said quietly.

He wasn't in the mood to turn somersaults, though he couldn't deny experiencing a sense of liberation. He was tired of being Dana Matherson's punching bag.

And while he felt guilty about making up the bogus cigarette story, Roy also couldn't help but think that putting Dana behind bars was a public service. He was a nasty kid. Maybe a hitch at juvenile hall would straighten him out.

'Hey, wanna do the skate park?' Garrett asked.

'Sure.'

Roy got on his borrowed skateboard and pushed off hard with his right foot. The whole way to the park, he never once checked over his shoulder to see if he was being stalked.

It felt good, the way Sundays ought to feel.

Curly awoke in his own bed, and why not?

The Mother Paula's vandal was finally in custody, so there was no reason to spend the night on guard at the trailer.

After Officer Delinko gave him a lift home, Curly had entertained his wife and mother-in-law with a blow-by-blow account of the exciting events. For dramatic purposes, Curly had jazzed up a few of the details.

In his version of the story, for instance, the surly young intruder disabled him with an expertly aimed karate chop (which sounded more serious than having dirt thrown in your face). Curly also decided it was unnecessary to mention that he'd tripped in an owl burrow and fallen. Instead he described the chase as a breathless neck-and-neck sprint. Officer Delinko's role in the capture of the fleeing criminal was conveniently minimized.

Curly's performance went over so fabulously at home that he was confident Chuck Muckle would go for it, too. First thing Monday morning, Curly would call Mother Paula's corporate headquarters to give the vice-president the details of the arrest, and of his own heroics. He couldn't wait to hear Mr Muckle choke out a congratulation.

After lunch, Curly sat down to watch a ball game. No sooner had he settled in front of the TV than a Mother Paula's commercial came on, promoting the weekend special: $6.95 for all the pancakes you could eat, plus free sausage and coffee.

The sight of Kimberly Lou Dixon playing Mother Paula made Curly think of the cheesy movie he'd rented, *The Last House on Witch Boulevard III*. He couldn't recall whether it was due back at Blockbuster that afternoon or the following day. Curly hated paying late fees on video rentals, so he decided to go to the trailer and get the tape.

On the drive there, Curly was distressed to remember that he'd left something else at the construction site: his gun!

During the night's commotion, he had somehow lost track of the .38 revolver. He didn't recall having it when he was riding in Officer Delinko's patrol car, so it must have slipped from his belt while he was scuffling with the kid outside the trailer. Another possibility was that he'd dropped it when he stepped in that darn owl hole.

Misplacing a loaded gun was a serious matter, and Curly was highly annoyed with himself. When he arrived at the fenced lot, he hurried to the area where he and the teenager had wrestled. There was no .38 lying around.

Anxiously Curly retraced his steps to the owl den and pointed a flashlight down the hole. No gun.

Now he was genuinely worried. He checked inside the trailer and saw that nothing had been disturbed from the night before. The door was too damaged to be reattached, so Curly covered the opening with two sheets of plywood.

Then he began a methodical search, back and forth across the property, eyes glued to the ground. In one hand he carried a heavy rock, just in case he encountered one of the poisonous moccasins.

Gradually a harrowing thought seeped into Curly's brain, chilling him like ice water: What if the teenaged burglar had swiped the revolver from his waistband while they were fighting? The kid could have stashed it in a Dumpster or tossed it in some bushes as he ran away.

Curly shuddered and pressed on with the hunt. After about half an hour, he'd worked his way down to the section of the property where the earthmoving equipment was parked in preparation for the site clearing.

By this time he'd almost given up hope of finding the gun. He was quite a distance from where he last remembered having it – and in the opposite direction from where the vandal had fled. Curly figured there was no possible way that the .38 could turn up so far from the trailer, unless an exceptionally large owl had picked it up and carried it there.

His eyes fixed on a shallow depression in a soft patch of sand: the imprint of a bare foot, definitely human. Curly counted the toes, just to make sure.

The foot appeared to be considerably smaller than Curly's own; smaller, too, than those of the husky teenaged burglar.

Farther ahead, Curly came across another footprint – and then another, and still another after that. The tracks led directly toward the row of earthmoving machines, and Curly advanced with a growing sense of unease.

He stopped in front of a bulldozer and shielded his brow from the sunlight. At first he didn't notice anything wrong, but then it hit him like a kick from a mule.

The driver's seat was gone!

Dropping the rock that he'd been carrying for protection, Curly dashed to the next machine in line, a backhoe. Its seat had disappeared, too.

In a snit, Curly stomped toward the third and last piece of equipment, a grader. Again, no driver's seat.

Curly spat out a cuss word. Without seats, the earth-moving machines were basically useless. The operators had to sit down in order to work the foot pedals and steer at the same time.

The foreman's mind was racing feverishly. Either the kid they'd caught last night had a hidden accomplice, or someone else had sneaked on to the property after Curly had departed.

But who? Curly wondered in exasperation. Who sabotaged my equipment, and when?

Fruitlessly he searched for the missing seats, his mood darkening by the moment. No longer was he looking forward to calling Mr Muckle at Mother Paula's headquarters; in fact, he was dreading it. Curly suspected that the grumpy vice-president would take great delight in firing him over the phone.

In despair, Curly headed for the portable latrines. Having guzzled almost a whole pitcher of iced tea during lunch, he now felt like his belly was about to burst. The stress of the situation wasn't helping, either.

Curly armed himself with the flashlight and entered one of the Travellin' Johnnys, leaving the door slightly ajar in case a hasty exit was required. He wanted to be sure nobody had booby-trapped the toilet with foul-tempered reptiles again.

Cautiously Curly aimed his flashlight down the dark hole of the commode. He gulped as the beam illuminated something shiny and black in the water, but upon closer scrutiny he saw that it wasn't an alligator.

'Perfect,' Curly muttered wretchedly. 'Just perfect.'

It was his gun.

Roy was aching to sneak over to the junkyard and visit Mullet Fingers. He wanted to find out what had happened last night at the Mother Paula's property.

The problem was Roy's mother. She invoked the Sunday rule as soon as he returned from the skateboard park, and a family outing was launched. Making good on his promise, Roy's father took them out the Tamiami Trail to an Indian tourist shop that offered airboat trips through the Everglades.

Roy ended up having a great time, even though the noise was so loud that it hurt his eardrums. The tall Seminole who was driving the airboat wore a straw cowboy hat. He said the engine was the same type used on small airplanes.

The rush of wind made Roy's eyes water as the flat-bottomed boat whisked across the sawgrass flats and weaved through the narrow winding creeks. It was cooler than a roller coaster. Along the way they stopped to look at snakes, bullfrogs, chameleons, raccoons, opossums, turtles, ducks, herons, two bald eagles, an otter, and (by Roy's count) nineteen alligators. His father got most of the action on video, while his mother took pictures with her new digital camera.

Although the airboat was very fast, the ride across the shallows was like gliding on silk. Again Roy was astounded by the immense flatness of the terrain, the lush horizons, and the exotic abundance of life. Once you got away from all the jillions of people, Florida was just as wild as Montana.

That night, lying in bed, Roy felt a stronger connection to Mullet Fingers, and a better understanding of the boy's private crusade against the pancake house. It wasn't just about the owls, it was about everything – all the birds and animals, all the wild places that were in danger of being wiped out. No wonder the kid was mad, Roy thought, and no wonder he was so determined.

When Roy's parents came in to say goodnight, he told them he'd never forget their trip to the Everglades, which was the truth. His mom and his dad were still his best friends, and they could be fun to hang out with. Roy knew it wasn't easy on them, either, packing up and moving all the time. The Eberhardts were a team, and they stuck together.

'While we were gone, Officer Delinko left a message on the answering machine,' Roy's father said. 'Last night he arrested a suspect in the vandalism at the construction site.'

Roy didn't say a word.

'Don't worry,' Mr Eberhardt added. 'It wasn't the young man you told me about, the one who ran away from the hospital.'

'It was the Matherson boy,' Mrs Eberhardt cut in excitedly, 'the one who attacked you on the bus. And he tried to convince the police he was you!'

Roy couldn't pretend not to know. 'Garrett told me all about it,' he admitted.

'Really? Garrett must have an inside source,' Roy's father remarked.

'The best,' said Roy. 'What else did the policeman's message say?'

'That's about it. I got the impression he wanted me to ask if you knew anything about what happened.'

'Me?' Roy said.

'Oh, that's ridiculous,' his mother interjected. 'How would Roy know what a hoodlum like Dana Matherson was up to?'

Roy's mouth was as dry as chalk. As close as he felt to his parents, he wasn't prepared to tell them that he'd mooned Dana, purposely lured him toward the Mother Paula's property, and then made up a story about a stash of cigarettes inside the trailer.

'It's certainly a strange coincidence,' Mr Eberhardt was saying, 'two different kids targeting the same location. Is it possible the Matherson boy hooked up with your friend, Beatrice's stepbrother—'

'No way,' Roy interjected firmly. 'Dana doesn't care about the owls. He doesn't care about anything but himself.'

'Of course he doesn't,' Roy's mother said.

As his parents were shutting the bedroom door behind them, Roy said, 'Hey, Dad?'

'Yes?'

'Remember how you said the pancake people could do whatever they wanted on that land if they had all the permits and stuff?'

'That's right.'

'How do I check up on something like that?' Roy asked. 'You know, just to make sure it's all legal.'

'I suppose you'd call the building department at City Hall.'

'The building department. OK, thanks.'

After the door closed, Roy heard his parents talking softly in the hallway. He couldn't make out what they were saying, so he pulled the covers up to his neck and rolled over. Right away he began drifting off.

Before long, someone whispered his name. Roy assumed he was already dreaming.

Then he heard it again, and this time the voice seemed so real that he sat up. The only sound in the bedroom was his own breathing.

Great, he thought, now I'm imagining things.

He lay back on the pillow and blinked up at the ceiling.

'Roy?'

He went rigid under the covers.

'Roy, don't freak out.'

But that's exactly what he felt like doing. The voice was coming from under his bed.

'Roy, it's me.'

'Me *who*?'

Roy's breath came in rapid bursts and his heart pounded like a bass drum. He could feel the presence of the other person beneath him in the darkness, under the mattress.

'Me, Beatrice. Chill out, man.'

'What are you doing here!'

'Shh. Not so loud.'

Roy heard her slide out from underneath the bed. Quietly she stood up and moved to the window. There was just enough moon in the sky to light up her curly blonde hair and cast a reflection in her glasses.

'How'd you get in our house?' Roy struggled to keep his voice low, but he was too rattled. 'How long have you been hiding here?'

'All afternoon,' Beatrice replied, 'while you guys were gone.'

'You broke in!'

'Relax, cowgirl. I didn't bust any windows or anything. The sliding door on your porch popped right off the track – they all do,' Beatrice said, matter-of-factly.

Roy hopped out from under the sheets, locked the door, and switched on his desk lamp.

'Are you completely wacko?' he snapped at her. 'Did somebody kick you in the head at soccer practice, or what?'

'I'm sorry about this, I really am,' Beatrice said. 'It's just, uh, things got kinda hairy at home. I didn't know where else to go.'

'Oh.' Roy was instantly sorry he'd lost his temper. 'Was it Lonna?'

Beatrice nodded gloomily. 'I guess she fell off her broom or somethin'.'

'That really sucks.'

'Yeah, her and my dad got in a huge fight. I mean huge. She threw a clock radio at his head, so he beaned her with a mango.'

Roy had always thought that Beatrice Leep wasn't afraid of anything, but she didn't look so fearless now. He felt bad for her – it was hard to imagine living in a house where the grown-ups behaved so idiotically.

'You can stay here tonight,' he offered.

'For real?'

'Long as my parents don't find out.'

'Roy, you're pretty cool,' Beatrice said.

He grinned. 'Thanks for calling me Roy.'

'Thanks for letting me crash here.'

'You take the bed,' he said. 'I'll sleep on the floor.'

'No way, José.'

Roy didn't argue. He gave Beatrice a pillow and a blanket, and she stretched out happily on the carpet.

He turned off the light and said goodnight. Then he

remembered something he meant to ask her. 'Hey, did you see Mullet Fingers today?'

'Maybe.'

'Well, he told me he had something planned for last night.'

'He's *always* got somethin' planned.'

'Yeah, but this stuff can't go on for ever,' Roy said. 'Sooner or later, he's gonna get caught.'

'I believe he's smart enough to know that.'

'Then we've gotta do something.'

'Like what?' Beatrice asked faintly. She was fading toward sleep. 'You can't stop him, Roy. He's too darn thickheaded.'

'Then I guess we've gotta join him.'

"Scuse me?'

'G'night, Beatrice.'

SEVENTEEN

Curly stared hard at the phone, as if staring would make it quit ringing. Finally he braced himself and picked up the receiver.

On the other end was Chuck Muckle, of course.

'Do I hear the sound of bulldozers, Mr Branitt?'

'No, sir.'

'Why not? It's Monday morning here in beautiful Memphis, Tennessee. Isn't it Monday morning in Florida, too?'

'I got some good news,' Curly said, 'and I got some bad news.'

'The good news being that you've found employment elsewhere?'

'Please, lemme finish.'

'Sure,' said Chuck Muckle, 'while you're cleaning out your desk.'

Curly hastily spilled his version of what had happened Saturday night. The part about the missing bulldozer seats definitely took some shine off the rest of the story. Not wishing to make things worse, Curly didn't mention that his pistol had somehow ended up submerged in a portable toilet.

A fuzzy silence lingered at the Memphis end of the conversation. Curly wondered if Mother Paula's vice-president for corporate relations had hung up on him.

'Hullo?' Curly said. 'You there?'

'Oh, I'm here,' Chuck Muckle replied tartly. 'Let me get this straight, Mr Branitt. A young man was arrested for attempted burglary on our property—'

'Right. Assault and trespassing, too!'

'—but then on the very same evening, another person or persons unknown removed the seats from the bull-dozers and backhoes and whatevers.'

'Yessir. That would be the not-so-good news,' Curly said.

'Did you report this theft to the police?'

'''Course not. I didn't want it to get in the newspaper.'

'Maybe there's hope for you yet,' said Chuck Muckle. He asked Curly if it was possible to operate the machines without driver's seats.

'Only if you're some kinda octopus.'

'So I'm correct in assuming there'll be no bulldozing today.'

'Or tomorrow,' Curly reported grimly. 'I got new seats on order from the wholesaler in Sarasota, but they won't be here till Wednesday.'

'What a happy coincidence,' Chuck Muckle said. 'That turns out to be the last day that Miss Kimberly Lou Dixon is available to us. Her mutant-insect movie begins shooting next weekend in New Mexico.'

Curly swallowed. 'You wanna do the groundbreaking this Wednesday? What about the site clearing?'

'Change of plans. Blame it on Hollywood,' said Chuck Muckle. 'We'll do the ceremony first, and as soon as everybody leaves you can crank up the machines – assuming they haven't been stripped down to the axles by then.'

'But it's just... Wednesday's the day after tomorrow!'

'No need to soil yourself, Mr Branitt. We'll arrange all the details from our end – the advertising, the press releases, and so forth. I'll get in touch with the mayor's office and the chamber of commerce. Meanwhile, your job is incredibly simple – not that you won't find a way to screw it up.'

'What's that?'

'All you've got to do is lock down the construction site for the next forty-eight hours. Think you can handle that?'

'Sure,' Curly said.

'No more alligators, no more poisonous snakes, no more stealing,' Chuck Muckle said. 'No more problems, period. *Comprendo?*'

'I got a quick question about the owls.'

'What owls?' Chuck Muckle shot back. 'Those burrows are abandoned, remember?'

Curly thought: I guess somebody forgot to tell the birds.

'There's no law against destroying abandoned nests,' the vice-president was saying. 'Anybody asks, that's your answer. "The burrows are deserted."'

'But what if one a them owls shows up?' Curly asked.

'What owls!' Chuck Muckle practically shouted. 'There are no owls on that property and don't you forget it, Mr Branitt. Zero owls. *Nada*. Somebody sees one, you tell him it's a — I don't know, a robin or a wild chicken or something.'

A chicken? Curly thought.

'By the way,' said Chuck Muckle, 'I'll be flying down to Coconut Cove so I can personally accompany the lovely Miss Dixon to our groundbreaking. Let's pray that you and I have nothing more to talk about when I arrive.'

'Don't worry,' Curly said, though he was plenty worried himself.

Beatrice Leep was gone when Roy awoke. He had no idea how she had slipped out of the house unnoticed, but he was glad she'd made it.

Over breakfast, Roy's father read aloud the brief newspaper account of Dana Matherson's arrest. The headline said: 'Local Youth Nabbed in Break-in Attempt.'

Because Dana was under eighteen, the authorities weren't allowed to release his name to the media — a fact that rankled Roy's mother, who believed Dana's mugshot should have been plastered on the front page. The story identified him only as a student at Trace Middle and said that the police considered him a suspect in several recent vandalisms. It didn't specifically mention Mother Paula's as the target.

Dana's arrest was the major buzz around school. Many kids were aware that he'd been picking on Roy, so they were eager to get Roy's reaction to the news that his tormentor had been nailed by the cops.

Roy was careful not to gloat or joke about it, or to draw any special attention to himself. If Dana blabbed about the imaginary cigarette stash, he might try to blame Roy for the bungled theft. The police had no reason to believe anything the kid said, but Roy wasn't taking any chances.

As soon as the bell rang ending homeroom, Garrett took him aside to share a weird new detail.

'Rat-traps,' he said, cupping a hand over his mouth.

'What are you talking about?' Roy asked.

'When they caught him, he had rat-traps stuck on his shoes. That's how come he couldn't run away.'

'I'm so sure.'

'Seriously, dude. The cops told my mom he stepped on 'em while he was sneakin' around the trailer.'

Knowing Dana, Roy could actually picture it.

'Broke three of his toes,' Garrett said.

'Oh, come on.'

'Absolutely! We're talkin' *humongous* rat-traps.' Garrett held his hands a foot apart to illustrate.

'Whatever.' Roy knew that Garrett was famous for exaggerating. 'Did the police tell your mom anything else?'

'Like what?'

'Like what Dana was after.'

'Smokes is what he said, but the cops don't believe him.'

'Who would?' said Roy, hoisting his book bag over his shoulder.

All morning he looked for Beatrice Leep between classes, but he never saw her in the hallways. At lunch hour, the girl soccer players were sitting together in the cafeteria, but Beatrice wasn't among them. Roy approached the table and asked if anybody knew where she was.

'At the dentist,' said one of her teammates, a gangly Cuban girl. 'She fell down some steps at home and broke a tooth. But she'll be ready for the game tonight.'

'Great,' said Roy, but he didn't feel so good about what he'd just heard.

Beatrice was such a phenomenal athlete that Roy couldn't imagine her falling down the stairs like some ordinary klutz. And after seeing what she could do to a bicycle tyre, he couldn't picture her breaking a tooth, either.

Roy was still thinking about Beatrice when he sat down in American history. He found himself struggling to concentrate on Mr Ryan's quiz, though it really wasn't that difficult.

The final question was the same one that Mr Ryan had asked him in the hallway on Friday: Who won the Battle of Lake Erie? Without hesitation, Roy wrote: 'Commodore Oliver Perry.'

It was the only answer that he was sure he got right.

On the bus ride home, Roy kept a wary eye on Dana Matherson's hulking friends, but they didn't glance once in his direction. Either Dana hadn't gotten the word out about what Roy had done, or his buddies didn't care all that much.

The police captain was reading the arrest report when Officer Delinko and the sergeant came in. The captain motioned for both men to sit down.

'Nice work,' he told Officer Delinko. 'You've made my life a whole lot easier. I just got off the horn with Councilman Grandy, and he's one happy camper.'

'I'm glad, sir,' Officer Delinko said.

'What do you make of this Matherson kid? What's he told you?'

'Not much.'

The interrogation of Dana Matherson hadn't gone as smoothly as Officer Delinko had hoped. In the training films, the suspects always caved in and confessed to their crimes. However, Dana had remained stubbornly un-cooperative, and his statements were confusing.

At first he'd said he was snooping around the Mother Paula's property in order to heist a load of Gladiator cigarettes. However, after speaking with a lawyer, the boy changed his story. He claimed he'd actually gone to the trailer to bum a cigarette, but the foreman mistook him for a burglar and came after him with a gun.

'Matherson's a hard case,' Officer Delinko told the captain.

'Yeah,' the sergeant said, 'he's been around the block a few times.'

The captain nodded. 'I saw his rap sheet. But here's what bothers me: The kid's a thief, not a practical joker. I can't picture him dumping alligators in port-a-potties.

Stealing port-a-potties maybe.'

'I wondered about that, too,' Officer Delinko said.

The Mother Paula's vandal had displayed a dark sense of humour that didn't fit the Matherson boy's dim-witted criminal history. He seemed more likely to strip the wheels from a patrol car than to paint the windshield black or hang his shirt like a pennant from the antenna.

'What's his motive for the funny stuff?' the captain wondered aloud.

'I asked him if he had a gripe against Mother Paula's pancakes,' Officer Delinko said, 'and he did say IHOP's were better.'

'That's it? He likes IHOP pancakes better?'

'Except for the buttermilks,' Officer Delinko reported. 'He had nice things to say about Mother Paula's buttermilks.'

Gruffly, the sergeant interjected: 'Aw, the kid's jerking our chain, is all.'

The captain pushed back slowly from his desk. He could feel another crusher of a headache coming on.

'OK, I'm making a command decision here,' he said. 'Considering we've got nothing better to work with, I intend to tell Chief Deacon that the Mother Paula's vandal has been apprehended. Case closed.'

Officer Delinko cleared his throat. 'Sir, I found a piece of a shirt at the crime scene – a shirt that's way too small to fit the Matherson boy.'

He didn't mention that the remainder of the shirt had

been tied, tauntingly, to the antenna of his squad car.

'We need more than a rag,' the captain grunted. 'We need a warm body, and the only one we've got is sitting in juvenile detention. So officially he's our perpetrator, understand?'

Officer Delinko and his sergeant agreed in unison.

'I'm going out on a limb here, so you know what that means,' the captain said. 'If another crime happens on that property, I'll look like a complete bozo. And if I end up looking like a bozo, certain people around here are going to spend the rest of their careers cleaning dimes out of parking meters. Am I making myself clear?'

Again Officer Delinko and his sergeant said yes.

'Excellent,' said the captain. 'So your mission, basically, is to make sure there's no more surprises between now and the Mother Paula's groundbreaking ceremony on Wednesday.'

'No sweat.' The sergeant rose to his feet. 'Can we tell David the good news?'

'Sooner the better,' said the captain. 'Officer Delinko, you're back on the road, effective immediately. In addition, the sergeant has written a letter commending the outstanding job you did in capturing our suspect. This will become part of your permanent file.'

Officer Delinko was beaming. 'Thank you, sir!'

'There's more. Because of your experience on this case, I'm assigning you to a special patrol at the Mother Paula's construction site. Twelve hours on, twelve hours off, beginning tonight at dusk. You up for that?'

'Absolutely, Captain.'

'Then go home and take a nap,' the captain advised, 'because if you doze off out there again, I'll be writing a much shorter letter for your file. A termination letter.'

Outside the captain's office, Officer Delinko's sergeant gave him a hearty slap on the back. 'Two nights and we're home free, David. You psyched?'

'One question, sir. Will I be on duty out there alone?'

'Well, we're hurting on the night shift right now,' the sergeant told him. 'Kirby got stung by a yellow jacket, and Miller's out with a sinus infection. Looks like you'll be riding solo.'

'That's OK,' Officer Delinko said, though he would have preferred to have a partner, under the circumstances. Curly probably would be staying at the trailer, though he wasn't the best company.

'You drink coffee, David?'

'Yes, sir.'

'Good. Drink twice as much as usual,' the sergeant said. 'I don't expect anything to happen, but you'd better be wide awake if it does.'

On the way home, Officer Delinko stopped at a souvenir shop along the main highway. Then he swung by the Juvenile Detention Center to take one more crack at Dana Matherson. It would be such a relief if the boy admitted to even one of the earlier vandalisms.

Dana was brought to the interview room by a uniformed guard, who took a position outside the door. The kid was dressed in a rumpled grey jumpsuit with the word INMATE stencilled in capital letters across the back. He wore only socks because his toes were still swollen from the rat-traps. Officer Delinko offered him a stick of gum, which the kid crammed into his cheeks.

'So, young man, you've had some time to think.'

''Bout what?' Dana blew a bubble and popped it.

'You know. Your situation.'

'I don't need to think,' the boy said. 'That's how come I got a lawyer.'

Officer Delinko leaned forward. 'Forget the lawyers, OK? I'll put in a good word with the judge if you'll just help me clear up some other cases. Are you the one who painted the windows of my patrol car?'

The boy snorted. 'Why would I do a dumb-ass thing like that?'

'Come on, Dana, I can make things easier for you. Just tell me the truth.'

'I got a better idea,' the boy said. 'Why don't you just kiss my big fat butt?'

Officer Delinko folded his arms. 'See, that's exactly the sort of disrespect for authority that got you here in the first place.'

'No, man, I'll tell you what got me here. That little dork Roy Eberhardt is what got me here.'

'Not this again,' Officer Delinko said, rising. 'Obviously we're wasting our time.'

Dana Matherson sneered. 'Duh-uh.'

He pointed at the small shopping bag that the patrolman had placed on the table. 'You finally bring me some smokes?'

'No, but I got you something else.' Officer Delinko reached into the bag. 'A little buddy to keep you company,' he said, casually dropping it in the boy's lap.

Dana Matherson howled and bucked and tried to knock it away, toppling his chair in the panic. He leaped up from the floor and scrambled out the door, where the guard clamped a brawny hand on his arm and led him off.

Officer Delinko was left alone to ponder the object lying on the linoleum tile – toothy, scaly and lifelike, except for the $3.95 price sticker glued to its snout.

It was a rubber alligator, which Officer Delinko had purchased at the tourist shop.

Dana Matherson's reaction to the harmless toy convinced the patrolman that he couldn't possibly be the Mother Paula's vandal. Anyone so freaked out by a puny fake wasn't capable of handling a real alligator, especially in the forbidding darkness of a Travellin' Johnny.

The true culprit was still out there somewhere, dreaming up a new scheme. Officer Delinko had two long, nervous nights ahead of him.

The Eberhardts owned a home computer, which Roy was allowed to use for homework assignments and for playing video snowboard games.

He was good at browsing the Internet, so with no difficulty he was able to Google up plenty of information about the burrowing owl. For instance, the type found in Florida went by the Latin name of *Athene cunicularia floridana* and had darker feathers than the Western variety. It was a shy little bird and, like other owls, was most active after dark. Nesting usually occurred between February and July, but fledglings had been observed in dens as late as October . . .

Systematically, Roy scrolled down the search items one by one until he finally hit the jackpot. He printed out two single-spaced pages, zippered them into his backpack, and hopped on his bicycle.

It was a quick ride to the Coconut Cove City Hall. Roy locked up his bike and followed the signs to the building-and-zoning department.

Behind the counter stood a pale freckle-faced man with pinched-looking shoulders. When the man failed to take notice of him, Roy boldly stepped forward and requested the file for Mother Paula's All-American Pancake House.

The clerk seemed amused. 'Do you have a legal description?'

'Of what?'

'The property.'

'Sure. It's the corner of East Oriole and Woodbury.'

The clerk said, 'That's not a legal description. It's barely even a proper address.'

'Sorry. It's all I've got.'

'Is this for a school project?' the clerk asked.

Why not? mused Roy. 'Yes,' he said.

He didn't see the harm in a tiny fib if it helped save the owls.

The clerk told Roy to wait while he cross-checked the street location. He returned to the counter carrying a fat stack of files in his arms. 'Now, which one of these did you want to see?' he asked with a slight smirk.

Roy stared in bewilderment. He had no idea where to begin.

'The one with all the construction permits?' he said.

The clerk pawed through the stack. Roy had a gloomy feeling that the forms and documents were written in such technical terms that he wouldn't be able to understand them, anyway. It would be like trying to read Portuguese.

'Hmm. That file's not here,' the clerk said, carefully tidying the tall pile.

'What do you mean?' Roy asked.

'The folder with all the permits and inspection notices – it's been checked out, I guess.'

'By who?'

'I'll have to talk to my supervisor,' the clerk said, 'and she's already left for the day. The office closes at four-thirty, and it's already, let's see, four-twenty-seven.' For emphasis he tapped the face of his wristwatch.

'OK, I'll be back tomorrow,' Roy said.

'Maybe you should choose another topic for your project.' The clerk's tone had an artificial politeness.

Roy smiled coolly. 'No thanks, mister. I don't give up that easy.'

From City Hall he rode his bike to a bait shop and, using a stash of leftover lunch money, bought a box of live crickets. Fifteen minutes later he was sneaking through the junkyard.

Mullet Fingers wasn't holed up in the ice-cream truck, though his rumpled sleeping bag was still there. Roy waited inside for a while, but without air conditioning it was unbearably hot and sticky. Before long, he was back on his bike, heading for the corner of East Oriole and Woodbury.

The gate was padlocked; there was no sign of the grumpy bald foreman. Roy walked along the outside of the fence, scouting for Beatrice's stepbrother or any clever surprises he might have left for the pancake-house people.

Roy wouldn't have noticed anything unusual had he not spooked one of the owls, which flared from its burrow and landed in the cab of the bulldozer. That's when Roy saw that the seat was missing. He immediately checked the other earthmoving machines and found the same thing.

So *that's* what the kid was up to the other night, Roy thought gleefully. That's why he told me to bring a wrench.

Roy walked back to the gate and opened the container of crickets and held it up to the fence. One at a time, the insects hopped out of the box, jumped through the chain-link holes, and landed on the ground. Roy was hopeful that the owls would find them once they came out of their dens for supper.

He probably should have left when he heard the first

honk, but he didn't. He knelt there patiently and waited until every last little cricket had vacated the box.

By then the honking had swollen to a steady blare, and the blue pickup truck was screeching to a stop. Roy dropped the box and jumped on his bike, but it was too late. The truck had blocked his escape.

The beet-faced bald guy vaulted from the cab and hoisted the bicycle by its seat, Roy pedalling furiously in suspension. His feet were a blur, but he wasn't going anywhere.

'What's your name! What're you doing here!' the foreman hollered. 'This is private property, don't you know that? You wanna go to jail, junior?'

Roy stopped pedalling and caught his breath.

'I know what you're up to!' the bald man snarled. 'I know your sneaky game.'

Roy said, 'Please, mister, let me go. I was only feeding the owls.'

The crimson drained from the foreman's cheeks.

'What owls?' he said, not so loudly. 'There ain't no owls around here.'

'Oh, yes, there are,' Roy said. 'I've seen them.'

The bald guy looked extremely nervous and agitated. He put his face so close that Roy could smell cooked onions on his breath.

'Lissen to me, boy. You didn't see no damn owls, OK? What you saw was a . . . was a wild chicken!'

Roy stifled a laugh. 'I'm so sure.'

'That's right. See, we got these dwarf chickens—'

'Mister, what I saw was an owl and you know it,' Roy said, 'and I know why you're so scared.'

The foreman let go of Roy's bicycle.

'I ain't scared,' he said stonily, 'and you didn't see no owls. Now get outta here and don't come back 'less you wanna go to jail, like the last kid I caught trespassin'.'

Roy carefully guided his bicycle around the pickup truck, then took off at full speed.

'They was chickens!' the bald guy bellowed after him.

'Owls!' Roy proclaimed triumphantly.

Up, up, up the steep mountainside he went – that's what he was imagining, anyway. That's what gave him the strength to push so hard.

In reality Roy was rolling along East Oriole Avenue, which was as flat as a Mother Paula's pancake. He was very worried that the construction foreman would change his mind and chase after him. Any second, Roy expected to hear honking behind him, curses in the wind; the pickup truck trailing so closely that he would feel the heat off its big V-8 engine.

So Roy didn't look back and he didn't slow down. He pedalled as fast as he could, his arms taut and his legs burning.

He wouldn't stop until he reached the crest of his imaginary Montana mountain and coasted downhill into the coolness of the valley.

EIGHTEEN

'Same scrawny brat I seen around here last week,' Curly complained to Officer Delinko, 'only this time I caught the little bugger!'

Officer Delinko offered to report the incident, but Curly assured him that it wasn't necessary.

'He won't come back, I guarantee you. Not after he got a faceful of me.'

It was nearly midnight at the construction site. The two men stood next to the patrolman's car, chatting casually. Both of them privately believed that the real Mother Paula's vandal was still on the loose, but they would not share their suspicions with each other.

Officer Delinko didn't tell Curly that the Matherson boy was too scared of alligators to be the vandal, because Officer Delinko didn't want the foreman to get all agitated again.

And Curly didn't tell Officer Delinko about the bulldozer seats being stolen while the Matherson kid was in custody, because Curly didn't want Officer Delinko to put the information in a police report that some nosy newspaper reporter might find.

Despite their secrets, both men were pleased not to be spending the night alone on the property. It was good to have a back-up nearby.

'Hey, I meant to ask,' Officer Delinko said, 'what

happened to those attack dogs you had watching the place?'

'You mean the psycho-mutts? Probably hightailed it all the way back to Berlin,' said Curly. 'Listen, I'm fixin' to turn in. Holler if you need anything.'

'You bet,' Officer Delinko said.

'And no naps tonight, right?'

'Don't worry.'

Officer Delinko was glad it was dark, so that the foreman couldn't see him blush. He'd never forget the sickening sight of his precious Crown Victoria, its windows painted as black as tar. Officer Delinko still dreamed of catching the offender and bringing him to justice.

After Curly retired to the air-conditioned comfort of the trailer, the patrolman began walking the property, following the line of his flashlight beam from one survey stake to the next. He intended to do this all night long, if necessary, to make sure the stakes weren't tampered with. He had packed five brimming thermos bottles of coffee in his car, so there would be absolutely no chance of running out.

Guarding a vacant lot wasn't the most glamorous police work, Officer Delinko knew, but this was an extremely important assignment. The chief, the captain, the sergeant – they all were relying on him to keep the pancake-house property free of mischief. Officer Delinko understood that if he did the job well, his career at the Coconut Cove Public Safety Department would once again be on the fast track. He could easily see a gold detective's badge in his future.

Trudging through the shadows, Officer Delinko pictured himself in a tailored suit instead of a starchy uniform. He would be driving a different Crown Victoria – the charcoal gray unmarked model reserved for detectives – and wearing a shoulder holster instead of a hip belt. He was daydreaming about getting an ankle holster, too, and a lightweight pistol to go with it, when he abruptly performed an involuntary somersault across the sandy scrub.

Oh, not again, the patrolman thought.

He groped around until he located his flashlight, but at first it didn't work. He shook it a few times and finally the bulb flickered on faintly.

Sure enough, he'd stepped in another owl burrow.

Officer Delinko got to his feet and smoothed the creases of his trousers. 'Good thing Curly's not awake to see this,' he mumbled.

'Heh,' came a small raspy voice in reply.

Officer Delinko slapped his right hand on the butt of his gun. With his left hand he aimed the flashlight toward the unseen intruder.

'Freeze!' the patrolman commanded.

'Heh. Heh. Heh.'

Back and forth went the yellow beam of light, revealing nothing. The runty, asthmatic-sounding voice seemed to come out of nowhere.

Officer Delinko carefully took two steps forwards and aimed the flashlight down the hole in which he'd tripped. An inquisitive pair of bright amber eyes peeked up from the blackness.

'Heh!'

The patrolman took his hand off his gun and cautiously dropped to a crouch. 'Why, hello there,' he said.

'Heh! Heh! Heh!'

It was a baby owl, no more than five or six inches tall. Officer Delinko had never seen anything so delicately perfect.

'Heh!' said the owl.

'Heh!' said the policeman, though his voice was too deep to do a proper imitation. 'I bet you're waiting for Momma and Poppa to bring supper home, aren't you?'

The amber eyes blinked. The yellow beak opened and closed expectantly. The little round head rotated back and forth.

Officer Delinko laughed aloud. He was fascinated by the miniature bird. Dimming the flashlight, he said, 'Don't worry, sport, I'm not going to hurt you.'

From overhead came a frenzied flutter, followed by a harsh *kssh! kssh! ksshhh!* The patrolman glanced up and saw, framed against the starlit sky, two winged silhouettes – the baby owl's parents, anxiously circling their frightened fledgling.

Officer Delinko slowly began backing away from the burrow, hoping that the grown-up birds would realize it was safe to land. In the blue-grey sky he could see their dusky shapes wheeling lower and lower, and he quickened his retreat.

Even after the two owls alighted, even after he watched them disappear like feathered ghosts into the ground, Officer Delinko continued moving away, backing up step by step until...

He bumped into something so big and so cold and so hard that it almost knocked the breath out of him. He spun around and switched on the flashlight.

It was a bulldozer.

Officer Delinko had clonked directly into one of Curly's earthmoving machines. He glared up at the steel hulk, rubbing his bruised shoulder. He didn't notice that the seat was gone, and even if he had, he wouldn't have given it a worry.

The policeman was grimly preoccupied with another concern. His gaze shifted from the massive bulldozer to the bird burrow, then back again.

Until that moment, Officer David Delinko had been so busy worrying about solving the Mother Paula's case and saving his own career that he hadn't thought much about anything else.

Now he understood what was going to happen to the little owls if he did his job properly, and it weighted him with an aching and unshakeable sorrow.

Roy's father had worked late, so Roy hadn't had a chance to tell him what he'd learned about the owls on the Internet, and that one of the pancake-house files had been removed from the building department. It seemed very suspicious, and Roy wanted to hear his father's theory about what might have happened.

But Roy went speechless the moment he sat down at

breakfast. There, smiling kindly at him from the back page of his father's newspaper, was Mother Paula herself!

It was a half-page advertisement under a banner of bold, patriotic-style lettering:

MOTHER PAULA'S
ALL-AMERICAN HOUSE OF PANCAKES, HOME OF THE WORLD-FAMOUS MOUTHWATERING LIQUORICE OATMEAL FLAPJACK, IS PROUD TO BECOME YOUR NEW NEIGHBOUR IN COCONUT COVE!

MOTHER PAULA WELCOMES YOU TO JOIN HER IN PERSON TOMORROW AT NOON FOR A GALA GROUNDBREAKING CEREMONY AT THE CORNER OF EAST ORIOLE AND WOODBURY, THE FUTURE LOCATION OF OUR 469th FAMILY-STYLE RESTAURANT IN THE UNITED STATES, CANADA, AND JAMAICA.

Roy dropped his spoon, launching a soggy wad of Froot Loops across the kitchen.

'What's wrong, honey?' his mother asked.

Roy felt sick to his stomach. 'Nothing, Mom.'

Then Mrs Eberhardt spotted the advertisement, too. 'I'm sorry, Roy. It's hard to think about those poor helpless birds, I know.'

Mr Eberhardt flipped the newspaper over to see what his wife and son were staring at. He frowned and said, 'Guess they're moving along pretty quickly with that project.'

Roy stood up in a dull fog. 'I better go. Don't wanna miss the bus.'

'Oh, there's plenty of time. Sit down and finish your breakfast,' his mother said.

Roy shook his head numbly. He grabbed his backpack off the chair. 'Bye, Mom. Bye, Dad.'

'Roy, wait. You want to talk?'

'Not really, Dad.'

His father folded the newspaper and handed it to him. 'Don't you have current events today?'

'Oh yeah,' said Roy. 'I forgot.'

Every Tuesday, Mr Ryan's history students were supposed to bring a topic for a current events discussion. On those days Roy's father always gave him the newspaper so that he could read it on the bus and pick out a timely article.

'How about if I take you to school today?' his mother offered.

Roy could tell she felt sorry for him because of the news about the pancake house. She thought the owls were doomed, but Roy wasn't ready to give up hope.

'That's OK.' He stuffed the newspaper into his backpack. 'Mom, can I borrow your camera?'

'Well...'

'For a class,' Roy added, wincing inwardly at the lie. 'I'll be real careful, I promise.'

'All right. I don't see why not.'

Roy carefully packed the digital camera among his books, gave his mother a hug, waved to his father, and streaked out the door. He jogged past his regular bus stop and kept going, all the way to the one on West Oriole, Beatrice Leep's street. None of the other Trace Middle kids had arrived yet, so Roy ran to Beatrice's house and waited on the front sidewalk.

He tried to cook up a good excuse for being there, in case Lonna or Leon noticed him. It was Beatrice who finally came out the front door, and Roy ran up so fast that he nearly knocked her down.

'What happened to you yesterday? Where's your brother? Did you see the paper this morning? Did you—'

She slapped a hand over his mouth.

'Easy, cowgirl,' she said. 'Let's go wait for the bus. We'll talk on the way.'

As Roy suspected, Beatrice had not broken a tooth falling down the steps. She'd broken it while biting a ring off one of her stepmother's toes.

The ring was made from a small topaz charm that

Beatrice's mother had left behind when she moved away. Lonna had pilfered the stone from Leon Leep's sock drawer and had gotten it made into a snazzy toe ring for herself.

Beatrice had taken exception to the theft.

'If my old man wanted Lonna to have it, he woulda given it to her,' she growled.

'So you gnawed it off her toe? How?' Roy was astounded.

'Wasn't easy.'

Beatrice made a chimpanzee face and pointed at a sharp stump where one of her incisor teeth used to be. 'Broke the tip off. They're gonna make me a fake one so it looks like brand-new,' she explained. 'Good thing my old man has dental insurance.'

'She was awake when you did this?'

'Yeah,' said Beatrice, 'but she probably wishes she wasn't. Anyway, tell me what was in the paper this morning that got you all freaked out.'

She groaned when Roy showed her the advertisement for the Mother Paula's groundbreaking extravaganza. 'Just what the world needs – another pancake joint.'

'Where's your brother?' Roy asked. 'You think he's heard about this?'

Beatrice said she hadn't seen Mullet Fingers since Sunday. 'That's when the you-know-what hit the fan. He was hiding in the garage, waitin' for me to get him some clean shirts, when my dad walked out for another case of Mountain Dew. The two of 'em were just standing around talkin', perfectly friendly, when Lonna shows up and pitches a major hissy.'

'What happened then?' Roy said.

'He ran off like a scalded dog. Meantime, Lonna and my old man get into this humongous fight—'

'The one you told me about.'

'Right,' said Beatrice. 'Dad wants my brother to come back and live with us again, but Lonna says no way, José, he's a bad seed. What the heck does that mean, Tex? "Bad seed." Anyway, they're still not speakin' to each other, Lonna and my dad. The whole house feels like it's about to explode.'

To Roy, Beatrice's situation sounded like a living nightmare. 'Need a place to hide out?' he asked.

'That's OK. Dad says he feels better when I'm around.' Beatrice laughed. 'Lonna told him I'm "dangerous and crazy". She might be half right.'

When they got to the bus stop, Beatrice hooked up with one of her soccer teammates and they started talking about the previous night's game, which Beatrice had won with a penalty kick. Roy held back and didn't say much, though he felt the curious stares from other kids. He was, after all, the boy who had defied Dana Matherson and survived.

He was surprised when Beatrice Leep ditched her teammates and sat next to him on the bus.

'Lemme see that newspaper again,' she whispered.

As she studied the Mother Paula's advertisement, she said, 'We've got two choices, Tex. We either tell him, or we don't.'

'I say we do more than just tell him.'

'Join him, you mean. Like you said the other night.'

'It's them against him. All alone, he doesn't have a chance,' Roy said.

'For sure. But we could all three of us end up in juvie hall.'

'Not if we're cool about it.'

Beatrice eyed him curiously. 'You got a plan, Eberhardt?'

Roy took his mother's camera out of the backpack and showed it to Beatrice.

'I'm listening,' she said.

So Roy told her.

He missed homeroom because he was summoned to the vice-principal's office.

The long, lonesome hair on Miss Hennepin's upper lip was even curlier and shinier than the last time Roy had seen her. Oddly, the hair was now golden blonde in colour, instead of jet-black as before. Was it possible that Miss Hennepin had dyed it? Roy wondered.

'We've been informed that a young man fled from the hospital emergency room Friday night,' she was saying, 'a young man who was registered falsely under your identity. What can you tell me about that, Mr Eberhardt?'

'I don't even know his real name,' Roy said flatly. Mullet Fingers had been wise not to reveal it; not knowing had saved Roy from telling another lie.

'You seriously expect me to believe that?'

'Honest, Miss Hennepin.'

'Is he a student here at Trace Middle?'

'No, ma'am,' said Roy.

The vice-principal was visibly disappointed. Obviously she'd hoped to claim jurisdiction over the missing runaway.

'Then where does your nameless friend attend school, Mr Eberhardt?'

Here goes, Roy thought. 'I think he travels a lot, Miss Hennepin.'

'Then he's home-schooled?'

'You could say that.'

Miss Hennepin peered narrowly at Roy. With a gaunt forefinger she stroked the lustrous strand above her mouth. Roy shivered in disgust.

'Mr Eberhardt, it's illegal for a boy your age not to be in school. The offence is called truancy.'

'Oh, I know.'

'Then you might wish to inform your fleet-footed friend of that fact,' the vice-principal said acidly. 'Are you aware that the school district has special police who go out searching for truants? They're very good at their jobs, I assure you.'

Roy didn't think the truancy police would have an easy time tracking Mullet Fingers through the woods and mangroves, but the possibility made him anxious, anyway. What if they had bloodhounds and helicopters?

Miss Hennepin edged closer, craning her stringy neck

like a buzzard. 'You let him use your name at the hospital, didn't you, Mr Eberhardt? You allowed this delinquent to borrow your identity for his own shady purposes.'

'He got bit by some bad dogs. He needed a doctor.'

'And you expect me to believe that's all there is to the story? Seriously?'

Roy could only shrug in surrender. 'Can I go now?'

'Until we speak again on this subject, you and I,' Miss Hennepin said. 'I know when I smell a rat.'

Yeah, thought Roy, that's because you're growing one on your lip.

At lunchtime he borrowed Garrett's bicycle and set out for the junkyard. Nobody saw him go, which was fortunate; it was strictly against the rules for kids to leave the school grounds without a note.

Beatrice's stepbrother was napping when Roy burst into the Jo-Jo's ice-cream truck. Shirtless and mosquito-bitten, the boy wriggled out of the sleeping bag and took the newspaper from Roy's hands.

Roy had expected an emotional reaction to the news of the groundbreaking ceremony, but Mullet Fingers remained surprisingly calm, almost as if he'd been expecting it. He carefully tore out the Mother Paula's advertisement and examined it as if it were a treasure map.

'Noon, huh?' he murmured quietly.

'That's only twenty-four hours from now,' Roy said. 'What are we going to do?'

'We who?'

'You, me and Beatrice.'

'Forget about it, man. I'm not draggin' you two into the middle of this mess.'

'Wait, listen to me,' Roy said urgently. 'We already talked about this, me and Beatrice. We want to help you save the owls. Seriously, we're locked and loaded.'

He unpacked the camera and handed it to the boy. 'I'll show you how this works,' Roy said. 'It's pretty easy.'

'What's it for?'

'If you can get a picture of one of the birds, we can stop the pancake people from bulldozing that lot.'

'Aw, you're full of it,' the boy said.

'Honest,' Roy said. 'I looked it up on the Internet. Those owls are protected – it's totally against the law to mess with the burrows unless you've got a special permit, and Mother Paula's permit file is missing from City Hall. What does that tell you?'

Mullet Fingers fingered the camera sceptically. 'Pretty fancy,' he said, 'but it's too late for fancy, Tex. Now it's time for hardball.'

'No, wait. If we give them proof, then they've got to shut down the project,' Roy persisted. 'All we need is one lousy picture of one little owl—'

'You better take off,' the boy said. 'I got stuff to do.'

'But you can't fight the pancake people all by yourself. No way. I'm not leaving until you change your mind.'

'I said, Get outta here!' Mullet Fingers seized Roy by one arm, spun him clockwise, and launched him out of the ice-cream truck.

Roy landed on all fours in the hot gravel. He was

slightly stunned; he'd forgotten how strong the kid was.

'I already caused enough trouble for you and my sister. This is *my* war from now on.' Beatrice's stepbrother stood defiantly in the doorway of the truck, his cheeks flushed and his eyes blazing. In his right hand was Mrs Eberhardt's digital camera.

Roy pointed and said, 'You keep it for now.'

'Get real. I'll never figure out how to use one a these stupid things.'

'Let me show you—'

'Nah,' said the boy, shaking his head. 'You go on back to school. I got work to do.'

Roy stood up and brushed the gravel off his pants. He had a hot lump in his throat, but he was determined not to cry.

'You done enough already,' the running boy told him, 'more than I had a right to expect.'

There were about a million things Roy wanted to say, but the only words he choked out were: 'Good luck tomorrow.'

Mullet Fingers winked and gave him a thumbs-up.

'Bye, Roy,' he said.

The newspaper contained several items that would have been excellent for current events.

A missing Green Beret soldier had been rescued in the mountains of Pakistan. A doctor in Boston had invented a new drug to treat leukemia. And in Naples, Florida, a county commissioner had been arrested for taking a

$5,000 bribe from the developer of a putt-putt golf course.

When Roy's turn came to address Mr Ryan's class, he didn't use any of those articles for his topic. Instead he held up the newspaper and pointed to the torn page where the Mother Paula's advertisement had been.

'Most everybody here likes pancakes,' Roy began. 'I know I sure do. And when I first heard that a new Mother Paula's was going to open here in Coconut Cove, I thought that was pretty cool.'

Several kids nodded and smiled. One girl pretended to rub her tummy hungrily.

'Even when I found out where they're going to build it – that big empty lot at the corner of Woodbury and East Oriole – I didn't see anything wrong with the idea,' Roy said. 'Then one day a friend of mine took me out there and showed me something that changed my mind totally.'

Now the other students stopped talking among themselves and paid attention. They'd never heard the new kid say so much.

'It was an owl,' Roy went on, 'about this tall.'

He held up two fingers, one eight or nine inches above the other, to show them. 'When my family lived out west we saw plenty of owls, but never one this small. And he wasn't a baby, either, he was full grown! He was so straight and serious, he looked like a little toy professor.'

The class laughed.

'They're called "burrowing" owls because they actually live underground,' Roy continued, 'in old holes made by tortoises and armadillos. Turns out that a couple of owl families hang out on that land at Woodbury and East Oriole. They made their nests in the dens and that's where they raise their babies.'

Some of the kids shifted uneasily. A few began whispering in worried tones and some looked at Mr Ryan, who sat thoughtfully at his desk, chin propped in his hands.

'Roy,' he said gently, 'this is an excellent subject for biology or social studies, but perhaps not for current events.'

'Oh, it's definitely a current event,' Roy countered. 'It's happening tomorrow at noon, Mr Ryan.'

'What is?'

'They're going to start bulldozing to make way for the pancake house. It's like a big party or something,' Roy said. 'The lady who plays Mother Paula on TV is going to be there. The mayor, too. That's what the paper said.'

A red-haired girl in the front row raised her hand. 'Didn't the paper say anything about the owls?'

'No. Not a word,' Roy said.

'So what's gonna happen to 'em?' called a freckle-faced boy from the back of the classroom.

'I'll tell you what's going to happen.' Roy looked at Mr Ryan. 'The machines are going to bury all those burrows, and everything inside.'

'No way!' the red-haired girl cried, and the class

erupted in agitated conversation until Mr Ryan asked everyone to please be quiet and let Roy finish.

'The grown-up owls might try to fly away,' Roy said, 'or they might just stay in the dens to protect their babies.'

'But they'll die!' the freckle-faced kid shouted.

'How can the pancake people get away with this?' demanded another.

'I don't know,' Roy said, 'but it's not legal, and it's not right.'

Here Mr Ryan interrupted firmly. 'Hold on, Roy, what do you mean it's "not legal"? You need to be careful when you're making those kinds of serious allegations.'

Excitedly Roy explained that the burrowing owls were protected by state and federal laws, and that it was illegal to harm the birds or disturb active burrows without getting special government permits.

'All right. Fine,' said Mr Ryan, 'but what does the pancake company have to say about this? I'm sure they got the proper permission—'

'The file is missing,' Roy cut in, 'and the foreman tried to tell me there weren't any owls on the property, not a single one. Which is a lie.'

The class started buzzing again.

'So tomorrow at lunch,' Roy continued, 'I'm going out there to...well, just because I want the Mother Paula's people to know that somebody in Coconut Cove cares about those birds.'

Mr Ryan cleared his throat. 'This is a sticky situation, Roy. I know how upset and frustrated you must feel, but

I've got to remind you that students aren't supposed to leave school property.'

'Then I'll get a note from my parents,' Roy said.

The teacher smiled. 'That would be the way to do it.' The class was expecting him to say more, but he didn't.

'Look,' said Roy, 'every day we've been reading about regular people, ordinary Americans who made history 'cause they got up and fought for something they believed in. OK, I know we're just talking about a few puny little owls, and I know everybody is crazy about Mother Paula's pancakes, but what's happening out there is just plain wrong. So wrong.'

Roy's throat was as dry as prairie dust, and his neck felt hot.

'Anyway,' he muttered, 'it's tomorrow at noon.'

Then he sat down.

The classroom fell quiet, a long heavy silence that roared in Roy's ears like a train.

NINETEEN

'I'm worried about the owls,' Officer Delinko told Curly.

'What owls?'

Darkness had fallen on the construction site and swallows were swooping back and forth, chasing mosquitoes. Tomorrow was the big day.

'Come on, I saw 'em with my own eyes,' the patrolman said. 'Isn't there a way to, like, move 'em someplace safe?'

Curly said, 'Want my advice? Don't think about it. Put it out of your mind, is what I do.'

'I can't. That's the trouble.'

Curly jerked a thumb toward the trailer. 'You wanna take a break? I rented the new Jackie Chan.'

Officer Delinko couldn't understand how the foreman could be so casual about burying the owl dens. He wondered if it was just a macho act. 'Did you tell them the birds were out here?' he asked.

'Tell who?'

'The pancake company. Maybe they don't know.'

Curly snorted. 'You kiddin' me? They know everything,' he said. 'Look, it ain't our problem. Even if we wanted to, there's nuthin' we could do.'

Curly went off to his trailer while Officer Delinko resumed patrolling the grounds. Whenever he passed a burrow, he shone his flashlight inside, but he saw no owls. He hoped the birds had already sensed that something awful was about to happen and had flown away, though it seemed improbable.

Shortly after midnight, Officer Delinko heard Curly come out and shout his name. The foreman claimed he'd been awakened by a noise like someone climbing the fence.

With his gun drawn, the policeman searched the area thoroughly; he checked the roof of the trailer and underneath it, too. All he found was a line of opossum tracks in the sand.

'Sounded way bigger'n a 'possum,' Curly said grumpily.

Later, as Officer Delinko was retrieving his third thermos of coffee from the squad car, he thought he saw a series of small white flashes at the other end of the property. It reminded him of the bright popping he'd seen at late-night car accidents while the police department's photographer was snapping pictures.

But when Officer Delinko ran to where he'd seen the flashes, he found nothing out of the ordinary. It must have been a burst of heat lightning, he thought, reflecting off the low clouds.

The rest of the night passed uneventfully. The patrolman stayed wide awake.

At breakfast Roy asked his mother if he could leave school during lunch. He figured she'd be more likely than his father to say yes, but she surprised him.

'I don't know if it's such a good idea for you to go to the Mother Paula's groundbreaking.'

'But, Mom—'

'Let's see what your dad thinks.'

Oh well, thought Roy, that'll be the end of that.

As soon as Mr Eberhardt sat down at the table, Mrs Eberhardt informed him of Roy's request.

'Sure, why not?' Mr Eberhardt said. 'I'll write him a note.'

Roy's jaw hung open. He had expected the opposite reaction from his father.

'But you've got to promise to behave,' Mr Eberhardt said, 'no matter how ticked off you get.'

'I promise, Dad.'

Later his father put Roy's bicycle in the trunk of his car and drove Roy to Trace Middle. As he dropped him off in front of the school, Mr Eberhardt asked, 'Think your friend will be at the ceremony today – Beatrice's stepbrother?'

'Probably,' Roy said.

'Pretty risky.'

'I know, Dad. I tried to tell him.'

'You be careful,' Mr Eberhardt said firmly, 'and be smart.'

'Yes, sir.'

Beatrice Leep was waiting outside Roy's homeroom. Her curly hair was damp, as if she'd just gotten out of the shower.

'Well?' she said.

'I got a note. How about you?'

Beatrice displayed a crumpled paper napkin that had been scrawled upon in red ink. 'I woke up my old man to ask him. He was so far out of it, he would've signed anything,' she said. 'I should've written myself a cheque for a thousand bucks.'

'So I guess we're all set for noon,' Roy said. He lowered his voice. 'I went to see your brother. He threw me out of the truck.'

Beatrice shrugged. 'What can I say. Sometimes he's impossible.'

She fished in her purse and came out with the camera belonging to Roy's mother. 'He dropped this off at the house late last night, after Lonna and Dad went to bed. He says he got the pictures you wanted. I tried to take a look but I couldn't figure out how to work the darn thing.'

Wordlessly Roy grabbed the camera and stashed it in his locker.

'Keep your fingers crossed,' Beatrice said, before melting into the stream of students and disappearing down the hall.

Roy spent the rest of the morning lost in excited distraction, wondering if his plan might actually work.

At ten-forty-five a.m., a black stretch limousine pulled up to the empty lot at Woodbury and East Oriole. The driver got out and opened one of the doors. Nothing happened for several moments, and then a tall man with wavy silver hair emerged, squinting into the sun. He wore pressed white trousers and a dark blue blazer with an emblem on the breast pocket.

The man glanced around impatiently behind enormous tinted sunglasses. Crisply he snapped his fingers at Officer David Delinko, who was unlocking his squad car.

The patrolman failed to notice he was being summoned. He was knocking off work after fourteen straight hours at the construction site – Curly had gone home to shower and shave, so Officer Delinko had stayed to keep an eye on the earthmoving machines, which had been refitted with new seats. Now that the foreman had returned – dressed up in a coat and tie, of all things! – the policeman was leaving the premises. He had no desire to hang around for the groundbreaking nonsense.

'Officer!' The silver-haired man beckoned insistently. 'Yo, Officer! Over here.'

Officer Delinko approached the limousine and asked what was wrong. The man introduced himself as Chuck E. Muckle, a vice-president of something-or-other for Mother Paula's All-American Pancake Houses, Inc. In a confidential tone, he added, 'We need some discreet assistance here.'

'Well, I'm off duty,' Officer Delinko told him, 'but I'd be glad to call for another unit.' He was so exhausted from lack of sleep that he barely had enough energy to carry on a conversation.

'Do you happen to know who's sitting in this car?'

Chuck Muckle asked, nodding toward the limo.

'No, sir.'

'Miss Kimberly Lou Dixon!'

'That's nice,' said Officer Delinko blankly.

'*The* Kimberly Lou Dixon.'

'Well, what d'ya know.'

Chuck Muckle thrust his ruddy face closer. 'You've got no idea who I'm talking about, do you, Officer?'

'Not a clue, sir. Never heard of the lady.'

The company vice-president rolled his eyes and proceeded to explain who Kimberly Lou Dixon was, and why she'd travelled all the way from Beverly Hills, California, to Coconut Cove, Florida.

'And right this minute,' Chuck Muckle said, 'she rather urgently needs a powder room.'

'A powder room,' Officer Delinko repeated quizzically.

'A place to powder her nose! A place to freshen up!' Chuck Muckle erupted in exasperation. 'Is this really such a difficult concept to grasp, Officer? Let me try to put this in language you can understand – she needs a potty, OK?'

'Gotcha.' Officer Delinko gestured toward Curly's trailer. 'Follow me.'

When Kimberly Lou Dixon got out of the limousine, Officer Delinko was startled by how young she looked compared with the wrinkled old granny she played on the TV commercials. Kimberly Lou had bright green eyes and rich auburn hair and smooth milky skin – a lovely and cultured woman, Officer Delinko thought.

Then she opened her mouth.

'I gotta tinkle,' she announced in a sandpaper voice. 'Lead the way, hotshot.'

The actress carried a leather tote bag over one shoulder, and she wore high heels, a black skirt and a pale silky blouse.

Curly was dumbstruck when he opened the door of the trailer. Without a word, Kimberly Lou Dixon stepped past him and made her way to the bathroom.

'Can I change in here?' she asked in a husky voice.

'Change what? You look pretty darned good the way you are.'

'Change into her Mother Paula's costume,' Officer Delinko interjected. 'She's with some guy; he wants to know if she can use your trailer as a dressing room.'

'Anytime,' Curly said with a dreamy smile.

A man's silhouette filled the doorway, followed by a gust of oily cologne. 'Why, you must be the one and only Leroy Branitt,' growled a familiar sarcastic voice.

Curly cringed. Officer Delinko stepped out of the way and said, 'This gentleman is from the pancake-house company.'

'I figured,' said Curly. He held out his right hand to Chuck Muckle, who stared at it as if it were a dead mudfish.

'Please tell me, Mr Branitt, that you have no bad news that would spoil this lovely tropical morning. Tell me everything's hunky-dory here in Coconut Cove.'

'Yessir,' Curly said. 'We stayed the last two nights on

the property, me and the policeman here, and it's been peaceful as a church house. Ain't that right, David?'

'Right-o,' Officer Delinko said.

Chuck Muckle whipped off his shades and eyed the patrolman dubiously. 'You wouldn't happen to be the same crackerjack lawman who fell asleep in his car while the vandal trashed our survey stakes, would you?'

As curious as Officer Delinko was to see Kimberly Lou Dixon dressed up as Mother Paula, he now wished that he were somewhere far, far away.

'The same genius,' Mr Muckle went on, 'whose careless sleep habits resulted in a newspaper article that unfairly smeared the good name and reputation of Mother Paula? Was that you?'

'Yeah, that would be him,' Curly said.

Officer Delinko shot the foreman a dirty look before addressing Mr Muckle. 'I'm really sorry about all that, sir,' the patrolman said, thinking: Sorrier for me than for you.

'It's rather astounding that you still have a job,' Chuck Muckle remarked. 'Your police chief must have a charitable heart. Either that or he's desperate for warm bodies.'

Curly finally came up with something positive to contribute. 'Officer Delinko is the one who helped me catch that burglar the other night!'

It was a shameless exaggeration of Curly's role in the capture of Dana Matherson, and Officer Delinko was about to set the record straight when Kimberly Lou Dixon came rocketing out of the bathroom.

'You've got, like, a major roach situation in there!' she exclaimed.

'They ain't roaches, they're crickets,' Curly said. 'I don't know where the heck they all came from.'

He elbowed his way past Officer Delinko and Chuck Muckle, and introduced himself to the actress. 'I'm the supervising engineer on this project, Miss Dixon, and I just want you to know that I seen all your movies.'

'All two of them, you mean?' Kimberly Lou Dixon patted his shiny scalp. 'That's all right, Mr Branitt, it's still a darling thing for you to say.'

'Hey, I can't wait for your new one, too – *Mutant Invaders from Saturn Eleven*. I really go for that sci-fi stuff.'

'*Jupiter Seven!*' Chuck Muckle cut in. 'It's called *Mutant Invaders from Jupiter Seven*.'

'Whatever,' Curly gushed, 'you're gonna make a fantastic grasshopper queen.'

'Yeah. I'm already writing my Oscar speech.' The actress glanced at her diamond-studded wristwatch. 'Listen, I'd better hurry up and start turning myself into adorable old Mother Paula. Can one of you sweethearts please fetch my suitcase out of the limo?'

TWENTY

A smaller limousine delivered the Coconut Cove mayor, Councilman Bruce Grandy and the chamber of commerce president to the construction site. A satellite truck from a Naples television station came next, followed by a newspaper photographer.

City workers tied red, white and blue streamers to the fence and hung a hand-lettered banner that said WELCOME, MOTHER PAULA.

At ten minutes to noon, Roy and Beatrice arrived; this time she rode the handlebars and he pedalled, the camera stowed safely in his backpack. They were startled to see that they weren't the only ones to show up – the freckle-faced boy, the red-haired girl, and at least half of Mr Ryan's history class were already there, along with a bunch of parents.

'What in the world'd you say to those kids yesterday?' Beatrice asked. 'You promise 'em free flapjacks or somethin'?'

'I just talked about the owls, that's all,' Roy said.

He got another pleasant surprise when a van from the Trace Middle School Athletic Department rolled up and Beatrice's soccer teammates piled out, some of them carrying posters.

Roy grinned at Beatrice, who shrugged as if it was no

big deal. They scanned the growing crowd but saw no sign of her runaway stepbrother.

There was no sign of the owls, either, which didn't surprise Roy; with so much noise and human commotion, the birds would likely stay underground where it was dark and safe. Roy knew that's what the pancake people were betting on: that the owls would be too frightened to venture out.

At quarter past twelve, the door of the construction trailer swung open. First to emerge was a policeman whom Roy recognized as Officer Delinko; then the bald construction foreman with the rotten temper; then a snooty-looking guy with silver hair and dorky sunglasses.

The last to come out was the woman who played Mother Paula on the TV commercials. She wore a shiny grey wig, wire-rimmed glasses, and a calico apron. A few people clapped in recognition, and she waved halfheartedly.

The group marched to a rectangular clearing that had been roped off in the centre of the construction site. A megaphone was handed to the silvery-haired guy, who said his name was Chuck E. Muckle, a vice-president from Mother Paula's company headquarters. He really thought he was hot snot, Roy could tell.

Ignoring the foreman and the police officer, Mr Muckle proceeded with great enthusiasm to introduce some local big shots – the mayor, a city councilman and the head of the chamber of commerce.

'I can't tell you how proud and delighted we are to make Coconut Cove the home of our 469th family-style restaurant,' Mr Muckle said. 'Mr Mayor, Councilman Grandy, all of you terrific folks who've come out on this gorgeous Florida day...I'm here to promise you that Mother Paula will be a good citizen, a good friend and a good neighbour to everybody!'

'Unless you're an owl,' Roy said.

Mr Muckle didn't hear it. Saluting the gathering of students, he said, 'I am truly excited to see so many of our fine young people here today. This is a historic moment for your town – *our* town, I should say – and we're happy you can take a short break from your classes and celebrate with us.'

He paused and manufactured a chuckle. 'Anyway, I expect we'll be seeing most of you again, once the restaurant opens and Mother Paula's busy in the kitchen. Hey, everybody, who likes liquorice oatmeal pancakes?'

It was an awkward moment. Only the mayor and Councilman Grandy raised their hands. The girl soccer players held their home-made signs with the blank side facing out, as they awaited directions from Beatrice.

Mr Muckle snickered nervously. 'Mother Paula, dearest, I think it's time. Shall we do the deed?'

They all posed side by side – the company VP, the mayor, Mother Paula, Councilman Grandy and the boss of the chamber of commerce – for the television crew and the news photographer.

Gold-painted shovels were handed out, and on Mr Muckle's signal all the dignitaries smiled, leaned over, and dug up a scoopful of sand. On cue, a smattering of city employees in the crowd cheered and applauded.

It was the most bogus thing Roy had ever seen. He couldn't believe anyone would put it on TV or in a newspaper.

'These people,' Beatrice said, 'need a life.'

As soon as the photo pose ended, Mr Muckle tossed down his gold shovel and snatched up the megaphone. 'Before the bulldozers and backhoes get rolling,' he said, 'Mother Paula herself wants to say a few words.'

Mother Paula didn't look overjoyed to have the megaphone shoved in her hand. 'You've got a real nice town,' she said. 'I'll see you next spring at the grand opening—'

'Oh no, you won't!'

This time the words came out of Roy's mouth as a shout, and nobody was more stunned than he. A tremor rippled through the audience and Beatrice edged closer, half-expecting somebody to come after him.

The actress playing Mother Paula seemed miffed, peering over her cheap wire-rimmed glasses into the crowd. 'Now, who said that?'

Roy found himself raising his right arm. 'I did, Mother Paula,' he called out. 'If you hurt a single one of our owls, I'm not eating any more of your stupid pancakes.'

'What're you talking about? What owls?'

Chuck Muckle lunged for the megaphone, but Mother Paula threw an elbow and caught him squarely in the gut. 'Back off, Chuckie Cheeseball,' she huffed.

'Go on, check it out for yourself,' Roy said, gesturing

around. 'Wherever you see one of those holes, there's an owl den underneath. It's where they build their nests and lay their eggs. It's their home.'

Mr Muckle's cheeks turned purple. The mayor looked lost, Councilman Grandy looked like he was about to faint, and the chamber-of-commerce guy looked like he'd swallowed a bar of soap.

By now, the parents in the crowd were talking loudly and pointing at the den holes. A few of the schoolkids started chanting in support of Roy, and Beatrice's soccer teammates began waving their hand-lettered signs.

One said: MOTHER PAULA DOESN'T GIVE A HOOT ABOUT OWLS!

Another read: BIRD KILLERS GO HOME!

And still a third sign said: SAVE THE OWLS, BURY THE BUTTERMILKS!

As the news photographer snapped pictures of the pro-testers, Mother Paula pleaded, 'But I don't want to hurt your owls! Really, I wouldn't hurt a flea!'

Chuck Muckle finally recaptured the megaphone and boomed a harsh scolding at Roy: 'Young fellow, you'd better get your facts straight before making such out-rageous and slanderous charges. There are no owls here, not one! Those old burrows have been abandoned for years.'

'Yeah?' Roy reached into his backpack and whipped out his mother's camera. 'I've got proof!' he shouted. 'Right here!'

The kids in the crowd hooted and hurrahed. Chuck

Muckle's face went grey and slack. He held out his arms and lurched toward Roy. 'Lemme see that!'

Scooting out of reach, Roy switched on the digital camera and held his breath. He had no idea what he was about to see.

He pressed the button to display the first photograph that Mullet Fingers had taken. The instant that the blurred, crooked image appeared in the viewfinder, Roy knew he was in trouble.

It was the picture of a finger.

Anxiously he clicked to the second frame, and what he saw was no less discouraging: a dirty bare foot. It appeared to be a boy's foot, and Roy knew whose it was.

Beatrice's stepbrother had many special talents, but nature photography obviously wasn't one of them.

In desperation Roy touched the button once more, and a third picture clicked into view. This time there was definitely *something* other than a human body part visible in the frame – a distant feathery form, unevenly illuminated by the camera's flash.

'Here!' Roy cried. 'Look!'

Chuck Muckle snatched the camera from him and examined the photo for all of about three seconds before bursting into cruel laughter. 'What's that supposed to be?'

'It's an owl!' Roy said.

And it was an owl, Roy was certain. Unfortunately, the bird must have swivelled its head just as Mullet Fingers snapped the picture.

'Looks more like a lump of mud to me,' Chuck Muckle said. He raised the camera so that those in the very front of the audience could see the viewfinder. 'Boy's got quite an imagination, doesn't he?' he added snidely. 'That's an owl, then I'm a bald eagle.'

'But it *is* an owl!' Roy insisted. 'And that picture was taken right here on this property last night.'

'Prove it,' Chuck Muckle gloated.

Roy had no response. He couldn't prove a thing.

His mom's camera was passed around the fringes of the crowd, and by the time it got back to Roy he knew that most people couldn't really tell it was a bird in the photograph. Even Beatrice wasn't sure, turning the viewfinder sideways and upside down as she tried in vain to identify a telltale part of owl anatomy.

Roy was crushed – the pictures taken by her stepbrother were worthless. The authorities in charge of protecting the burrowing owls would never block construction of the pancake house based on such fuzzy evidence.

'Thank you very much for coming,' Mr Muckle told the crowd through his megaphone, 'and thanks also for your patience during this rather...*inconsiderate* delay. We'll see all you pancake lovers next spring for a big hearty breakfast. In the meantime, this event is now officially over.'

The kids from Trace Middle stirred restlessly and looked toward Beatrice and Roy, who no longer had much of a plan. Roy could feel his shoulders sagging in defeat, while Beatrice's face had become a mask of grim resignation.

Then a young voice rose up: 'Wait, it ain't over! Not by a mile it ain't.'

This time it wasn't Roy.

'Uh-oh,' said Beatrice, lifting her eyes.

A girl in the rear of the crowd let out a shriek, and everybody wheeled at once to look. At first glance the object on the ground could have been mistaken for a kickball, but it was actually...a boy's head.

His matted hair was blond, his face was caramel-brown, and his eyes were wide and unblinking. A kite string led from his pursed lips to the handle of a large tin bucket a few feet away.

The bigshots came hurrying out of the crowd, with Beatrice and Roy on their heels. They all stopped to gape at the head on the ground.

'What now?' moaned the construction foreman.

Chuck Muckle thundered: 'Is this somebody's idea of a sick joke?'

'Good heavens,' cried the mayor, 'is he dead?'

The boy wasn't the least bit dead. He smiled up at his stepsister and winked slyly at Roy. Somehow he'd fitted his entire skinny body down the opening of an owl burrow, so that only his noggin stuck out.

'Yo, Mother Paula,' he said.

The actress stepped forward hesitantly. Her wig looked slightly crooked and her make-up was beginning to melt in the humidity.

'What is it?' she asked uneasily.

'You bury those birds,' Mullet Fingers said, 'you gotta

bury me, too.'

'But no, I love birds! All birds!'

'Officer Delinko? Where are you!' Chuck Muckle motioned for the policeman to come forward. 'Arrest this impertinent little creep right now.'

'For what?'

'Trespassing, obviously.'

'But your company advertised this event as open to the public,' Officer Delinko pointed out. 'If I arrest the boy, I'll have to arrest everybody else on the property, too.'

Roy watched as a vein in Mr Muckle's neck swelled up and began to pulse like a garden hose. 'I'll be speaking to Chief Deacon about you first thing tomorrow,' Mr Muckle hissed under his breath at the patrolman. 'That gives you one whole night to work on your sorry excuse for a résumé.'

Next he turned his withering gaze upon the forlorn foreman. 'Mr Branitt, please uproot this...this stringy *weed*.'

'Wouldn't try that,' Beatrice's stepbrother warned through clenched jaws.

'Really. And why not?' Chuck Muckle said.

The boy smiled. 'Roy, do me a favour. Check out what's in the bucket.'

Roy was happy to oblige.

'What do you see?' the boy asked.

'Cottonmouth moccasins,' Roy replied.

'How many?'

'Nine or ten.'

'They look happy, Roy?'

'Not really.'

'What do you think's gonna happen if I tip that thing over?' With his tongue Mullet Fingers displayed the string that connected him to the bucket.

'Somebody could get hurt pretty bad,' Roy said, playing along. He had been mildly surprised (though relieved) to see that the reptiles in the bucket were made of rubber.

Mr Muckle stewed. 'This is ridiculous – Branitt, do what I told you. Get that kid outta my sight!'

The foreman backed away. 'Not me. I don't much care for snakes.'

'Really? Then you're fired.' Once again the vice-president turned to confront Officer Delinko. 'Make yourself useful. Shoot the damn things.'

'No, sir, not around all these people. Too dangerous.'

The policeman approached the boy and dropped to one knee.

'How'd you get here?' he asked.

'Hopped the fence last night. Then I hid under the backhoe,' the boy said. 'You walked right past me about five times.'

'You're the one who painted my patrol car last week?'

'No comment.'

'And ran away from the hospital?'

'Double no comment,' the boy said.

'And hung your green shirt on my antenna?'

'Man, you don't understand. The owls got no chance against those machines.'

'I *do* understand. I honestly do,' Officer Delinko said. 'One more question: You serious about the cotton-mouths?'

'Serious as a heart attack.'

'Can I have a look in the bucket?'

The boy's eyes flickered. 'It's your funeral,' he said.

Roy whispered to Beatrice: 'We've gotta do something quick. Those snakes aren't real.'

'Oh, great.'

As the policeman approached the tin bucket, Beatrice shouted, 'Don't do it! You might get bit—'

Officer Delinko didn't flinch. He peeked over the rim for what seemed to Roy and Beatrice like an eternity.

Jig's up, Roy thought glumly. No way he won't notice they're fake.

Yet the patrolman didn't say a word as he backed away from the bucket.

'Well?' Mr Muckle demanded. 'What do we do?'

'Kid's for real. If I were you, I'd negotiate,' said Officer Delinko.

'Ha! I don't negotiate with juvenile delinquents.' With a snarl, Chuck Muckle snatched the gold-painted shovel from Councilman Grandy's hands and charged toward the bucket.

'Don't!' hollered the boy in the owl hole, spitting the string.

But the man from Mother Paula's was unstoppable. With a wild swing of the shovel he knocked over the bucket, and commenced flailing and hacking at the snakes in a blind, slobbering fury. He didn't stop until they were in pieces.

Little rubber pieces.

Exhausted, Chuck Muckle leaned over and squinted at the mutilated toy snakes. His expression reflected both disbelief and humiliation.

'What in the world?' he wheezed.

During the violent attack on the cottonmouths, the crowd had *oooh*-ed and *aaah*-ed. Now the only sounds to be heard were the *click-click-click* of the news photographer's camera and the panting of the Mother Paula's vice-president.

'Hey, them snakes're fake!' Curly piped. 'They ain't even real.'

Roy leaned toward Beatrice and whispered, 'Another Einstein.'

Chuck Muckle pivoted in slow motion. Ominously he pointed the blade of the shovel at the boy in the owl burrow.

'You!' he bellowed, stalking forward.

Roy jumped in front of him.

'Outta my way, kid,' Chuck Muckle said. 'I don't have time for any more of your nonsense. Move it *now*!'

It was clear that the Mother Paula's bigshot had totally lost his cool, and possibly his marbles.

'What're you doing?' Roy asked, knowing he probably wouldn't get a calm, patient answer.

'I said, *Get outta my way!* I'm gonna dig that little twerp out of the ground myself.'

Beatrice Leep darted forward and stood next to Roy, taking his right hand. An anxious murmur swept through the crowd.

'Aw, that's real cute. Just like Romeo and Juliet,' Chuck Muckle taunted. He dropped his voice and said, 'Game over, kiddies. On the count of three, I'm going to start using this shovel – or better yet, how about I get Baldy over here to crank up the bulldozer?'

The foreman scowled. 'Thought you said I was fired.'

Out of nowhere, somebody grabbed Roy's left hand – it was Garrett, his skateboard tucked under one arm. Three of his skateboarding homeys were lined up beside him.

'What're you guys doing?' Roy said.

'Skippin' school,' Garrett replied merrily, 'but, dude, this looks like way more fun.'

Roy turned to see that Beatrice had been joined by the entire soccer team, linking arms in a silent chain. They were tall, strong girls who weren't the least bit intimidated by Chuck Muckle's blustery threats.

Chuck Muckle realized it, too. 'Stop this foolishness right now!' he begged. 'There's no need for an ugly mob scene.'

Roy watched in wonderment as more and more kids slipped out of the crowd and began joining hands, forming a human barricade around Beatrice's self-buried stepbrother. None of the parents made a move to stop them.

The TV cameraman announced that the demonstration

was being broadcast live on the noon news, while the photographer from the paper swooped in for a close-up of Mr Muckle, looking drained, defeated, and suddenly very old. He braced himself on the ceremonial shovel as if it were a cane.

'Didn't any of you people hear me?' he rasped. 'This event is over! Done! You can all go home now.'

The mayor, Councilman Grandy and the man from the chamber of commerce stealthily retreated to their limousine, while Leroy Branitt plodded off to his trailer in search of a cold beer. Officer Delinko leaned against the fence, writing up a report.

Roy was in an eerie yet tranquil daze.

Some girl started singing a famous old folk song called 'This Land Is Your Land.' It was Beatrice, of all people, and her voice was surprisingly lovely and soft. Before long, the other kids were singing along, too. Roy shut his eyes and felt like he was floating on the sunny slope of a cloud.

'Excuse me, hotshot. Got room for one more?'

Roy blinked open his eyes and broke into a grin.

'Yes, ma'am,' he said.

Mother Paula stepped between him and Garrett to join the circle. Her voice was gravelly, but she could carry a tune just fine.

The demonstration went on for another hour. Two other TV crews showed up, along with a couple of extra Coconut Cove police cruisers, summoned by Officer Delinko.

Chuck Muckle exhorted the newly arrived lawmen to arrest the protesters for trespassing, truancy and disturbing the peace. The suggestion was firmly rejected, a sergeant informing Mr Muckle that handcuffing a bunch of middle-school kids wouldn't be good for the public safety department's image.

The situation remained fairly stable until the flamboyant arrival of Lonna Leep, who'd spotted her son on the TV news. She was all dressed up like she'd been invited to a party, and she wasn't the least bit shy about sticking her nose in front of the cameras. Roy overheard her tell a reporter how proud she was of her boy, risking his freedom to save the poor helpless owls.

'He's my brave little champion!' Lonna crowed obnoxiously.

With a phoney squeal of affection, she charged towards the wall of humanity that encircled her son. Beatrice ordered everyone to lock arms, blocking Lonna's path.

There was one hairy moment when Lonna and her stepdaughter stood glowering at each other, eye to eye, as if they were about to tangle. Garrett broke the stand-off with a phenomenal fake fart that sent Lonna reeling backward in horror.

Roy nudged Beatrice. 'Look up there!'

Overhead, a small dusky-coloured bird was flying in marvellous daring corkscrews. Roy and Beatrice watched in delight as it banked lower and lower, finishing with a radical dive toward the burrow at the centre of the circle.

Everybody whirled to see where the bird had landed.

All of a sudden the singing stopped.

There was Mullet Fingers, trying not to giggle, the daredevil owl perched calmly on the crown of his head.

'Don't worry, little guy,' the boy said. 'You're safe for now.'

TWENTY-ONE

Napoleon?

'Napoleon Bridger.' Roy read the name aloud.

'It's certainly colourful,' his mother remarked.

They were at the breakfast table, Mrs Eberhardt carefully clipping articles and photographs from the morning newspaper.

The front page featured a picture of Roy, Beatrice and Mother Paula clasping hands in the circle at the demonstration. The head of Beatrice's stepbrother could be seen in the background, looking very much like a fallen coconut with a blond toupee.

The caption beneath the photograph revealed Mother Paula as an actress and former beauty queen named Kimberly Lou Dixon. Beatrice's stepbrother was identified as Napoleon Bridger Leep.

'Is he back home now?' Roy's mother asked.

'I don't know if he'd call it that,' Roy said, 'but he's back with his mom and stepfather.'

At the scene of the student protest, Lonna Leep had pitched a weepy spluttering fit and demanded to be reunited with her son. Not knowing any better, police officers had led her out of the crowd toward Mullet Fingers, spooking the bold little owl away from the boy.

'My champ! My brave little hero!' Lonna had

swooned for the cameras as he wriggled out of the burrow. Roy and Beatrice had watched in helpless disgust as she'd locked Mullet Fingers in a smothering, melodramatic hug.

Mrs Eberhardt clipped out the newspaper photo of Lonna posing with the boy, who looked extremely uncomfortable.

'Maybe things'll be better between the two of them,' Roy's mother said hopefully.

'No, Mom. She just wanted to be on TV.' Roy reached for his backpack. 'I'd better get going.'

'Your father wants to see you before school.'

'Oh.'

Mr Eberhardt had worked late the previous night, and Roy had already gone to sleep by the time he'd gotten home.

'Is he mad?' Roy asked his mother.

'I don't think so. Mad about what?'

Roy pointed at the paper, chequerboarded with scissor holes. 'About what happened yesterday. About what me and Beatrice did.'

'Honey, you didn't break any laws. You didn't hurt anybody,' Mrs Eberhardt said. 'All you did was speak out for what you believed was right. Your dad respects that.'

Roy knew that 'respects' wasn't necessarily the same thing as 'agrees with'. He had a feeling his father was sympathetic on the owl issue, but Mr Eberhardt had never come out and said so.

'Mom, is Mother Paula's still going to build the pancake house?'

'I don't know, Roy. Apparently this Mr Muckle fellow lost his temper and tried to strangle a reporter when she asked the same question.'

'No way!' Roy and Beatrice had left before the impromptu press conference was over.

Mrs Eberhardt held up the clipping. 'Says so right here.'

Roy couldn't believe how much space the newspaper had devoted to the owl protest. It must have been the biggest story to hit Coconut Cove since the last hurricane.

His mother said, 'The phone started ringing at six this morning. Your dad made me take it off the hook.'

'I'm really sorry, Mom.'

'Don't be silly. I'm making a whole scrapbook, honey, something to show your children and grandchildren.'

I'd rather show them the owls, Roy thought, if there are any left by then.

'Roy!'

It was his father, calling to him from the den. 'Could you please get the door?'

A thin young woman with short-cropped black hair greeted Roy on the front steps. She was armed with a spiral notebook and a ballpoint pen.

'Hi, I'm from the *Gazette*,' she announced.

'Thanks, but we've already got a subscription.'

The woman laughed. 'Oh, I don't sell the newspaper. I write it.' She extended a hand. 'Kelly Colfax.'

On her neck Roy noticed several bluish, finger-sized marks that resembled the bruises that Dana Matherson had left on him. Roy figured that Kelly Colfax was the reporter whom Chuck Muckle had tried to choke.

'I'll go get my father,' he said.

'Oh, that's not necessary. It's you I wanted to speak with,' she said. 'You *are* Roy Eberhardt, right?'

Roy felt trapped. He didn't want to act rude, but he certainly didn't want to say anything that might cause more trouble for Mullet Fingers.

Kelly Colfax began firing questions:

'How'd you get involved in the demonstration?'

'Are you friends with Napoleon Bridger Leep?'

'Were you two involved in the vandalism incidents on the Mother Paula's property?'

'Do you like pancakes? What kind of pancakes?'

Roy's head was whirling. Finally he broke in and said, 'Look, I just went there to stand up for the owls. That's all.'

As the reporter jotted down Roy's words, the door swung open, and there stood Mr Eberhardt – shaved, showered, and neatly dressed in one of his grey suits.

'Excuse me, ma'am, may I have a word with my son?'

'Absolutely,' said Kelly Colfax.

Mr Eberhardt brought Roy inside and closed the door. 'Roy, you don't have to answer any of her questions.'

'But I just want her to know—'

'Here. Give her this.' Roy's father clicked open his briefcase and removed a thick Manila folder.

'What is it, Dad?'

'She'll figure it out.'

Roy opened the folder and broke into a grin. 'This is the file from City Hall, isn't it?'

'A copy,' said his father. 'That's correct.'

'The one with all Mother Paula's stuff. I tried to find it, but it wasn't there,' Roy said. 'Now I know why.'

Mr Eberhardt explained that he had borrowed the file, xeroxed every page, and then taken the material to some lawyers who were experts on environmental matters.

'So does Mother Paula's have permission to bury the owl dens or not?' Roy asked. 'Was it in the file?'

His father shook his head. 'Nope.'

Roy was exultant but also puzzled. 'Dad, shouldn't you be giving this to somebody at the Justice Department? Why do you want me to hand it over to the newspaper?'

'Because there's something there that everybody in Coconut Cove ought to know.' Mr Eberhardt spoke in a hushed and confidential tone. 'Actually, it's what *isn't* there that's important.'

'Tell me,' Roy said, and his father did.

When Roy opened the front door again, Kelly Colfax was waiting with a perky smile. 'Can we continue our interview?'

Roy smiled brightly in return. 'Sorry, but I'm running real late for school.' He held out the file. 'Here. This might help with your story.'

The reporter tucked her notebook under one arm and

snatched the folder from Roy's hands. As she thumbed through the documents, the elation on her face dissolved into frustration.

'What does all this stuff mean, Roy? What exactly am I looking for?'

'I think it's called an EIS,' Roy said, reciting what his father had told him.

'Which stands for...?'

'Environmental Impact Statement.'

'Right! Of course,' the reporter said. 'Every big construction project is supposed to do one. That's the law.'

'Yeah, but Mother Paula's EIS isn't in there.'

'You're losing me, Roy.'

'It's *supposed* to be in that file,' he said, 'but it's not. That means the company never did one – or they lost it on purpose.'

'Ah!' Kelly Colfax looked as if she'd just won the lottery. 'Thank you, Roy,' she said, embracing the folder with both arms as she backed down the steps. 'Thank you very, very much.'

'Don't thank me,' Roy said under his breath. 'Thank my dad.'

Who obviously cared about the owls, too.

EPILOGUE

During the following weeks, the Mother Paula's story mushroomed into a full-blown scandal. The missing Environmental Impact Statement made the front page of the *Gazette* and ultimately proved to be the fatal blow to the pancake-house project.

It turned out that a thorough EIS *had* been completed, and that the company's biologists had documented three mated pairs of burrowing owls living on the property. In Florida the birds were strictly protected as a Species of Special Concern, so their presence on the Mother Paula's site would have created serious legal problems – and a public-relations disaster – if it had become widely known.

Consequently, the Environmental Impact Statement conveniently disappeared from the city files. The report later turned up in a golf bag owned by Councilman Bruce Grandy, along with an envelope containing approximately $4,500 in cash. Councilman Grandy indignantly denied that the money was a bribe from the pancake people; then he rushed out and hired the most expensive defence lawyer in Fort Myers.

Meanwhile, Kimberly Lou Dixon quit her TV role as Mother Paula, declaring she couldn't work for a company that would bury baby owls just to sell a few flapjacks. The climax of her tearful announcement came when she displayed her life membership card from the Audubon Society – a moment captured by *Entertainment Tonight*, *Inside Hollywood* and *People* magazine, which also published the picture of Kimberly Lou, Roy and Beatrice hand-in-hand at the owl protest.

It was more media attention than Kimberly Lou Dixon had received as the Miss America runner-up, or even as the future star of *Mutant Invaders from Jupiter Seven*. Roy's mother kept track of the actress's soaring career in the show business columns, where it was reported that she'd signed a deal to appear in the next Adam Sandler movie.

By contrast, the owl publicity was a nightmare for Mother Paula's All-American Pancake Houses, Inc., which found itself the subject of an unflattering front-page article in the *Wall Street Journal*. Immediately, the price of the company's stock began sinking like a stone.

After going wacko at the groundbreaking ceremony, Chuck E. Muckle got demoted to the post of assistant junior vice-president. Although he did not go to jail for choking the newspaper reporter, he was forced to take a class called 'How to Manage Your Anger,' which he failed. Soon afterward, he resigned from the pancake company and took a job as a cruise director in Miami.

In the end, Mother Paula's had no choice but to abandon its plan to put a restaurant on the corner of East Oriole and Woodbury. There were the nagging headlines about the missing EIS, the embarrassing resignation of Kimberly Lou Dixon, the TV footage of Chuck Muckle throttling Kelly Colfax... and, last but not least, those darn owls.

Everybody was upset about the owls.

NBC and CBS sent film crews to Trace Middle School to meet with the student protesters, as well as with faculty members. Roy lay low, but he later heard from Garrett that Miss Hennepin had given an interview in which she praised the kids who took part in the lunchtime protest and claimed she'd encouraged them to participate. Roy was always amused when grown-ups lied to make themselves look more important.

He wasn't watching TV that evening, but his mother burst in to report that Tom Brokaw was talking about him and Beatrice on the network news. Mrs Eberhardt led Roy to the living room just in time to hear the president of Mother Paula's promise to preserve the Coconut Cove property as a permanent sanctuary for burrowing owls and to donate $50,000 to the Nature Conservancy.

'We want to assure all our customers that Mother Paula's remains strongly committed to protecting our environment,' he said, 'and we deeply regret that the careless actions of a few former employees and contractors may have put these unique little birds in jeopardy.'

'What a crock,' Roy muttered.

'Roy Andrew Eberhardt!'

'Sorry, Mom, but the guy's not telling the truth. He knew about the owls. They all knew about the owls.'

Mr Eberhardt muted the television set. 'Roy's right, Lizzy. They're just covering their butts.'

'Well, the important thing is you *did* it,' Roy's mother told him. 'The birds are safe from the pancake people. You should feel great about that!'

'I do,' Roy said, 'but it wasn't me who saved the owls.'

Mr Eberhardt came over and put a hand on his son's shoulder. 'You got the word out, Roy. Without you, nobody would've known what was happening. Nobody would have showed up to protest the bulldozing.'

'Yeah, but it all started because of Beatrice's step-brother,' Roy said. 'He's the one who should've been on Tom Brokaw or whatever. The whole thing was his idea.'

'I know, honey,' Mrs Eberhardt said, 'but he's gone.'

Roy nodded. 'Sure looks that way.'

Mullet Fingers had lasted less than forty-eight hours under the same roof with Lonna, who'd spent most of that time on the telephone trying to drum up more TV interviews. Lonna had been counting on her son to keep the Leep family in the limelight, which is the last place he wanted to be.

With Beatrice's assistance, the boy had snuck out of the house while Lonna and Leon were arguing about a new dress that Lonna had purchased for seven hundred dollars in anticipation of appearing on *The Oprah Winfrey Show*. Nobody from Oprah's programme ever called Lonna back, so Leon had demanded that she return the dress and get a full refund.

When the Leeps' shouting reached the same approxmate decibel level as a B-52, Beatrice lowered her stepbrother out of a bathroom window. Unfortunately, a nosy neighbour had mistaken the escape for a burglary in progress and had notified the police. Mullet Fingers made it only two blocks before speeding patrol cars surrounded him.

Lonna had been furious to learn her son was up to his old runaway tricks. Out of spite, she told the officers that he'd stolen a valuable toe ring from her jewellery box, and demanded that he be locked up in juvenile detention to teach him a lesson.

There the boy had lasted only seventeen hours before breaking out, this time with an unlikely accomplice.

Hiding in the laundry basket with his new best friend, Dana Matherson undoubtedly had no clue that he'd been specially selected to join the jailbreak, that the scrawny blond kid knew exactly who he was and knew all the rotten things he'd done to Roy Eberhardt.

Being of simple mind, Dana probably had thought only of his unexpected good fortune as the laundry basket was loaded into the laundry truck, which was then driven out the gates of the detention centre. Even the approaching sirens probably hadn't worried him until the truck braked and the back doors flew open.

It was then the two young fugitives leaped from the smelly bundle of dirty clothes and made a run for it.

Later, when Roy heard the story from Beatrice, he knew instantly why her stepbrother had chosen Dana Matherson as an escape partner. Mullet Fingers was fleet and slippery while Dana was sluggish and sore-footed, still not fully recovered from his encounter with the rat-traps.

The perfect decoy – that was Dana.

Sure enough, the police had easily caught up with the big thug, though he shook off two officers before eventually being tackled and handcuffed. By then, Beatrice's stepbrother was a distant blur, a bronze-coloured wisp vanishing into a snarled tree line.

The police never found him, nor did they search particularly hard. Dana was the prize catch, the one with the rap sheet and the bad attitude.

Roy couldn't find Mullet Fingers, either. Many times he'd ridden his bicycle to the junkyard and checked the Jo-Jo's ice-cream truck, but it was always empty. Then, one day, the truck itself vanished, dragged off and pressed into a rusty cube of scrap metal.

Beatrice Leep knew where her stepbrother was hiding, but he'd sworn her to secrecy. 'Sorry, Tex,' she'd told Roy, 'I made a blood promise.'

So, yes, the kid was gone.

And Roy knew he'd never see Napoleon Bridger again, unless he wanted to be seen.

'He'll be all right. He's a survivor,' Roy said, for his mother's benefit.

'I hope you're right,' she said, 'but he's so young—'

'Hey, I've got an idea.' Roy's father jangled his car keys. 'Let's go for a ride.'

When the Eberhardts arrived at the corner of Woodbury and East Oriole, two other vehicles were already parked at the fence gate. One was a squad car, the other was a blue pickup truck; Roy recognized both of them.

Officer David Delinko had stopped on his way home from the police station, where he'd received another commendation from the chief – this time for aiding in the recapture of Dana Matherson.

Leroy 'Curly' Branitt, who was temporarily between jobs, had been driving his wife and mother-in-law to the outlet mall when he'd decided to make the brief detour.

Like the Eberhardts, they'd come to see the owls.

As dusk fell, they waited in a friendly and uncomplicated silence, though there was plenty they could have talked about. Except for the fence with its fading streamers, the land bore no sign that the pancake-house people had ever been there. Curly's trailer had been towed, the earthmoving machines hauled away, the Travellin' Johnnys returned to the toilet-rental company. Even the survey stakes were gone, uprooted and carted off with the trash.

Gradually the night air filled with the buzz of crickets, and Roy smiled to himself, remembering the boxful he'd released there. Obviously the owls had plenty of other bugs to eat.

Before long, a pair of the birds popped out of a nearby burrow. They were followed by a wobbly-legged youngster that looked as fragile as a Christmas ornament.

In unison, the owls rotated their onion-sized heads to stare at the humans who were staring at them. Roy could only imagine what they were thinking.

'I gotta admit,' Curly said with a fond grunt, 'they're kinda cute.'

One Saturday, after the Mother Paula's scandal had died down, Roy went to watch Beatrice and her friends play a soccer game. It was a sweltering afternoon, but Roy had resigned himself to the fact that there was no change of seasons in South Florida, only mild variations of summer.

And though he missed the crisp Montana autumns, Roy found himself daydreaming less often about the place. Today the sun lit up the green soccer field like a neon carpet, and Roy was happy to peel off his T-shirt and bake.

Beatrice scored three goals before she noticed him sprawled in the bleachers. When she waved, Roy gave her two thumbs up and chuckled, because it was pretty funny – Beatrice the Bear waving at Tex, the new kid.

The high sun and the steaming heat reminded Roy of another bright afternoon not so long ago, in a place not so far off. Before the soccer match ended, he grabbed his shirt and slipped away.

It was a short ride from the soccer field to the hidden creek. Roy chained his bike to a gnarly old stump and picked his way through the tangled trees.

The tide was very high, and only a weather-beaten wedge of the *Molly Bell's* pilothouse showed above the waterline. Roy hung his sneakers on a forked limb and swam out toward the wreck, the warm current nudging him along.

With both hands he grabbed the lip of the pilothouse roof and hoisted himself up on the warped bare wood.

There was scarcely enough space for a dry perch.

Roy lay on his belly, blinked the salt from his eyes, and waited. The quiet wrapped around him like a soft blanket.

First he spotted the T-shaped shadow of the osprey crossing the pale green water beneath him. Later came the white heron, gliding low in futile search of a shallow edge to wade. Eventually the bird lighted halfway up a black mangrove, squawking irritably about the high tides.

The elegant company was welcome, but Roy kept his eyes fastened on the creek. The splash of a feeding tarpon upstream put him on alert, and sure enough, the surface of the water began to shake and boil. Within moments a school of mullet erupted, sleek bars of silver shooting airborne again and again.

Atop the pilothouse, Roy scooted forward as far as he dared, dangling both arms. The mullet quit jumping but assembled in a V-shaped squadron that pushed a nervous ripple down the middle of the creek toward the *Molly Bell*. Soon the water beneath him darkened, and Roy could make out the blunt-headed shapes of individual fish, each swimming frantically for its life.

As the school approached the sunken crab boat, it divided as cleanly as if it had been sliced by a sabre. Quickly Roy picked out one fish and, teetering precariously, plunged both hands into the current.

For one thrilling moment he actually felt it in his grasp – as cool and slick and magical as mercury. He squeezed his fingers into fists, but the mullet easily jetted free, leaping once before it rejoined the fleeing school.

Roy sat up and gazed at his dripping, empty palms.

Impossible, he thought. *Nobody* could catch one of those darn things bare-handed, not even Beatrice's step-brother. It must have been a trick, some sort of clever illusion.

A noise like a laugh came out of the dense knotted mangroves. Roy assumed it was the heron, but when he looked up, he saw that the bird had gone. Slowly he rose, shielding his brow from the sun's glare.

'That you?' he shouted. 'Napoleon Bridger, is that you?'

Nothing.

Roy waited and waited, until the sun dropped low and the creek was draped in shadows. No more laughing sounds came from the trees. Reluctantly he slid off the *Molly Bell* and let the falling tide carry him to shore.

Robotically he got into his clothes, though when he reached for his shoes he saw that only one was hanging from the forked bough. His right sneaker was missing.

Roy put on the left sneaker and went hopping in search of the other. He soon found it half-submerged in the shallows beneath the branches, where he figured it must have fallen.

Yet when he bent to pick up the shoe, it wouldn't come loose. The laces had been securely entwined around a barnacle-encrusted root.

Roy's fingers trembled as he undid the precisely tied clove-hitch knots. He lifted the soggy sneaker and peeked inside.

There he spied a mullet no larger than a man's index finger, flipping and splashing to protest its captivity. Roy emptied the baby fish into his hand and waded deeper into the creek.

Gently he placed the mullet in the water, where it flashed once and vanished like a spark.

Roy stood motionless, listening intently, but all he heard was the hum of mosquitoes and the low whisper of the tide. The running boy was already gone.

As Roy laced on his other sneaker, he laughed to himself.

So the great bare-handed mullet grab wasn't a trick. It wasn't impossible after all.

Guess I'll have to come back another day and try again, Roy thought. That's what a real Florida boy would do.

Turn the page for an exclusive extract from Carl Hiaason's brilliant new adventure, *Squirm*.

ONE

This one kid, he got kicked out of school.

That's not easy to do—you need to break some actual laws. We heard lots of rumors, but nobody gave us the straight story.

The kid's name was Jammer, and I got his locker.

Who knows what he kept in there, but he must've given out the combination to half the school. Kids were always messing with my stuff when I wasn't around.

So I put a snake inside the locker. Problem solved.

It was an Eastern diamondback, a serious reptile. Eight buttons on the rattle, so it made some big noise when people opened the locker door. The freak-out factor was high.

Don't worry—the rattlesnake couldn't bite. I taped its mouth shut. That's a tricky move, not for rookies. You need steady hands and zero common sense. I wouldn't try it again.

The point is I didn't want that rattler to hurt anyone. I just wanted kids to stay out of my locker.

Which they now do.

I set the diamondback free a few miles down Grapefruit Road, on the same log where I found him. It's important to exit the scene fast, because an adult rattlesnake can strike up to one-half of its body length. Most people don't know that, and why would they? It's not a necessary piece of information, if you live a halfway normal life.

Which I don't.

"What does your dad do?"

I hear this question whenever we move somewhere new.

My standard answer: "He runs his own business."

But the truth is I don't know what my father does. He sends a check, Mom cashes it. I haven't seen the guy since I was like three years old. Maybe four.

Does it bother me? Possibly. Sure.

I've done some reading about this, how it can mess up a person when his parents split, especially when one of them basically vanishes from the family scene. I don't want to be one of those screwed-up kids, but I can't rule out the possibility.

Mom doesn't say much about Dad. The checks always show up on time—the tenth of the month—and they never bounce. We might not be rich, but we're definitely not poor. You wouldn't believe how many pairs of shoes my sister owns. God, I give her so much grief.

The way I look at it, Mom doesn't get a free pass just because she doesn't want to talk about my father. That's not what you'd call a healthy, open approach to an issue. So I stay on her case, though not in a mean way.

"What does he do for a living?" I'll say, like I've never asked before.

"Well, Billy, I'm not exactly sure what he does," she'll begin in the same tight voice, "but I can tell you what he *doesn't* do."

Over time, based on my mother's commentary, I've scratched the following professions off my Phantom Father list:

Astronaut, quantum physicist, lawyer, doctor, heavy-metal guitarist, veterinarian, architect, hockey player, NASCAR driver, jockey, plumber, roofer, electrician, pilot, policeman, car salesman, and yoga instructor.

Mom says Dad's too claustrophobic to be an astronaut, too lousy at math to be a quantum physicist, too shy to be a lawyer, too squeamish to be a doctor, too uncoordinated to play the guitar, too tall to be a jockey, too hyper for yoga, and so on.

I don't like this game, but I'm making progress, information-wise. Mom's still touchy about the subject, so I try to take it easy. Meanwhile, my sister, Belinda, acts like she doesn't care, like she's not the least bit curious about the old man. This fake attitude is known as a "coping mechanism," according to what I've read.

Maybe my father is a psychiatrist, and one day I'll lie down on his couch and we'll sort out all this stuff together. Or not.

At school I try to keep a low profile. When you move around as much as my family does, making friends isn't practical. Leaving is easier if there's no one to say goodbye to. That much I've learned.

But sometimes you're forced to "interact." There's no choice. Sometimes staying low-profile is impossible.

The last week of school, some guy on the lacrosse team starts pounding on a kid in the D-5 hallway. Now, this kid happens to be a dork, no question, but he's harmless. And the lacrosse player outweighs him by like forty pounds. Still, a crowd is just standing around watching this so-called fight, which is really just a mugging. There are dudes way bigger than me, major knuckle-draggers, cheering and yelling. Not one of them makes a move to stop the beating.

So I throw down my book bag, jump on Larry Lacrosse, and hook my right arm around his neck. Pretty soon his face goes purple and his eyes bulge out like a constipated bullfrog's. That's when a couple of his teammates pull me off, and one of the P.E. teachers rushes in to break up the tangle. Nobody gets suspended, not even a detention, which is typical.

The dorky kid, the one who was getting pounded, I didn't know his name. The lacrosse guy turns out to be a Kyle something. We've got like seven Kyles at our school, and I can't keep track of them all. This one comes up to me later, between sixth and seventh period, and says he's going to kick my butt. Then one of his friends grabs his arm and whispers, "Easy, dude. That's the psycho with the rattler in his locker."

I smile my best psycho smile, and Kyle disappears. Big tough jock who likes to beat up kids half his size. Pathetic.

But lots of people are terrified of snakes. It's called *ophidiophobia*. The experts say it's a deep primal fear. I wouldn't know.

During seventh period I get pulled out of class by the school "resource officer," which is what they call the sheriff's deputy who hangs out in the main office. His name is Thickley, and technically he's in charge of campus security. He's big and friendly, cruising toward retirement.

"Billy, I'm going to ask you straight up," he says in the hallway. "There's a rumor you've got a snake in your locker. A rattlesnake."

"A live rattler?" I laugh. "That's crazy."

"Can we have a look?"

"No problem. Who's *we*?"

"Me. Just myself."

"Sure, Officer Thickley. You don't need to ask first."

"Oh, I always ask," he says. "See, if I show respect for the students, they'll show respect for me. It's a two-way street."

"Be my guest," I tell him. "You can just pop the lock, right?"

"I'd like you to come along with me."

"But I really can't miss this class," I say. "Mrs. Bowers is reviewing for the final."

"Please, Billy. I'm not a fan of snakes."

We walk down the hallway to my locker. Thickley stands at least ten feet behind me while I open the door.

"Here you go," I say.

"Holy crap!"

"It's not real, man." I dangle the rubber snake, its tail jiggling. "See? Just a toy."

The color returns to Thickley's face. I bought the joke

285

snake for like three bucks at a party store. It's black and skinny, and doesn't look anything like a diamondback rattler. They had it on the same aisle with the fake vomit and dog poop.

"Billy, why have you got that thing in there?"

"Because other kids keep breaking in and messing with my stuff. You knew Jammer, right? This was his locker before he got expelled."

"Oh," says Thickley. "Then we should get you a different one."

"*No necesito.*"

"But the locker still smells like Jammer's . . . stuff."

"Is that what stinks so bad?"

Thickley says, "I'll get you a can of Febreze."

You're probably thinking: *This is a disturbed young man.*

Based on what happened with me and the rattler, right?

But I've been catching snakes since I was a little kid, and I know what I'm doing. Usually I don't handle the poisonous ones, because a split-second mistake will put you in an ambulance, speeding to the E.R. You might not die from the bite, but from what they say, the pain is extreme.

Right now at home I've got a corn snake, a king snake, two yellow rat snakes, and a banded water snake, all non-venomous. I can't say "harmless" because the water snake is mean and nasty. Honestly, the rattler was way easier to handle.

I never keep a snake for more than a week or two. They

stay out in the garage, inside dry aquarium tanks with lids that screw down tight. My mother isn't thrilled about the arrangement, but she's gotten used to it. She says it's safer than wakeboarding or BASE jumping, neither of which is on my list of future hobbies.

A wild snake won't hurt anybody, as long as you give it some space. That's true for rattlers, same as the others.

"What is *wrong* with you," my sister often says. This is never a question. "These aren't normal pets."

"They're not pets, Belinda. I don't *own* them."

"At least a puppy gives you love. A snake gives you nothing but a blank stare." My sister, the comedian.

In a few months she's leaving for college—Cornell University in Ithaca, New York. Big-time school. Good for her.

Belinda says she's looking forward to northern winters, but she hasn't got a clue. Like me, she has spent her entire life in Florida, the place everybody up north wants to be every January.

She didn't know about the rattlesnake, of course. Neither did Mom. They steer clear of my aquarium tanks in the garage.

I'm holding the king snake when Mom pokes her head out the door and says, "What happened at school today, Billy? Put that creepy thing away and come inside."

Turns out the dorky kid—Chin is his last name—he friended my mother on Facebook. Who does that? He sent her a message thanking me for saving him from the beatdown in D-5. He said nobody's ever stuck up for him before.

See, this is why I'm not on social media. Way too much human contact.

"Why didn't you tell me about this?" Mom asks.

"'Cause it was no big deal."

"Fighting is too a big deal. You've got a week left of school before summer. Can you please try not to get kicked out?"

"They won't kick me out, Mom. I've got straight A's."

"But what if you'd hurt that other boy?"

"Only thing I hurt was his shiny blond ego."

She sighs. "We've had this discussion, Billy."

"What—I'm supposed to turn the other way when I see something bad going down?"

"No, of course not, no. What you should do is immediately report it to a teacher. Or run to the office and tell somebody. That's how cases of bullying are supposed to be handled. It says so in the school Code of Conduct."

I have to chuckle. I'm not trying to disrespect my mother, but seriously—the Code of Conduct? Kyle the lacrosse star was punching that poor kid in the head. Come on.

Next day, I notice Chin eating by himself in the cafeteria. He's got a bruised eye and white gauze taped over one ear. He never looks up from his lunch tray, so he doesn't see me.

I walk straight to the lacrosse kids' table, sit down next to Kyle, and start eating my ham-and-fried-egg sandwich. He just glares at me. It's not what you'd call a bonding moment.

One of Kyle's jock friends tells me to move to another table.

"Aw, but you guys are so cool," I say. "I want to be just like you. Talk the same cool way. Wear the same cool clothes. Hang with the same cool girls. It's truly an honor to sit with you here at your special cool table. Seriously, this lunch is the high point of my entire life."

And they thought *they* were pros at sarcasm.

"Move it, Snake Boy!" the kid barks.

I can't help but laugh. Is this what they're calling me now?

"So, you guys are into reptiles, too?" I put down the sandwich, whip out my phone.

Kyle's angry, but nervous at the same time. Doesn't say a word.

I google a picture of a wild-hog hunter who got bitten by a diamondback over near Yeehaw Junction. That's a real place, you can look it up. The hog hunter's arm is swollen thick as a pine stump. His fingers look like boiled purple sausages. I hold up the phone so that Kyle and his all-jock posse can see the photo.

"That's what can happen," I say, "when you're not careful."

Kyle goes pale and edges back his chair. "Dude, you *are* a total psycho."

"Can I have the rest of your Doritos?" I ask pleasantly.

They all get up, snatch their trays, and walk off, Kyle in the lead.

FYI, that hog hunter didn't die from the snakebite. He was back in the woods a month later—but way more careful.

Kyle won't bother Chin again. That's my guess.

The night before the last day of school, Mom's in the kitchen working on the household budget. She has a yellow notebook, two sharpened pencils, and a calculator. I notice the monthly check from my father on the table. His name is printed on it, but no address.

Mom doesn't care if we see the check, but she always cuts up the mailing envelope and throws away the pieces—which I later dig out of the garbage can and try to tape back together.

Usually it's impossible, because the snipped pieces are as small as confetti, but on this particular night she must have been in a hurry with the scissors. When she's not looking, I collect the fragments of the envelope and smuggle them to my room. This time they fit together like a miniature jigsaw puzzle, and it's easy to read the return address printed in the upper left-hand corner.

So I walk back to the kitchen and say, "Mom, how much is a plane ticket to Montana?"

"What are you talking about?"

I show her the taped-together envelope.

She frowns. "We can't go anywhere this summer. I've got a brand-new job here, remember?"

"They've got Uber cars in Montana."

"I doubt that," Mom says. "Uber tractors, maybe."

My sister and I don't approve of her working for a car-service app, because it's so dangerous on the roads. Florida has possibly the worst drivers in the universe. Also the most trigger-happy.

But Mom said she was bored with accounting and wanted a job where she could meet new people every day.

"Let me fly out there by myself," I tell her. "I can pay for it from my savings."

"And where would you stay?"

"With Dad. Where else?"

"But he didn't invite you, Billy."

"I'm inviting myself."

Mom looks sad. "He's got a whole new life now, honey."

"That's bull," I say. "Just because you get a new zip code doesn't mean you get a new life. Look at *us*."

She closes her eyes for a moment, then says: "I wish I could let you go, but it's not a great idea. He got remarried."

"Doesn't he still ask about me and Belinda?"

"I send him pictures."

"That's it?"

"Let's not talk about this now, Billy."

Back in my room, I go online to check the balance of my bank account: $633.24. This is what I've saved up from Christmases and birthday presents, and also from working at Publix for five weekends until I couldn't stand it anymore. Bagging groceries requires friendly conversation with strangers, which I'm not especially good at.

Truthfully, I'm surprised I've got so much cash in the bank. There's a travel site offering $542 round-trip tickets from Orlando to Bozeman, Montana, so I write Mom a check and slip it into her handbag after she goes to bed.

Then I "borrow" her credit card to order the plane ticket off the airline's website.

The last day of school is short because I've got only one final exam, in algebra. I'm done at noon, and Mom is waiting in the parking lot. She found my check in her purse, and she's angry.

"You are *not* going to Montana," she declares.

"It's a nonrefundable ticket."

"Don't be a smart-ass, Billy. I don't even have your father's phone number!"

"Then how do you know he's married?"

"He told me in a letter. This was a few years ago."

"Were you mad?"

"I'm mad he doesn't call you guys. That's all."

"And you seriously have no idea what he does for a living?"

Mom sighs. "He says he's working for the government—whatever that means."

"How come you never told me?"

"Because I was embarrassed I didn't know more."

I reach over and squeeze her arm. "If he doesn't want to see me, I'll come straight home. That's a promise."

She says, "This is all my fault."

"Please don't cry. It's just a plane ride."

But she knows better than that. So do I.

Too much time has passed. I need to talk to the man.

That evening, I take the snakes out of their tanks and put

them in pillowcases, which I knot snugly at the open ends. My mother drives me down Grapefruit Road until I find the right place to stop. She stays in the car, as any normal person would, while I walk into the trees, open the pillowcases, and free the snakes.

I'd waited until dark so they could crawl away safely. Most hawks don't hunt at night, another piece of information you'll probably never need.

The next morning, Mom takes me to the airport. I've told her I spoke to my father and he's excited about my visit.

Not true. I'd spent an hour on the internet but couldn't find a phone number anywhere. All I have is the return address on that envelope.

And now I'm getting on an airplane, flying across the country to meet a man who might not even want to see me.

Brilliant.

ABOUT THE AUTHOR

Carl Hiaasen was born and raised in Florida, where he still lives with his family. His books include the Newbery Honor winner *Hoot,* as well as *Flush, Scat, Chomp,* and *Skink–No Surrender.*

Hiaasen writes a column for the *Miami Herald* and is the author of many bestselling novels for adults, including *Bad Monkey, Star Island,* and *Razor Girl.*

Read more about Hiaasen's work at carlhiaasen.com or follow him on Twitter at @Carl_Hiaasen.

New York Times bestselling
CARL HIAASEN

SQUIRM

A wickedly funny adventure
about families, nature and
figuring out what's really important,
from the award-winning Carl Hiaasen.